THE RIGHT HAND

OF THE FATHER

PAUL TRIPI

Paul Tripi

Chapter 1

It was a normal August day in St. Louis, hot. The mercury was climbing along with the humidity and both read ninety-four. Tony Russo, age thirty-nine, a native of St. Louis, was on his way downtown to meet his brother Joseph, a partner in a well-to-do law firm in Clayton, Missouri. Joe was in possession of his company's season baseball tickets and was treating his brother to one of the more sought after events of a St. Louis summer, a St. Louis Cardinal-Chicago Cubs baseball game.

Tony was excited. Joe's company seats, called club seats, were among the best seats in the house. Of the 50,000 seats at Busch stadium fewer than 200 were club seats. These premium priced seats came with very special amenities. Festivities begin with a luxurious pre-game dinner in the members-only dining room closely situated near the Cardinals locker room beneath the stands. After dinner, members were seated directly behind home plate, so close to the field that conversations between catchers and batters could be heard. Last but not least, these seats came with their own waiters, allowing occupants to order any food or beverage they desire from a broad menu as often as they wished, all included in the ticket price. To Tony, a huge sports fan, life didn't get any better than this.

"My bro," said Tony as he hugged the handsome man who resembled him.

"My brother," came the response. "You ready for this?"

"Like a woman who's ten months pregnant waits for the baby to be born."

"I don't get it," responded Joe.

"You don't get it?"

"Yes, I get it you dope. But what kind of analogy is that for crying out loud?"

Tony retorted, "Why do you always have to be so serious? Lawyers!"

Joe raised the tickets up in the air and yelled, "I've got one for sale here."

"Give me that ticket or I'm telling mom."

"Oh yeah, pull the I'm-telling-mom-card again."

Both brothers laughed, hugged again and headed into the stadium.

The game ended with a Cardinal loss but it was a victory for the Russo brothers. After all, they spent time together, got to watch the Cards play the Cubs, and ate and drank to their hearts' content.

After the game as they were saying their goodbyes, Tony asked his brother, "You and the family coming over for Sunday sauce?"

"Does a man with a cold have to blow his nose?" came his answer.

"What kind of answer is that? You're sick," Tony said just before he burst out laughing. "Does that mean yes?"

"Shut up. See you Sunday. Love ya."

"Me too, thanks bro, today was great. Tell Sally and the kids hi for me."

"See you all Sunday."

The Russos, like many Italian families, usually have pasta sauce on Sundays; it's an Italian tradition. Someone in the family makes the spaghetti sauce, a family recipe handed down through generations, and the entire family goes to whoever's turn it is that week to cook it. It was always at their parents' home until their dad and mom retired and moved to Florida.

Tony left the stadium, slipped into his new red Ford Explorer, rolled up the highway and fell into place with the horde of other Cardinal fans trying to get home.

The St. Louis highway system design was an easy configuration and made travel a piece of cake. Of course when 50,000 people enter the highway system all at once, a piece of cake was not the terminology Cardinal fans used.

Tony lived in Ballwin, a western suburb about twenty miles from the city, with his wife, Gina, and their nine-year-old daughter Molly. They lived in a lovely brick ranch home with three bedrooms, two and a half baths and a two-car attached garage. The house sat on a large lot with beautiful mature trees and was landscaped to perfection. Tony took pride in his property and it definitely showed.

Another feature of their home was that directly behind the house sat a private little two-acre lake stocked with fish, for the sole use of the subdivision residents. Not many used it. Tony, on the other hand, utilized it to the fullest, and spent many hours walking the banks and casting. Not so much catching, just enjoying the outdoors and atmosphere. He loved it out there, plus it was a great place to take his little girl for some quality private time. Tony loved his little daughter with all his heart. He lit up just talking about her. She was a beautiful girl with long dark hair like her mother's and a smile that simply melted the hearts of any and all around her. She was a good student, loved music, reading, and talking on the phone, the usual combination for a

Paul Tripi

nine-year-old fourth grader.

Tony was a good sized man, standing six foot one and about 225 pounds on a sturdy frame. He had the curse of most middle-aged men, a beer belly. His thick black hair was thinning on top a bit, but his beard was heavy, giving him the appearance of a man constantly in need of a shave. His green eyes seemed to change color when the sun hit them just right, and due to his Italian heritage, he looked like he had a perpetual tan.

His only flaw is a not too obvious scar over his left eye, which he received as a youngster fighting in the Missouri Golden Gloves Boxing Tournament. It was twenty-five years ago but he still talked about it as though it was yesterday. He wore that scar like a badge of honor. All in all, Anthony Michael Russo was a handsome man.

Tony was born and raised on the Hill in St. Louis. His dad, Anthony, no middle name, and his mom, Maria, maiden name Telesco, had three children. Tony was the oldest, his brother Joseph came next, and the baby was sister Elizabeth, known to the family as Betty. It was a loving family and along with his wife and daughter it was the heart of Tony's life.

The Hill is an area in southwest St. Louis where many Italian immigrants settled and is now almost entirely populated by people of Italian decent. Because of that the area has all the stores and restaurants necessary for Italian Americans to function. The Hill is easily recognizable; all fire hydrants are painted in the colors of the Italian flag—red, white and green.

Tony's wife Gina was born in Chicago, Illinois, the only daughter

6

of Babe and Regina Rancuso, two wonderful parents who love their daughter, granddaughter, and son-in-law immensely. Babe Rancuso moved his family to St. Louis from Chicago more than twenty-five years ago, and now considered himself a St. Louisian. Although he can't help rooting for the Chicago Bears football team, Babe was a die-hard St. Louis Cardinal baseball and St. Louis Blues hockey fan.

He and Regina had two children. Gina, thirty-seven, and their son Thomas, forty-five, who lived with his family in Downers Grove, Illinois, a suburb just west of Chicago. Babe owned and operated two upscale furniture stores; he ran the one nearest his home and Tom operated the one near Chicago. Both are called "Rancuso's." According to the way Babe set up the deal with his son, Tom owned seventy-five percent of that store. One more year like they had last year and he'd own that store outright. Babe and Tom had been after Tony to join the family business for years. However, Tony loved the freedom of his job as a business forms broker, buying and selling printing in the St. Louis area.

Now comes Gina. Gina can only be described as beautiful. She might be considered a tad short standing five foot two but her height was not what people first noticed. Her face was mesmerizing. She had dark hair and the deepest brown eyes imaginable. They're so dark they're almost black.

Her body has the right curves in all the right places, including breasts that could feed the babies in a small nursery. She could afford to lose a few pounds but nothing a few weeks on a simple diet wouldn't cure. She worked out, but she being of Italian descent found food a big part of her life. It's a battle most Italians love to fight. Gina's full-time job was homemaking and she was good at it. She kept her house meticulously clean and cooked like a gourmet chef. Her floors were so clean you could eat off them and with her cooking you'd be happy to do it.

7

The most important thing in Gina Russo's life was her family. The only person on earth who she loved more than Tony was Molly. There is a bond between mother and daughter the depth of which most fathers may think they know, but only mothers really do. Molly was the perfect daughter; Tony and Gina consider her a gift from God. They were told after years of trying that it was highly unlikely they would ever be able to have any children, but through the grace of God, Molly was conceived. She, however, was born two months premature and weighed only three pounds; her chance for survival was put at twenty percent. No one could guess that now. She was as healthy and vibrant as any child her age, with a bubbling personality, energetic and outgoing as can be.

God certainly had blessed Tony Russo. According to Tony it all happened the day a cocky young teenage boy from the Hill met a pretty suburbanite who just transferred from a high school in Chicago. For Tony it was lust at first sight. At least that's what he always said. But the truth of the matter is the first time Tony Russo laid eyes on Gina Rancuso he was caught. Hook line and sinker.

The day they met was just another standard St. Louis summer day. Hot as hell and no relief in sight. Tony and a couple of his Christian Brothers College High School buddies decided to go out to the 'burbs to Kohler Pool, a large community swimming pool loaded with young girls working on their tans.

Tony, Vito Grimaldi, and Frankie Paladino grabbed a corner of the pool area and like the true hunters they were, waited for the prey. There was a virtual smorgasbord of girls to talk to but Tony was content with just looking, and jumping in the pool to cool off every once in a while. He was drying off after a refreshing plunge when a new crop of girls arrived; one of them, a petite black-haired beauty, walked past Tony and smiled. Tony melted, his blood pressure shot up, and he was totally infatuated. He had to meet her but he had to be cool about it. He wasn't.

He waited as long as he could, about a minute, and walked over to where the girls were stretching out their towels, preparing to catch some rays.

"Excuse me miss," he said to the lovely black-haired girl, using the best smile he could muster up. "I have never done anything like this in my entire life but I feel compelled to tell you that you are the most beautiful girl I have ever seen and I was wondering if you would consider becoming my wife."

"What a nice offer but I'm already married," she replied.

"I'm so sorry, I didn't mean, I mean I didn't think, I mean I'm sorry."

"What DO you mean?" she asked.

"I don't know what I mean, I mean I didn't realize, I thought," he stuttered, dropped his head, and started to walk away.

"I can't believe you fell for that. I'm only fifteen years old for heaven sakes!" she said laughingly.

"Well how was I supposed to know that?"

"Maybe because I'm with a whole bunch of girls from high school."

"Wait, just wait a second. Can I have a chance to start again?" Tony asked but started without waiting for an answer.

"My name is Tony, I'm a junior at CBC high, I think you're cute and I wanted to get your name."

"Alright, if you put it that way, hi, my name is Gina, I'm a freshman at Parkway South, now please leave."

"OK, I will but I'm sorry I'm gonna stay here and keep bothering you until you tell me your last name."

"You are bothering me; now don't make me call the police!"

"What police? We're at the pool."

"Alright, if I tell you my last name, will you leave us alone?"

"Yes, I promise."

9

"My last name is Rancuso."

"You have got to be kidding me! My last name is Rancuso."

"No way." She said with a stunned look on her face.

Tony laughed. "I can't believe you fell for *that*. My name is Russo, Tony Russo. I'm leaving now but you will hear from me again. I hope that's alright with you?"

"It's a free country. Now goodbye Russo, Tony Russo," she said as she giggled and returned talking to her girl friends.

Tony turned and walked away, a little embarrassed but victorious. He did get what he wanted, her name.

It was a storybook romance. It started with a few dates, then it became a little more serious, and by the time they got to college it was hot and heavy. It all led to a wonderful wedding at Tony's life-long church, St. Ambrose on the Hill. Their love and respect for one another was obvious. They shared everything. The first years of their marriage they were inseparable and as the years went on that didn't change. The only thing missing from their lives was the pitter-patter of little feet. Even though it looked like that wouldn't happen for them, they keep on hoping. Hope springs eternal and never giving up sometimes pays off. Molly was born and Tony and Gina's life became complete.

There you have it. Tony, Gina, and Molly Russo, a near perfect and extremely happy family.

Chapter 2

"Honey, what time did Joe say they'd be here?" asked Tony as he stirred the pot of pasta sauce he was preparing for Sunday dinner.

"He said about noon. He wants to catch the first pitch of the Cardinal game on TV, but Sally and the kids won't get here until after church. They're going to twelve o'clock mass," Gina replied.

"What about my sister's family? Are they coming late or not coming at all? I know my nephew Bobby has a ball game at 2:00, so Betty didn't know if they were coming or not."

Gina smiled, saying, "Betty, Sam, and the boys are coming after Bobby's game. Betty said you could put the water on around 3:30. They'll definitely be here by 4:00."

Putting the water on means just that, placing a giant pot of water on the stove until it boils, and then dropping in the pasta. Tony has to boil enough water to cook about three pounds of pasta. It takes about twenty to twenty-five minutes to bring that much water to a boil and another twelve for the pasta to cook.

The pasta sauce is filled with meatballs and a slab of pork ribs;

11

both used for flavoring. Usually the women are the cooks in the Russo family, but when it comes to cooking the pasta sauce that's an Italian male domain. Tony, his brother Joe, and their brother-in-law Sam Cota, all make delicious tomato sauce. They're all different, but the whole family loves them all. All three of the guys think their sauce is the best.

Joe arrived at noon. He and Tony grabbed a beer and started watching the Cards beat up on the Cubs. At the end of the first inning they went into the kitchen, and made themselves a meatball sandwich. Joe's wife Sally, their two daughters, Sarah and Sandy, and their son Anthony, arrived at 1:30. Tony's sister Betty, her husband Sam, and their boys Bobby and Steven made it just in time to sit down to dinner. Gina and Molly made their special cannoli dessert, an Italian delicacy made with a ricotta cheese mixture stuffed into a hard shell and sprinkled with powdered sugar and chocolate bits. Aah! Sunday sauce, a tradition that will probably be passed through the Russo families forever.

After dinner Tony set the kids up with some of his old fishing equipment and the children headed to the pond. Molly showed them the ropes. The women cleaned up the kitchen and the men relaxed on the patio.

"Hey Tony," said Joe. "Are you guys having another kid?"

"Of course not," exclaimed Tony. "Who told you that?"

"Nobody said anything. I was referring to that potbelly of yours. It looks like you're about seven months along." Joe laughs.

Tony smiles, "Look who's talking, is that your ass or do you have a pillow stuck in the back of your pants?"

Sam joins in the fun. "I don't know why I'm laughing; it's time the three of us did something about this weight. I don't know about you guys, but it's not just the weight for me, I'm really out of shape to boot. I get winded taking out the garbage."

Tony agrees. "You're right, Sam. What are you guys doing in the morning? Do you want to check out some gyms?"

"I heard the new YMCA in Ballwin is supposed to be great. I don't have to be in court until 11:00 so I can check it out in the morning," Joe answers.

"I'd love to but I can't," says Sam. "I've got to be in the office early tomorrow. You guys go and if you like it, count me in."

"Joe, why don't you meet me at the donut shop on Manchester at 7:30 and we'll have a look-see. You guys could use the exercise and I could use the laughs," Tony adds.

Tony was at the donut shop when Joe arrived. "Hey bro, what's your pleasure? I'm buying."

"Hey Tony, how about coffee and a long john."

The waitress brought the coffee and donuts. Tony picked up his donut and asked, "Joe, would it bother you if I dunk my donut?"

Joe answered, "Who cares?"

With that Tony dunked his donut right into Joe's coffee and with a big smile on his face he says "Thanks, I hate to get crumbs in my own coffee."

Joe burst out laughing. "You're completely out of your mind bro, but that was funny."

Tony, still laughing himself, ordered Joe a fresh cup of coffee; they drank them, and headed over to check out the Y. It was a great facility with all kinds of amenities—a workout rooms loaded with equipment, a roomful of free weights, an Olympic-size swimming pool, a large gymnasium, an indoor track, a hot tub, a steam room, and a boxing area complete with a small ring and both types of punching bags.

It didn't take much time for them to decide that they loved the place and on top of everything else, the price was right; they joined.

Joe headed to court in Clayton. Tony headed home. He has his office there. It's a great set-up. He has his own business forms brokerage company. He represents a number of printing manufacturers, which include printing on paper, plastic, and labels. He doesn't get paid as an employee of the companies he represents. He actually purchases the printing and then invoices his customers, adding a fair mark-up. In this way he controlled profitability. Tony has a substantial customer base and does quite well financially. He is a good businessman who is trusted and respected in the industry, and has been for almost twenty years. He's on the board of the MBFA (Missouri Business Forms Association) and has served as the vice president of the St. Louis branch for the last five years. He enjoys the flexibility of having his own company, and has always been able to take the good with the bad.

As Tony headed home his thoughts were on working out and getting back in shape. He was quite impressed with the facilities at the Y and was especially interested in trying out the punching bags and some other equipment in the boxing room. The smell of canvas and feel of the ropes in the boxing ring brought back some mixed memories.

Pulling into the driveway, he didn't get out of the car. His mind wandered back to boyhood boxing days long since past.

He heard the crowd roar as he stepped into the ring for his first preliminary qualify bout in the Missouri Golden Gloves Boxing Tournament.

"In the blue corner, wearing white trunks, weighing 156 pounds, fighting for the Butler Murry Boys Club, Anthony Russo," yelled the announcer from the middle of the ring

"In the red corner, wearing the red trunks, weighing 155 pounds, fighting out of the Missouri Gym, Tommy Callahan.

Two sixteen-year-old boys stared at each other and waited for the bell to ring, signifying the first round in both of their careers.

Before boys can officially enter the Golden Gloves tournament they have to fight two preliminary bouts. These are usually between inexperienced fighters, who have never fought in a tournament. It takes both wins to qualify for the Golden Gloves event. Tony's first fight was with Thomas Sean Callahan. Tommy was a kid with visions of boxing grandeur; with only one obstacle standing in his way, an Italian kid from the Hill, Tony Russo.

Both boys were tough as nails but neither had any ring experience. Tony decided to try his hand at boxing the first time he walked into the Butler Murry Boys Club boxing facility. The main reason, because that's when and where he met Jerry (Pop) Merlo.

Pop Merlo was the St. Louis University boxing coach and extremely well respected in the boxing community. He loved the fight game and spent a lot of his free time teaching youngsters the art of pugilism at the Butler Murry Boys Club, situated smack-dab in the heart of the Hill.

Pop Merlo showed Tony many skills; including but not exclusive to the one that Tony enjoyed mastering the most, the speed punching bag. The air-filled speed bag is the smaller of the two punching bags used by fighters when training. It's used to develop hand speed and timing. The second is the heavy bag usually filled with sand. Its purpose is to develop power in the punch. Tony started his first lesson on the speed bag slowly. "Dun dun" was the sound the bag made as it swung back and forth against the wooden board it hung on. Dun dun dun, dun dun dun, dun dun dun, faster and faster and louder and louder went the bag as Tony started finding the rhythm. It was mesmerizing. He took to the speed bag like fish take to water. Before he knew it, he was training for the Golden Gloves Tourney.

Suddenly and without the proper amount of time needed to hone his skills, he found himself standing in the middle of a boxing ring, listening to the referee bark out the rules and waiting for the bell.

Ding went the bell; Tommy came running across the ring with both arms flailing away like a windmill. It was obvious that neither boxer had ever fought in a ring. Tony stayed out of Tommy's reach, although a couple of punches got through, landing but not doing damage. Callahan threw a left hook at Tony's head and missed, finding himself vulnerable to Tony's right-hand cross. Bang! A hard right to Tommy's head. Bang! Left hook to the ribs. Bang! Another right to the head, and Tommy stumbled. The referee stepped in. He looked into Tommy's eyes and gave him a standing eight count. With the referee shouting out the count, Tony was elated. He felt he was invincible! All he needed was a few more seconds and he'd have Tommy down and out. The ref waved his arm signaling the fight to continue. Now Tony was the one who rushed across the ring anxious to land a few more blows that he thought would end the fight. Callahan wasn't as hurt as Tony thought and surprised the unsuspecting combatant with a straight right of his own, smack in the middle of Tony's face!

Tony mumbled through his mouthpiece as he danced to his left, staying away from Tommy's right hand. They were both staying away from each other as the bell rang, ending round one of the three-round bout.

Pop said, "You did real good. Be patient. You can take this guy if you stay focused and just stay calm."

"Is my nose broken?"

"No, just a little red. Listen up. The next time he throws that big left hook counter with a right, left, right, left combination and you can end this fight. Rinse out your mouth, spit out the water, take a deep breath, get in there and fight," Pop directed.

The bell rang signaling the start of round two. Once again Tommy came rushing across the ring. Tony danced and jabbed and stayed away from the ropes. Callahan kept throwing haymakers trying to end the fight with one blow but Tony was too fast for him. Tommy was punching thin air. Then it happened, Callahan threw that big left hook and missed. Pow! Tony landed a big right to Callahan's jaw, a left and right to his mid section, and a perfectly thrown left hand to his head, Tommy went down.

"One, two, three," counted the ref. "Four five six," he yelled with his hand waving in the air with every number. "Seven eight nine ten, you're out," he barked. He waved both hands over his head, then walked over to Tony and raised his right hand. Tony Russo won his first qualifying match! And, he won it by knockout.

His second qualifying bout was just a few days later. His opponent was a short, stocky, fifteen-year-old Italian boy named Al Greccio. Al had trained with Pop Merlo for a while at the boys club until his dad got interested in Al's progress and he started training his son.

Gino Greccio, Al's dad, was a boxing wannabe. He pushed his son like he was training for the middleweight championship of the world. It's a shame when parents live their lives vicariously through their children. After all, this was a boxing match between two young men who are just trying to break into a new sport.

Pop was aware of Mr. Greccio's feeling and planned a strategy for Tony.

"Stick and move. Frustrate him. He's going to come out like a

17

raging bull," Pop advised. "Stay away from him and jab whenever you can."

"How do you win when you're running away?"

"You're not running away, Tony. You're bidding your time.

"When he can't hit you he'll get frustrated, and that leads to mistakes. Just stick and move. You don't have to knock a man out to win a fight. You'll be scoring with every jab. Just go out there and out-point this guy. But if he gives you an opening, nail him."

The fight started out just as Pop predicted. Al chased Tony around the ring for the entire first round, but all he got for his effort was about twenty left jabs in his face. The second round was a copy of the first, Tony easily out pointing Al with an accurate left hand. Al had landed a couple of punches, but was missing with almost everything he threw, and he found himself in a big hole way behind in points.

"What the hell are you doing out there?" screamed Gino Greccio, as he removed Al's mouthpiece and threw a sponge full of water in his son's face.

"You've gotta knock this kid out now or you're out of this tournament. Go out there and knock his block off."

"You're fighting a smart fight, Tony. Keep your eyes open; he's going to throw everything he's got at you," Pop said, wiping sweat from Tony's eyes.

"Hold onto him in the clinches. Time is on your side. Three more minutes and you're in like Flynn."

The third round bell rang; the two fighters touched gloves. Pow! Al landed a hard right to Tony's jaw. He followed that with a left right combination.

"Get away from him!" shouted Pop from the corner.

Tony danced sharply to his left. Al was in quick pursuit and threw a mighty left hook. He missed and when he did, he threw himself off balance. Tony countered with a heavy right hand.

Bang! Went Tony's right to Al's forehead. Pow! Went a left right combination to the ribs. Tony charged forward, left jab, left jab, straight right hand, left hook. Al Greccio was in trouble.

"Grab him," screamed Gino Greccio as loud as he could. But it was too late; Tony was in the midst of landing two more right hands that sent Al dropping to the canvas. There was no count. The referee ran over to Al, took a look in his eyes, waved his arms over his head and yelled, "It's over!"

Tony jumped into the air and immediately ran over to his corner to hug the man that made it all possible, his mentor and trainer, Pop!

Pop responded, "Stay calm, this is just the beginning, Tony. You're in the big show, the tournament now. Next bout you'll be fighting an experienced fighter. Don't get too cocky over these wins. You've got a lot of work in front of you. For tonight, enjoy this victory. You fought a great fight, kid. I'm proud of you!"

The next two weeks, Tony trained as hard and as often as he could—jumping rope, punching the speed bag, punching the heavy sand bag, and shadow boxing. He was running five miles a day. In his mind he was a lean, mean, invincible fighting machine!

Seeds determine the matches in the tournament. The highest seed in the weight class faces the lowest. Tony was the fifteenth seed out of sixteen middleweights. Making his opponent the number two seed, Chase Walker.

Chase Walker, sixty-six wins and eight losses as an amateur fighter, finished second in his weight class in last year's tournament. He hadn't had an official fight since he lost in the finals of the Gloves a year earlier, but he always kept himself in top-notch shape. Chase was a family man with two young sons, ages three and eighteen months. He had spent the last year working on an oil pipe crew in Benton, Texas. He

19

hated to leave the kids for that length of time, but the money was too good for him to pass up. He was a tough, tough man with the savvy and know-how needed to make the pros. The only thing needed to make the jump was a big win and winning the Missouri Golden Gloves could be his shot.

It was obvious that Tony didn't realize the difference between the two fights he won and the sixty-six fights Chase won. He had been bragging like he had just won the World middleweight title, and fighting Chase Walker was just a formality.

Anthony Russo, Tony's dad, sat nervously on the edge of his seat as he waited for his son to step into the ring. Seated next to him were his fourteen-year-old son Joey and most if not all of Tony's friends. Tony had them convinced they were about to see the next Sugar Ray Robinson, and they couldn't wait to see their buddy in action.

Tony slid between the ropes into the ring. He was talking trash for two weeks, but now that he looked across the ring at a twenty-four-year-old man who was built like Adonis, he wasn't so confident. In fact he was a little scared.

Tony was proud when the ring announcer called out his name. His family and friends couldn't wait for the bell.

"Listen to me now, Tony," said Pop, looking into Tony's eyes. "This guy is good. He's fast and can take you out with either hand. You're going to have to stay away but keep throwing out your left as fast and as often as you can. Keep circling to your right, that will take away some of the power from his right hand. Stick and move, stick and move, and keep your hands up."

Pop wiped some Vaseline over Tony's face. He slipped in his mouthpiece, tapped his gloves together and finished his prefight talk saying, "If he knocks you down, stay down till you hear the ref say 'eight'. Now go get him, tiger!"

Walker came out slow. He watched every move Tony made before he threw one punch. They both danced around until they met in the middle of the ring. Left, left, left, left, every punch landing on Tony's forehead. Tony throws out a left jab but misses. Left, left, left, left, again Walker lands four lefts so fast Tony couldn't do a thing about it. Tony throws a big right hand and misses badly, taking a short but powerful left hook to the jaw for his effort. Tony danced, that's a polite way of saying he was running around the ring trying to stay away from the quite evident better fighter. In the next ten seconds, Tony's life changed. Tony wasn't sure how many times he got hit in those ten seconds by the lighting punches of Chase Walker, but he figured it had to be in the vicinity of 2,000. The final punch was a devastating straight right hand that opened a cut above Tony's left eye. Tony had no idea he was bleeding, because at that moment he was flying across the ring and landing on his back. Tony would never forget the burning feeling he experienced as the sweat ran down his back into the brush burn created when he slid on the rough surface of the canvas. "Seven, eight," yelled the referee, but he might as well have been speaking French. Tony couldn't understand what he was saying because Tony was in no man's land. The next thing Tony remembered was the ref holding up Chase's hand and the announcer calling out, "At one minute and thirty-three seconds of the first round, the winner by knock out, Chase Waaaaalker!"

"What the hell did I tell you?" Big Tony said to his son as they drove to the doctor's office from the Kiel Center after the fight. "I'm proud of you for your effort, but what did I tell you about these fighters who fight year after year in these things. You did a great job just getting into the tournament, and I hope you learned a lesson, but as far as I'm concerned, you're done."

"OK Dad. I admit it. I didn't have any idea I was going to be out-classed so badly.

Count on this, it will be a cold day in hell before I ever step foot into a boxing ring again!"

"What a flash back," Tony said out loud as he rubbed the scar over his left eye. He got out of the car and walked into the house.

"Gina, honey, I'm home. Great news. We're the newest members of the Ballwin YMCA."

Chapter 3

Gina was excited about the Y membership. To her, it seemed like ever since she turned thirty-five, she'd had a difficult time keeping her figure. She owned a few exercise videos and would use one every now and again, but not as often as she'd like. She needed a concerted effort and the aerobics class offered at the Y was perfect for her. She couldn't wait to get started. She'd fit her workouts around Tony's schedule for the next week or so until Molly started back to school, and then she should be able to have it a little more regimented.

Gina was standing in the kitchen when the phone rang. She had a short conversation, hung up the phone and shouted up to her husband.

"Tony, do you care if Molly goes swimming at Jackie Warrens?"

"Did the Warrens ask or did the kid?" Tony yelled from his office at the top of the stairs.

"Maryanne Warrens called and said that she told Jackie she could have a couple of friends over, but we need to pick Molly up at 4:00. Can you pick her up when you get back from your appointment downtown?"

"Where are you going to be?" asked Tony.

"I told Betty I'd meet her for lunch and then we're going to Dad's furniture store."

"What in the world is she buying now?"

"She wants to get rid of that old blue recliner they have in the family room."

"That's Sam's favorite chair," exclaimed Tony.

"I said that. Then I asked if she said anything about it to Sam." She said she told him "Sam, I don't care what you say, the chair is going. It smells like old peoples' feet. It goes or I go.

"You know what your brother-in-law said to that," continued Gina. "He asked if he could have a couple of minutes to make up my mind."

"I love that guy." Tony laughed.

"Well, can you pick her up?" asked Gina again.

"Sure honey. I should be back here in the office by 3:00. I won't have any problem picking her up. Have a nice time and tell my sister I said hello."

Molly had heard the conversation between her parents and was already in her swimsuit when her mother walked into her room.

"Well, I guess there's no reason to ask you if you want to go over to Jackie's, since you have you suit on already."

"Oh yes Mom, I can't wait to go," said Molly. "I'm really glad they called. I am sooooo bored."

"I'll take you in a few minutes," Gina said, "but first I want you to eat some lunch."

"I'm not hungry," answered Molly.

"I don't care. You eat some lunch or you're not going."

"Can I just have a bowl of cereal?"

"I don't call that lunch, but OK," said Gina with a smile.

It was noon when Gina and Molly arrived at the Warrens'. Molly was pretty excited because she hadn't seen her friend since Jackie went to her grandmothers in Cleveland two weeks ago.

"Hi Molly!" said Jackie as Molly opened the car door.

"Jackie, I missed you."

"I missed you too. Come on in."

"Bye Mom, I love you!" said Molly as she grabbed her towel and started towards the front door.

"Molly, don't forget your father will be here at 4:00 to pick you up. Please be ready; you know how he is when you make him wait. Have a nice time, be careful, behave yourself, and Molly, I love you too honey, bye."

Gina left to meet Betty for lunch; Molly and Jackie rushed into the yard to go poolside. A few minutes later three more girls arrived, Lisa, Annabella, and Nancy. You could tell by their shrieks of joy they were all thrilled to be reunited with their companions. They were having withdrawals from not speaking to one another for two whole weeks and were eager to be filled in on Jackie's trip to Cleveland. Jackie told them about the Rock and Roll Hall of Fame, and the Cleveland Indians baseball game they went to, and how her uncle took everyone out on his yacht in Lake Erie. She told them that she had a wonderful time but that she missed them and she was glad she was home.

When it was Molly's turn she told the girls about the super fun she had at the Lake of the Ozarks with her mom and dad. She said that her dad rented a wave runner and even though it was against the rules and maybe even the law he let her drive it. He was sitting right behind her but she was doing the driving. What a riot! She continued by telling them all about her learning to water ski and what a ball she had tubing

25

and last but not least she giggled about all the fishing she and her dad did. She shared a big secret, too. One morning when she and her dad were out fishing he told her that he was the luckiest man in the world because she was his daughter. She said that she felt really neat about it and she thought her dad was super cool.

Lisa said all she did was sit around the house and was bored to the max. Nancy added a simple ditto. Anna spent her time watching her little sister. The only good thing about it was her parents gave her $20.00 a week.

After the gossip Jackie was quick to yell, "Last one in the pool is it."

Tony arrived at the Warrens' on time. Went to the front door, rang the bell, and much to his surprise Molly was ready to go. Tony told Molly to thank Mrs. Warner, and they headed to the car.

"Did you have fun, baby?" asked Tony

"Yes, Dad. Guess what, Jackie went to the Rock and Roll Hall of Fame, and it was neat."

"That's sounds great. How would you like to go there sometime?"

"Sometime, I guess, but there's a bunch of other places I'd like to go to first," said Molly. She continued, "Hey Dad, can we stop at Dairy Queen on the way home?"

"Molly, you know we're going to be eating dinner in a little while and your mother will kill me if we do."

"Please."

"OK," said Tony, "but whatever you get has to be a small and don't tell your mother."

"Thanks Dad, you're the best, and I won't, it will be our little secret."

Tony and Molly got back to the house about the same time as Gina. After asking Molly if she had a good time she asked Tony what he wanted for dinner.

He responded, "Surprise me."

While they sat enjoying a beautiful meal consisting of thinly sliced fried veal cutlets breaded in Italian breadcrumbs laced with a variety of Gina's magic spices (that's what she called them), a nice tomato and onion salad, and fresh corn on the cob, Tony interrupted the meal.

"Gina? Do you think we can get someone to watch Molly for four or five days starting the middle of next week?"

"What are you talking about?" she replied with an over acted puzzled look on her face.

"I thought we'd take a little vacation before school starts and I didn't think Molly would want to go."

"Could you speak English please 'cause I don't have a clue what you're talking about," she added with a sly look on her face.

"Well, I already bought three tickets but then I thought it over and decided, nah, Molly would hate it there."

"I want to go Daddy, where Daddy?"

"No honey it wouldn't be any fun for you."

"Yes it would, Dad."

"You don't even know where I'm talking about. How could you say it would be fun?"

"Well, tell me where and I'll tell you if it would be any fun or not."

"I don't know. You might say it sounds like fun and then when we get there you'd be complaining the whole time and your mother and I couldn't have any fun."

"Dad, I'm not a little girl anymore and I think I'm capable of making a decision if a place would be fun or not."

"What do you think Gina, should we let her decide?"

"OK, but whatever you decide Molly, that's final."

"Fine, where?"

In unison Tony and Gina said, "DISNEYLAND!"

Molly leaped from her seat and threw her arms around her father's neck and hugged him until she started to cry.

"We'll take that as a yes," said Gina.

With that said Molly swung over to hug her mother even harder.

A tear of joy rolled down Tony's face as he watched the sheer happiness on both of his girls' faces.

"That settles that. We leave on Wednesday," he said.

Tony and Gina, of course, had planned all of this the day Tony found out he had to go to Los Angeles on business. It just worked out so well with Molly still off of school and all. They were going to spend a few days just loafing around on the beaches down there and a few days watching their daughter have the time of her life at Disney.

They arrived at LAX early Wednesday morning, what with the time difference and all, got settled into their hotel room, had some lunch, and were lounging around on the beach by 2:00. Molly was in her glory as she shoveled sand all over Tony trying to cover everything but his head.

"Do you have to spoil her to this degree?" asked Gina. "That sand is going to get everywhere and I do mean everywhere."

"So what? The kid's having the time of her life and the sand will wash away as soon as I hit the surf."

"That's what you think."

With that said, Tony jumped up from under his sand blanket, grabbed his little girl under his arm, and ran towards the water.

"Don't Dad, the water's gonna be cold."

Too late; Tony was galloping like a horse in the shallow surf until it was over his knees and then splash . . . Molly hit the water. She came up laughing and so was Tony.

When they were finished playing in the water they walked hand in hand in the sand back to the blanket where Gina was sitting and watching. Gina looked like a movie star sitting there. In that moment Tony looked over at the smile on his daughter's face and then up at his beautiful wife and reality stuck him hard, he couldn't be any happier.

"Have I told you lately that you are the most beautiful woman in the world?"

"Don't try any of those swarthy Italian lines on me Mr. Russo. It's just a waste of time," she said smiling.

"Lines, lines, I mean it."

"I meant it's a waste of time 'cause if you think you're going to get lucky tonight, well, let me put it this way. You are."

Tony knelt down and kissed Gina full on the lips.

"DAD, people are watching."

Disneyland, well all you can you say is it's a paradise for kids of all ages. Tony and Gina had almost as much fun as Molly, *almost*. They squeezed in every ride they could in the two days and were able to go on a few of their favorites numerous times. Their favorite ride of all was Space Mountain. Space Mountain is a roller coaster ride with a twist— it's completely in the dark. You have no idea when you're going to climb or fall or jerk left or right but whenever you do you scream. The days flew by and before they knew it they were back in good old Saint Louis driving home from the airport.

No words were said as they pulled up the driveway. Gina and Tony looked up at each other and knew what the other was thinking. Mission accomplished.

The next day was business as usual. Tony went to work trying to make some money to pay for the trip. Gina was busy as usual, after all a homemaker's work is never done, and Molly was off telling her friends about everything. You know, living life.

29

Tony got home a little early, around 3:00, and thought he'd run off to the Y for a work out before dinner. He packed up a gym bag and off he went. Gina started dinner and Molly went down stairs to the basement to play.

It'd been awhile since Tony was in a gym working out, but he felt right at home. He started out simply, walking on a treadmill for a mile or so. Then he moved over to the lifting equipment. Here reality met embarrassment. He thought that he was pretty strong until he started following an older woman around the machines. He was lowering the weight on every piece of equipment he tried. He smiled to himself as he walked over to the boxing area. There he settled in and felt at home. He started out jumping rope, and man was he rusty. From the rope he went over to the speed bag, his favorite piece of equipment the YMCA had to offer. He started out slow, then tried to speed up but his timing was too far off he couldn't really get it going like he used to. He hit it pretty well but he figured it would take a few times before he could get back to form. He also had to admit that his arms, hell his whole body was sore with a capital S.

His next stop was the whirlpool bath. Ecstasy was the only word that could come to Tony's mind as he slipped into the water. He soaked for a good while and let the jets beat on every sore spot on his body, which was just about everywhere. The whole time he was soaking he couldn't help but think what a good move it was to get back into shape. He knew it would take hard work but nothing worthwhile ever comes easy. When he finally pulled himself from the whirlpool he went directly to the steam bath. He felt drained but he wanted to try everything.

He took a shower and was getting dressed when a young man who was holding a basketball said, "Excuse me mister but are you a fighter?"

"I used to be," replied Tony. "I sort of fooled around with the sport a couple hundred years ago."

"Did you ever fight anyone I might have heard of?" asked the inquisitive youth.

"Well," said Tony, "have you ever heard of Joe Frazier the ex-heavyweight champion of the world?"

"Yes! Who hasn't?"

Tony said, "Well, I lost a pretty close fight to his mother in a grocery store parking lot not too long ago."

The kid started laughing and so did Tony. Then, Tony told the kid about the Golden Gloves Tournament years ago, showing him his scar.

"It's a dumb sport," said Tony, "but it's a great way to get back into shape, and that's all I'm trying to do."

"I didn't mean to be noisy. I just saw you working out in the boxing room and there's hardly ever anyone working out in there. I just thought you might be somebody."

"No, I'm nobody, buddy, just an old out-of-shape salesman trying to get in a workout," said Tony as he finished tying up his shoes.

Tony grabbed his bag and had to push himself up. He was tired and sore as he headed home.

Approaching the corner to his street he noticed a commotion and sped up just a bit. Tony turned the corner and his heart dropped. There was a fire engine and an ambulance parked in front of his house. He stopped his car leaving it in the middle of the street and grabbed a firefighter who was sitting on the edge of the hook-and-ladder that was blocking the driveway.

"I'm Anthony Russo! This is my house! Where are my wife and kid? Is everybody safe? Is everybody alright?"

The fireman looked up, hesitated for a moment, pointed to the ambulance parked in the driveway and said, "Your wife."

31

Paul Tripi

That's as much as he got out before Tony took off toward the ambulance. Gina was lying on a stretcher. She was covered with soot and her hands were wrapped in bandages. She was out cold. Paramedics were administering oxygen when Tony stuck his head in the ambulance.

"Oh my God! Oh my God! Oh my God!" screamed Tony as he tried to scrambled into the back of the ambulance.

"Gina! Gina! Are you alright, honey?"

"Are you her husband?" asked one of the paramedics pushing Tony back away from the gurney and out of the ambulance.

"Yes," replied Tony as he wiped the tears from his eyes.

"Your wife is suffering from smoke inhalation and her hands and arms are severely burned. She is breathing on her own, and we expect her to be coming around soon." The paramedic placed his hand on Tony's shoulder.

"My daughter! My daughter! Was my little girl in the house?" he asked frantically. "Where is my daughter?"

Before he could answer, the fire chief standing behind Tony cleared his throat, asking, "Are you Mr. Russo?"

"Yes," replied Tony with a look of fear on his face.

"Mr. Russo, we believe that the water heater in the basement exploded which started the fire. Your daughter was apparently very close to the heater when it blew.

"Mr. Russo, we regret having to tell you that your daughter lost her life in the explosion."

"Noooooooooooooo!" screamed Tony. He dropped to his knees and wept. The life he once knew draining from his body with every tear.

Chapter 4

Tony sat looking catatonic in the emergency room waiting area of St. Paul Medical Center when his brother came running in. Tony and Gina's next-door neighbor Adrienne Jurkowski called Joe as soon as she found out where the ambulance was taking Gina. Joe was crying when he saw Tony. He rushed to his brother's side.

"My baby" is all Tony got out of his mouth before he broke down.

Joe tried to console his brother. He hugged him. He really couldn't say a word. He was crying too hard.

They stood there for a couple minutes, two rough tough rugged men, just holding each other, crying, not speaking. Joe gathered himself and asked. "Gina, how is Gina?"

"Her hands are burned pretty badly, and she swallowed a lot of smoke," Tony answered taking little breaths in between each word. "She's on a respirator in there." He pointed to the room directly across from where they were sitting.

"They asked me to wait here, and said they'd come out in a few minutes and let me know her condition."

"Was she able to talk? Did you talk to her in the ambulance? Does she know?" asked Joe.

Before he could answer, Tony's head dropped. He started to sob uncontrollably. Joe stood there a second then turned and yelled to a nurse who was just walking by.

"Nurse, nurse, please, can you help my brother."

Before she answered, the door to the room Gina was in, opened and a young doctor dressed in scrubs emerged and walked directly into the waiting room.

"Tony," said Joe as he rubbed Tony's back. "Tony, the doctor's here."

Tony lifted his head up but it was pretty obvious that Tony Russo was not in any shape to talk to the doctor.

"Just rest here a minute, Anthony," said Joe. "I'll take care of things here and I'll tell you everything in just a minute."

"Doctor, I'm Gina Russo's brother-in-law Joseph. This is my brother sitting right here. He is so distraught. It's probably better if I get the information and the instructions from you," said Joe.

Dr. Ito Row, first year intern, informed Joe that they had treated Gina for second-degree burns on both hands and on her right arm. He said that her breathing was smoke impaired but she was breathing on her own. They didn't believe that there was any damage to her lungs. They were aware of the details of the loss, and that due to Mrs. Russo's mental state, they presently had her sedated.

"We want to keep her for a little while for observation. She definitely would not be released today," said Dr. Ito.

"OK, thank you doctor. I'll take care of any of the necessary paperwork at the desk. But my brother, I'm worried about my brother. Can you give him something to calm him down?"

"It would be better to contact his personal physician, Mr. Russo. We would have to admit him before I could administer any medication. I would need his history and medication record before I could give him anything anyway," said the doctor.

"OK, I'll call Dr. Uhler right after I fill out the paperwork for Gina. Thank you again, doctor."

Just then Betty walked through the emergency room doors, spotted Joe, and ran to his side. Tears fell from her eyes as they hugged, and then Betty started sobbing.

"Oh my God, Joe," Betty cried.

"Betty, Betty, I know what kind of tragedy we're dealing with here, but you've got to try and pull yourself together. Please for Tony's sake." "Gina is alright. She's burned on her hands and one arm, and they're going to hold her overnight."

"It's our brother who I'm worried about."

"Sis I'm worried that he's having some kind of breakdown or something."

"I need you to keep yourself together, and go over there and stay with Tony while I fill out whatever it is I'm supposed to fill out."

"OK Joe, it's just that—" and with that Betty started to cry again. "Dear Lord."

"Betty, please."

Betty pulled herself together as best as she could, wiped her eyes, blew her nose, kissed her brother Joe, and said, "Where is Anthony?"

"He's there in the waiting room. Be strong Betty."

Betty walked into the waiting room and saw Tony bent over in a chair with his head in his hands. She tried to be strong but her heart was broken.

"Tony, honey," she said and she sat next to her brother.

"Oh Betty, my baby girl, my baby girl is dead," Tony choked out as he sobbed and sobbed.

Betty held her brother as tight as she could as he violently shook with emotion. She tried as hard as she could to keep her composure but couldn't and she burst out crying, the sadness was overwhelming. She sat there with her brother trying to console him while Joe completed Gina's paperwork.

Within fifteen minutes Gina's parents Babe and Regina Rancuso arrived, followed closely by Joe's wife Sally, and Betty's husband Sam. They all sat in the waiting room while they waited for Gina to be moved into a room. Joe gave the details concerning Gina's condition to the Rancusos, Sally, and Sam, nothing else was said. Tony quietly sat in the room while Joe talked. He just sat there staring into space. It was evident to everyone that Tony was in shock.

Joe went up to the ER desk. This time a nurse came to check on Tony. She checked his eyes and took his blood pressure and said everything checked out OK. She told Joe and Betty to keep an eye on him and get him something to help him sleep. Most importantly, don't leave him alone. While this was going on Regina and Babe sat on the other side of the room, crying. The loss of their little granddaughter and the condition of their daughter was too much to bear.

Sam traveled back and forth from each side of the room trying to be strong for everyone. He was helping. It appeared that he was in control of his emotions but if you were to look into his face you would see that even though he was trying to be the voice of reason tears were dropping from his eyes and at a pretty good pace.

The nurse who had checked on Tony came back ten minutes later to inform the family that Gina had been moved to room 115 in the east wing. She said Gina was heavily sedated. They did not expect her to be awake for the rest of the evening. If anyone wanted to stay, there was a waiting room at the end of her hall.

"Thank you," said Joe who had obviously taken charge.

"Tony, I think it would be a good idea if you went someplace and tried to get some sleep," said Joe as he looked over to Betty. "Why don't you go over to Betty's? I'll take care of things here. Nothing is going to happen with Gina until morning anyway."

"Thanks Joseph, but I'm not going anywhere."

"Tony, the nurse said you needed to get some rest and the doctor said that you should call Dr. Uhler. Have him prescribe something that will help you rest."

"No," said Tony, "I'm staying right here."

Joe grabbed Tony by the shoulders, stared right into his eyes and said. "Tony we are going to need every bit of strength we have to get through this. We are going to stand by each other and do whatever is necessary. What's necessary right now is that you get some rest. Please go home with Betty."

"Look Joe, I'm listening to everything that you're saying and I will never be able to thank you for what you're doing right now. Let me just stay here a while just so I can be near her," Tony responded with a look that said thank you brother I love you.

"Whatever you want Tony," answered Joe. "I'll stay with you. But at some point tonight you're coming home with me."

"OK, thank you Joseph," Tony said and hugged his brother tightly.

Sally sat quietly mourning in a chair next to Betty. She got up and called her husband over to her. They embraced. She, too, was being as strong as she could but it was her turn to lose it.

"I'm sorry Joe, I just can't help it," she said as she buried the side of her face into his chest and cried.

"Everything will be alright honey. God just wanted Molly to be with him," Joe said, ever weakening from the ordeal.

Babe and Regina sat next to Tony, holding each other's hand, not saying a word. Sometimes silence says everything. After a while Babe went over to the nursing station to verify everything that they had been told thus far. The desk nurse reiterated what Gina's nurse had said and convinced Babe that it would be better if they went home and got some rest themselves. When they come back in the morning their daughter would be awake and lucid.

Babe called Joe over and shared the nurse's words with him. "What are you going to do Joe?" asked Babe.

"I'm going to stay here with my brother until we are both convinced that Gina's alright."

"Do you want me to stay with you boys?"

"Of course you can, but I think you'd better stay with your wife right now Babe. Tonight is going to be hell on her."

"It will be hell on us all."

Shortly afterwards, Babe walked over to Joe and quietly said, "Regina wants everybody to come to the house when we leave here for something to eat. What do you think about that?"

"Thank you Babe, I think that's a good idea."

"I know that everyone would probably like to stay here. But, the only purpose that would serve is we'd all be together."

"I think you're house is a perfect place for all of us right now," Joe said gratefully. "I'll try and talk my brother into going over to your place now and then in a little while coming back here and check on Gina. Then I plan on taking him home with me."

"OK, Joe that sounds like a good idea."

"We'll leave now and get some food ready."

"Babe don't have Regina go to any trouble, some coffee would be just fine," replied Joe.

"It won't be any trouble Joe, plus being busy might help her get some of this off her mind."

Joe called everyone over to where Tony was sitting and conveyed the Rancuso's invitation.

"Ma, you don't have to do that, just go home and rest," Tony told his mother-in-law.

"Never you mind, we all need to eat something to keep up our strength. Now you are all coming. I won't take no for an answer," said Regina convincingly.

"Do you have any liquor in the house?" Tony asked Babe.

"All you want, son, all you want," answered Babe as he and his wife hugged everybody and got ready to leave.

Regina, Sally, and Betty sat in the kitchen of the Rancuso's elegant town house in the St. Louis suburb of Town and Country, Missouri. The large kitchen had two bay windows overlooking a lovely flower garden created by Regina's green thumb.

The house, a palatial three story, was magnificently decorated and furnished exquisitely.

Of course, what else would be expected? They did own a furniture store. They had a library off of the dining room that would put a law office to shame, and an elegantly furnished den just off that. Their home and its surrounding spoke volumes about the success of the Rancuso's.

Babe, Tony, Joe, and Sam were sitting in the den, drinking Irish coffees when Babe said to Tony, "When you leave the hospital with Gina tomorrow, we would like you to move in with us for awhile. At least until the insurance company has a chance to do the repairs on your home.

39

"Mom can take care of Gina and you can setup shop in my office up stairs. Please don't say no," pleaded his father-in-law.

Joe spoke before Tony had a chance to answer.

"Tony, I think your father-in-law is making a whole lot of sense." "We'll bring Gina here tomorrow and then either you, me, and Sam or just me and Sam can take care of the insurance people and—" Joe stopped for a second before he finished. "And the arrangements."

Tony lowered his head and started to cry again. Joe didn't want to broach the subject but it had to be discussed.

"Joe why don't you take care of Tony and Gina and the house stuff, Betty and I will take care of the other thing that has to be taken care of," said Sam as he watched Tony sink deeper into his chair.

"Alright Sam. We'll talk in the morning and work out some of the details," replied Joe.

Tony composed himself, took a deep breath, and answered. "Dad, thank you, I think it would be best for us to stay with you.

"Sam, I don't think I can help you with, with, that, with—" He stopped and started sobbing.

Betty rushed in from the kitchen, sat on the arm of Tony's chair, and put her arms around her brother. She didn't say a word. Joe thought this might be a good time for Betty to talk to Tony alone and signaled the others to leave the room. He nodded to Betty and went into the kitchen.

"Are you alright Anthony?" questioned Betty in a loving tone.

"I can't believe this. I can't believe this is really happening. What am I going to do Betty?" answered Tony. "What am I going to do?"

"Well, first you're going to take care of Gina," answered Betty, "Then the two of you are going to have to get on with your lives." She continued.

"Get on with our lives!" Spurted Tony. "Get on with our lives! What lives? I died today Betty." Tony hesitated and said, "I have no reason to live."

"Anthony, you have a beautiful loving wife who is going to need every bit of support and love you can give her right now. You have a family that loves you and will stand by you no matter what happens. No one will forget what happened today. We'll never forget it as long as we live.

"But life goes on. Be brave for her!" She kissed her brother on the forehead.

Joe and Sam came back into the den and sat on the couch by Tony's chair. Sam reluctantly asked Tony a few questions concerning Molly's arrangements. Tony replied by simply saying, "Sam, I trust your judgment. Do whatever you think is necessary. I don't care about the cost. I don't even want to know anything about it.

"Sam, thank you, brother."

Sam got up, took Betty by the hand and they walked out of the den.

"Tony, do you think we should go back to the hospital now?"

"We'll check on Gina and then we'll go back to my place and crash," said Joe. "Do you want to go by the house first?"

Tony looked into his brother's face and said slowly and succinctly, "I'll never step foot in that house again. I mean it Joe. Never."

Chapter 5

The limousine carrying Gina and Tony pulled out of the cemetery and headed, along with fifty other cars, to the Alaina's of Chesterfield restaurant for a breakfast prepared in Molly's memory. The room was quiet. Most people exchanged greetings, had a little to eat, expressed their sympathies, and left. The Russo family was of course the last to leave.

Babe paid the bill, walked back to the family table and suggested, "Why don't we all go back to the house? I don't know about you but I could use a drink."

Tony's mom and dad told everybody to go ahead and go to the Rancuso's without them they would take all the children over to Joe and Sally's and see everyone there later.

"Thanks, Mom." Tony kissed his mother.

Tom, Gina's brother, was doing the pouring in the den while Judy, his wife, prepared the coffee in the kitchen. As usual the men gathered in one room and the women in another. Gina was staring out the kitchen widow, not really looking at anything when her mother said. "Honey, let me take a look at your hands."

"I'm fine, mother."

"I didn't ask you how you felt; I said I need to check your bandages."

"OK Mom, but everything is fine."

"I think it might be a good idea if you were to lie down for just a bit?" suggested Regina as she eyed the bandages on her daughter's hands.

"Not right now Mom, maybe in a while."

Betty and Sally moved into the den sitting next to their husbands. Babe and Tom drifted out of the den into the library.

"Dad, what can I do to help Gina and Tony with all this," asked Tom.

"I don't know what to tell you son. This is something I never thought that I'd have to deal with."

"I know what you mean Dad, it's unbelievable. How has Sis been handling it so far?"

"She's trying to be brave but she's had periods of non stop crying. Who could blame her?"

"What about Tony?"

"I'm really worried about Tony, son. He's staying completely to himself, and I've never seen him drink like this. He and your sister haven't been communicating at all. He's withdrawing into some kind of cocoon or something."

"Have you tried talking to him?"

"Not really Tom, it's too soon, and I don't know what to say."

"What about their home? What's going on with that?"

"Joe and Sam are taking care of the house, as far as the insurance and the repairs are concerned. I'll tell you this. I don't think Tony cares one bit about the house, in fact he's been saying he'll never go there again, and I believe him."

"What about Gina? What's she saying?" Tom asked with a worried voice.

"I don't know. She really hasn't said anything other than she's leaving all the decisions to Tony. I'm not seeing them doing much talking though."

"That's terrible," exclaimed Tom, "Just terrible."

The Rancuso house was quiet after the Russo family left. Gina went up stairs to lie down. Tony sat with Tom in the den. Tony was getting pretty deep into a bottle of scotch and Tom wasn't about to stop him. Even though he knew it wasn't going to help.

"I met a few of your customers this morning," said Tom. "They think highly of you, Tony."

"Yeah, Tom, I'm a lucky man," replied Tony as sarcastically as he could.

Tom got the hint and left Tony to his bottle. Judy was sitting on the patio with her in-laws when Tom came out the back door. "I tried to talk to Tony but I couldn't. I didn't know what to say."

"I told you we've been really worried about him," said Babe.

"Gina has been unbelievably sad, but consistent," said Regina. "But Tony, he's staying to himself and he's becoming a very angry man."

"I can understand that," said Judy. "All we can do is give them support and love, I hate saying this but time does heal all wounds," continued Judy.

"Some wounds just don't heal," said Regina, and she started to cry.

When Gina got up from her nap, she and Tony went over to Joe's to continue the worst day of their lives. Big Tony asked his son and daughter-in-law to come back with them to Florida. He thought it would be good for them to get away for a while. Just to get out of their environment while Joe and Sam took care of the house and stuff. Gina hugged them, told them how much they loved them, and declined the invitation. She said maybe they would come for a visit in a few months. Right now there were just too many decisions that had to be made.

Maria, Tony's mom, put up a little fight but in the end she understood. Tony and Gina stayed a respectable amount of time, hugged and kissed all, and left. They drove back to Gina's folk's house without speaking a word to one another. There just wasn't anything to say.

After a few days, Big Tony and Maria returned to Florida, Tom and Judy to Chicago. Babe went back to work at the store. Tony, now working from his in-law's home, made a few business calls but his heart wasn't really in it. Regina was caring for her daughter as if it was a full time job, and Gina was recuperating nicely. On the surface it seemed like things were getting back to normal. In reality Tony was screwed up and drinking heavily.

Tony was sitting in the corner of Braden's Saloon on Manchester Road in Ballwin. He was digging in pretty good when Joe walked in.

"What's up," said Joe. He grabbed a stool and sat next to Tony.

"Nothing Joe, I just wanted to have a few drinks with my brother," answered Tony.

"Well it seems as though you've got a head start on me," Joe said sarcastically.

"Yeah, I've been here a while," retorted Tony. "What'll you have?"

"Ah, I think I'll have a beer."

"Hey Matt, when you get a chance, a long neck for my brother and give me a refresher."

Joe gave Tony a good looking over, and shook his head.

"Look at you, what are you doing to yourself? What's with all this drinking?"

"Nothing, it's nothing, I'm just having a couple of drinks," replied

Tony as he took a long pull on his scotch and water.

"I wish you'd slow down. This is getting to be just too much! You're getting sloshed every night!"

"Mind your own damn business," responded Tony in a loud voice.

"This is my business, and don't raise your voice to me," Joe responded in a calm but firm tone.

"I'm sorry, I'm sorry Joe, I'm just sick of everybody talking to me about my drinking. I need it right now, OK, I need it," Tony said as he dropped his head down on his arms.

"Look Tony, it's just that you've got everybody so damn worried."

"I'll be fine, I'll be fine."

After three beers Joe was ready to go. But, it was evident that Tony wasn't going anywhere. Joe felt that if he tried to talk Tony into leaving with him it would just start a loud argument and that's not at all what he wanted. After all, who knew Tony better than Joe? No one was going to talk Tony Russo into doing something he didn't want to do. When Tony got up to go to the men's room, Joe called Matt over. He paid the tab and said.

"Matt, here's an extra twenty, when my brother gets ready to leave make sure it's in a cab and here's my home number just in case he won't listen."

Tony came back, Joe gave him some brotherly advice and left. The bar was starting to fill as it got later into the evening. The people kind of stayed out of Tony's corner. He was drinking hard, crying, and not caring a bit who saw him. It was three younger guys who crossed the imaginary line between Tony and the rest of the bar. Tony didn't care, as long as they left him alone. And they did for a little while, and then it happened. One of the guys said something about the drunk in the corner, and Tony's ears perked up.

"Who is this guy," the tall one asked the heavyset one.

"I don't know but he's in our part of the bar."

"Yeah, he's cramping our style," he replied as he walked over to where Tony was sitting.

"Excuse me pal, but this part of the bar is reserved, move!" said the young man in an unfriendly tone.

"You talking to me?" Tony asked staring right through the guy.

"Who do you think I'm talking to old man?"

"Look you little punk you say one more word to me and I'll drop you like a bad habit." Tony stood up.

The guy didn't know what to say. He turned around and walked back to his group. Within seconds the toughest looking one of the three strolled over to Tony and said, "Hey, moron," and grabbed at Tony's shirt.

Before he could get another word out of his mouth Tony threw a short right hand and caught the kid flush on the jaw.

He went down and Tony showed him no mercy. He kicked him square in the face and turned to face the other two who were already on their way. The tall one threw a shot at Tony's face but Tony saw it coming. He lowered his chin so the kid ended up punching Tony right on the top of his hard head. Not fazing Tony at all but hurting the hell out of the tall guy's hand. Tony threw a combination at the heavyset guy and all three punches landed, dropping him where he stood. The tall guy grabbed a beer bottle and yelled something at Tony. Tony looked right into the kid's face and said, "Drop that bottle kid, or I'll kill you. Did you hear what I just said, I won't just beat the hell out of you, I will kill you."

Matt was over the bar by now and was keeping everybody back.

"Drop the bottle Richard, he's not kidding."

"Drop it right now," Matt yelled.

He jumped in between the two combatants. Richard dropped the bottle and started explaining to Matt what happened. Tony didn't even pay attention and went back to his drink on the bar.

"What are you talking about Richard, I saw the whole thing," yelled Matt.

"Tony do you want me to call the police? Do you want to press charges?"

"No, just get them out of my face.

"And hey Dick or whatever your name is, you ever say another word to me again and I'll bust you up so bad you'll be eating soup for a month. You got that? Now pick up your buddies and get them out of my sight!"

Within ten minutes of Matt's call, Joe came running in the bar.

"Tony, are you alright? What the hell happened?"

"Nothing, I had a slight altercation. It's all over now," said Tony calmly.

"I knew I shouldn't have left you alone," exclaimed Joe.

"What are you talking about? It's nothing. It's over," retorted Tony

"I'm talking about your drinking. That's what I'm talking about. Your drinking's the cause of all this," shouted Joe.

"Will you stop with the drinking crap talk? I drink, so what?" he continued.

"Tony, let me just take you home, will ya. Haven't you had enough for one night?"

"Alright Joe, let's go."

When Tony walked into the house Gina was waiting for him. It was time they had a talk.

The drinking and the late nights were becoming a daily event and Gina was worried.

"Tony, this has got to stop," said Gina.

"What's the big deal, I just had a few drinks, that's all," responded Tony.

"The big deal is that it's more than a few drinks and it's every night. It's got to stop."

"Leave me alone, Gina! Just leave me alone!"

"I can't leave you alone Tony! You're my husband and I love you. I can't leave you alone!

"She was my daughter too, I know what you're going through," she sobbed. "We can't let this break up our family."

"Our family died, don't you understand that?" Tony screamed

"For crying out loud Tony! Our daughter died, not our family, unless you kill what's left," Gina said as she stood up and left the room.

Tony sat at the kitchen table put his head in his hands and just cried.

The next morning Babe walked into the kitchen and was startled by the sight of his son-in-law sleeping with his head lying on the table. He walked over to Tony and shook him.

"For crying out loud Tony. What are you doing to yourself?" said a concerned father-in-law.

"I don't know what the hell I'm doing," said Tony.

"Let me get you some help," replied Babe.

"What kind of help can you give me Dad? Nobody can help me."

"I know a guy who helps people deal with tragedies like this. I think it would be good if both you and Gina made an appointment to see the guy," said Babe.

"I don't know Dad, maybe. It's just that right now I don't feel like talking to anybody about anything."

"I just don't like seeing you like this son, and quite honestly your drinking's got us worried," said Babe.

I'm alright Dad," said Tony as he stood up and hugged his father-

49

in-law. "I just want to thank you for everything."

Two days later Tony was back in his usual bar stool at Braden's when Gina walked through the front door. She spotted her husband, walked over, and sat on the barstool next to him.

"Tony, come home."

"Gina, I'm sorry. I can't, if you haven't notice I'm having a tough time dealing right now."

"I just don't think that drinking is helping anybody," replied Gina.

"It helps me," responded Tony.

"Helping you ruin our marriage?"

"If that's what you think then why don't you just get the hell out of my life."

Gina looked at Tony in astonishment. Got up from her seat and walked out.

"The hell with it," said Tony and he guzzled down another scotch.

Tony was a sad, confused, and angry man when the two leather-jacketed men came into Braden's and sat next to him. Tony was eyeing down the duo kind of sizing them up when one of the long hairs said, "What are you looking at?"

Tony came back with his usual, "You talking to me."

"Who the hell you think I'm talking to?" answered the stranger.

"You looking for a fight buddy?" asked Tony.

"Maybe, old man."

"Then why don't you stick your head up my ass and fight for air?" replied Tony as he positioned himself in the corner so he wouldn't be as vulnerable when both guys came at him. And he knew they were coming. He was right. The longhaired one threw the first punch and it caused some damage as it landed plum in the middle of Tony's face. Tony's nose started bleeding immediately. Tony got a good shot of his own off, trying to incapacitate mister long hair with the most deadly of all punches, a throat punch. It landed high on the guy's chest but not close enough to the throat to drop him. By this time his friend had joined in and Tony was in a lot of trouble. Tony was punching away as fast as he could throw his hands and he was landing but not enough to keep them at bay. He was taking a pretty good beating. Mathew was not working that night, the new bartender had called the cops as soon as the fight broke out but didn't do much to stop the fight. The biker guys left before the cops arrived, leaving Tony lying on the ground in a pool of his own blood. The cops questioned Tony as he cleaned himself up. He wasn't seriously hurt but he looked terrible. He gave the police a description of the two men, which by the way could have been anybody in the city wearing leather jackets. He didn't care what they did with them. He wasn't going to pursue the matter. He just wanted to go home. The police offered to take Tony to the hospital to be checked out, he thanked them and declined.

Tony left the bar but instead of going to his in-laws', he drove to his brother Joe's.

"Oh my God," shouted Joe as soon as he laid eyes on his brother. "What the hell happened?"

"I was just in the wrong place at the wrong time," answered Tony.

"What bar were you in?" asked Joe. "

"Braden's," said Tony.

"Let me take a look at you. I think we ought to take you to the hospital. Your eye is starting to close."

"I can see fine, out of both eyes. I'm alright," answered Tony. "I just came over here because," he hesitated for a moment "because I had some words with Gina tonight, and I couldn't face her."

"That's all!" said Joe as frustrated as could be. "That's it! This crap has got to stop! I mean it Tony. You call this a life?" Joe shook as he spoke.

51

Tony sat down on the couch and began sobbing.

"And I'm sick of the damn crying too," shouted Joe. "Be a man for crying out loud!"

Tony took a few deep breaths, stood up and headed towards the door.

"Wait a minute! Where are you going? Wait Tony! I'm sorry! Tony, Tony! I'm sorry!"

It was too late; the door closed. Tony was gone.

Chapter 6

It was brutally hot. In fact the heat was rising from the asphalt when the doorbell rang at the Russo's Florida home. Maria was flabbergasted to see the disfigured face of her son standing on the other side of the door.

"Oh sweet Jesus, Anthony, what happened to you? What are you doing here? Oh my God, what happened?"

"Mom, Mom everything is alright, I'm fine, really I'm fine," answered Tony.

"What happened? What are you doing here? Is everything alright?" his mother frantically asked.

"Mom, everything is fine. I had a little fight, that's all. I'm fine. I just needed to get away from everything for a little while so I came down here for a short visit," Tony said calmly.

"Oh my son, *Mi bella Bedu,*" she said as she hugged her son. "Sit down. I'll make you something to eat."

"In a little while Mom, Just make some coffee now. Where's

Dad?"

"He's golfing, but he should be home any minute," she answered as she poured water into the coffee maker. "Tell me what happened. Where is Gina?"

"Look Mom, we've been having a tough time since the baby died. It's me. I can't cope with it. I'm making it worse for everyone and I know it. I just don't know what to do," Tony said pouring out his heart.

"Well, first thing tomorrow morning we'll go to church and we'll talk to Father Polino."

"Sorry Mom but to me there is no God! No God would take an innocent little girl's life for no reason. I'll never go to church again. So don't ask me," Tony said firmly.

"*Dio mia* , Anthony, how could you say such a thing?" She made the sign of the cross touching her head, her heart and both shoulders. "God wanted my granddaughter with him. That's where she is now, in a better place, with God," said his mother so sweetly.

"Well, I wanted her here with me, and I don't want to hear about any heaven crap," Tony exclaimed as the door opened and his father walked in.

"Anthony, what are you doing here? What the hell happened to you?"

"I'm fine Dad. I had a little scrap, that's all. You should see the other guy," Tony said as he hugged his father.

"I just came down to see you guys, and to get away for a bit."

"Good, it's good to see you son," said Big Tony. "Marie, make the boy something to eat."

"I'm not hungry right now, Dad but mom is making coffee. You want some?"

"Yeah, I'll have a cup. Have a seat Anthony, tell me what's happening."

Tony felt better just being around his parents and out of St. Louis. He sat with them in their screened in porch and explained about the troubles he was having coping with the loss of his daughter. He didn't go deeply into his drinking, which even he was starting to recognize as a problem. He told them about the problem that was developing between he and his wife and he told them about walking out on his brother Joe.

"Son, it sounds to me like you need some professional help. You can't allow yourself to lose everything you've worked so hard for!"

"I think you're right dad, I'll tell you what, I'm feeling better just being here with you and mom right now. When I get home I'll talk to someone."

"Thank God," said Maria

"God doesn't have anything to do with it, Mom."

"Anthony, please son. Don't say stuff like that."

"OK, sorry Mom, but that's just how I feel."

"Tony, did you tell anybody you were coming here?" asked big Tony.

"Not really Dad," answered Tony.

"Go call Gina right now."

"OK, Dad."

Tony called Gina. The conversation was a short one, she was glad he was safe but she didn't want to talk. Tony went back out to the screen room to sit with his parents. About an hour later the phone rang, it was Joe. Tony apologized to his brother immediately. Joe responded with an apology of his own.

He told Tony he thought it was a good idea going to Florida. He told him he had some good news. He had an offer on the house and

55

wanted to know what Tony wanted to do about it. Tony thought the offer was fair and since he wanted out of that house really at any cost, he told Joe to take the offer and run. Tony reminded Joe that he had power of attorney and that he trusted him emphatically. He told him to confer with Gina. Joe said he already had.

"What did Gina say?" said Tony.

"She said it was OK with her if it was OK with you," replied Joe.

"Then dump it," said Tony.

"Alright, Anthony, consider it done," responded Joe.

"Joe, thank you. I love you brother."

"I love you too, Tony. Have a nice time with the folks and I'll see you when you get home. Let me say hello to mom and dad."

The Russos lived in a lovely retirement community. They had a network of friends that they do everything with. There are a few couples so close they might as well be joined at the hip.

It was Tuesday. Every Tuesday the group goes to dinner at the Seafood Hut restaurant. It's all you can eat seafood buffet night, for $12.95. It has become a ritual for the Russo's and their friends.

Lefty Stephens and his wife Donna were the first to arrive at the Russo's door.

"Hello, in the house!" shouted Lefty as he stuck his head in the door.

"Lefty, come on in," said Big Tony. "Is Donna with you?"

"Of course" said Lefty. "You guys ready to go?"

"*Minga*," responded Big Tony. "I forgot it was Tuesday."

"I don't think we're going tonight, Lefty. My son's here from St. Louis visiting."

"Wait a minute, Dad," Tony said as he walked into the kitchen. "If you're talking about going out to dinner, I'm in. I'm celebrating, I just sold the house.

"I'd love to take you and mom out for dinner, let's go," Tony said using a tone of voice he hadn't used since the tragedy.

"Good," responded his father "I would love for you to meet our friends, starting with this crazy guy, Lefty Stephens. "Lefty, I'd like to introduce you to my oldest son Anthony."

"Lefty," said Tony sticking out his hand to meet his father's friend. "I can't tell you how much my father has told me about you."

"Don't believe everything you hear, Anthony," said Lefty. "If he told you about the trouble I'm in, I swear to you she told me she was sixteen."

Tony laughed out loud for the first time in a long while. Marie strolled into the kitchen holding Donna's hand.

"Donna, this is my handsome son, Anthony. As you can see he's all boy. I know what you're thinking but all he said to me was you should have seen the other guy."

No questions were asked concerning Tony's facial condition.

"It's a pleasure to meet you, Tony. I have to tell you, we love your parents so much that you're like family to us. We are so happy to finally meet you," said the attractive elderly woman.

"Donna, the pleasure is mine," responded Tony "Now, come on, let's get something to eat." He put his arm around his mother.

"Andy and Russell have already gone ahead," said Lefty. "They said they'd save us a table."

"Good, if everybody's ready, let's go," said Big Tony.

Andy and Terri Winter had already arrived at the restaurant and were sitting with Russ and Colleen La Motta when Big Tony's small group strolled in. Marie took care of the introductions and everyone ordered a drink.

"Some guy said my mother wasn't the best cook in the world so what else could I do." Said Tony humorously, dodging any questions that may have come up concerning his war wounds.

"Well in little Tony's honor, I would like to tell a joke," said Lefty.

"No, please spare us!" said Russ.

"Spare you, for crying out loud I'm about to dazzle you," said Lefty with a big smile.

"There's nothing we can do about this so let him tell it so we can get this over with," said Donna and she gave the floor to her husband.

"OK, get ready to laugh," said Lefty. "There were three blondes walking down the street," started Lefty

"No dumb blonde jokes," said Colleen, the only blonde at the table.

"Come on Colleen you know there isn't one of you lovely ladies that can remember what your real hair color is, anyway," answered Lefty.

"You're right. Proceed," said Colleen with a giant smile.

"OK, there were these three dumb blondes walking down the street. All of a sudden one of them said in a disgusted tone. "Oh my God look at that dog across the street with only one eye.

"The other two dumb blondes covered up one of their eyes and looked across the street at the dog."

Everyone at the table burst out laughing. Lefty was a funny guy and he had a great delivery. Everything Tony had heard about these people was true. It made him feel happy for his parents. These folks were wonderful and it was quite obvious they were all very close friends.

"Did you hear about the dumb blonde and the moron who were walking down the street," continued Lefty.

"I think we're about to!" said Andy.

"Well it seems that this moron was walking down the street with this dumb blonde when the moron says to the blonde, "If you can guess how many quarters I've got in my pocket, I'll give you both of them. The blonde thought for a second and said three?"

"Stop it, you're killing me," said Big Tony sarcastically.

Tony looked over at his dad, winked, and said to Lefty. "I'll tell you what Lefty, as a personal gift to you for being my dad's friend I'm going to tell you the funniest joke I've ever heard. You are going to get a lot of miles out of this joke, guaranteed because it has to do with getting older and since you live in a retirement community, well, you'll see."

Tony started by saying, "Did you know when you get older, people tend to lose their hearing a little? Well it seems an older couple went to their doctor for their yearly physicals, together, and while the woman was busy with the nurse the husband told the doctor that he was really worried about his wife's hearing and asked if there was some kind of a test he could give her at home to check it out? 'Yes,' answered the doctor, "You can give her the twenty, ten, five test and let me know the results."

"I will Doc but I don't know what that test is."

"Well, you get about twenty feet from her and start a conversation. If there is no reply, move to ten feet. No reply again, move to five, and if that's the case call my office immediately and set up an appointment for her to be tested for hearing aids."

"I'll do it as soon as we get home," said the worried husband.

When they arrived home the woman went into the kitchen to start dinner. The husband calculated what was twenty feet away and in a clear voice asked.

"Honey, what's for dinner?'

No response—he shook his head a little and moved to ten feet. He asked again, "Honey, what's cooking?"

Again no response—he shook his head even more and he moved to five feet. He asked again with an extremely worried voice, "Honey what's for dinner."

She replied in a very loud voice, *"Turkey—for the third time."*

Lefty laughed so hard his drink came shooting out of his nose. He hadn't laughed that hard in a long time. You couldn't tell if the rest of the group was laughing at the joke or at how hard Lefty was laughing, but everyone was in tears with laughter.

When Lefty caught his breath he said to Tony. "That's it. I give up. I have no reason to tell another joke. I give."

"Thank you," said Tony as he stood up and took a bow.

Driving home, Tony was truly pleased to see how much his mom and dad were enjoying their retirement. It was obvious that they had a wonderful circle of friends and it sounded like they had an almost endless social calendar. For the first time in a very long time Tony felt contentment. He felt good about himself knowing that he had made the right decision to visit his parents in Florida. He also knew his mission was accomplished and he wouldn't have to stay long. He felt better. He had needed that escape.

Sunday morning, Marie and Big Tony went to church but they couldn't talk Tony into joining them. When they returned they found their son had packed up the few things he had brought and was ready to go. He told them he felt much better and he thought he was ready to go home and get back down to business. They hugged each other and Tony started to leave. Turning, he said, "Thank you Mom and Dad. I needed this. I feel better! I love you both so much," he completed his turn and walked out the door. Tony felt like it was going to be more than a trip home. He felt like it was the beginning of his journey back.

Chapter 7

Gina was stunned when she left Braden's the night Tony told her to get out of his life. She knew he was having a horrible time and was unable to cope with their loss of their daughter. But, she had enough of his drinking, and his attitude. What was he thinking that she wasn't suffering? Her daughter! The absolute love of her life! Her baby, gone. She needed Tony more now than she ever needed him before. And what does she get from him? Understanding, support, no. All she got was, if you don't like it get out of my life. She went home and cried herself to sleep. The next morning she awoke with a new philosophy of living. The man she loved! The man she married. He was gone and she wasn't going to deal with the man who took his place. She had to take him up on his offer. She was getting out of his life.

Tony stepped off the plane at Lambert Field. As soon as he did the sinking feeling he had been living with these past months came back and hit him like a ton of bricks. He hesitated. He was going to pick up the phone and call Gina. Instead he picked up his car and started driving around. He ended up at Braden's. After a few pick me ups, he called his brother Joe and asked him if he wanted to join him for a drink. Joe really didn't want to, but he agreed and said he'd be there in a few minutes.

"Hey, Joe!" Tony said as Joe pulled up a stool. "How are you my brother?" he continued.

"I'm fine. The question is how are you?"

"It was good to get with the folks. It did get my mind off everything a little. I feel rested."

"But!" said Joe.

"But it just seems like my life is so screwed up right now a few days away has only postponed everything," said Tony with a dejection in his voice that scared Joe.

"What do you mean everything? What are you talking about?"

"For one thing, my business is hurting, Joe. I've neglected it. Worst than that, I've stepped on so many toes. I don't know if I can save it," Tony confessed. "But most importantly, Gina has made it clear that she had enough of me."

"What are you talking about? I just talked to her about the house and she didn't say anything nor did she imply anything concerning your relationship."

"Trust me Joe, why do you think I'm in this bar right now? Don't you think I'd have gone straight home to my wife?"

"Some things were said, and it's more than that. Ever since Molly died it hasn't been the same between us," said Tony staring at the ground.

"For crying out loud, Tony," was the only response Joe had.

Joe was aware that the drinking caused by his grief was engulfing Tony's life, but he had not assumed it had deteriorated to this.

"What did Gina say?"

"It's not what she said so much, although when we talked the other day it was pretty obvious to me that she didn't care what I was saying or doing."

"It all stems from what I said to her," said Tony.

"Oh God, what did you say?" asked Joe with a disgusted look.

"She was giving me trouble about my drinking, and I let her have it," said Tony. "I don't know exactly how I said it, but basically, I told her to get out and stay out of my life."

"Oh my God, Tony," Joe said shaking his head. "Get in your damn car right now, go over to your in-laws, get down on your knees and beg that woman to forgive you. You stupid idiot."

"I can't face her."

"Well, if you don't, you're going to lose the best thing that ever happened to you. Don't screw this up Anthony, I promise you, you'll regret it the rest of your life."

"What if she won't listen to me?"

"Make her listen, plead, beg, whatever it takes. Just make her listen."

"But what if she won't?"

"If she's that mad don't argue with her, just give her time to cool off. Come over to the house and stay with us until the time is right," suggested Joe.

"Thanks, you're the best brother in the world."

"Yeah, yeah, yeah, I know, I know, now just go home to your wife."

"OK I'm going right now, thanks again."

"You can thank me by not showing up at my door," said Joe as they both got up and left.

Tony walked up to the front door, and knocked. Gina answered the door.

"We have to talk," said Tony.

"Yes, we do Tony. But not here. Let me grab my purse and we'll go out for a cup of coffee."

They never made it to the restaurant, in fact the car never moved. What started out as a civil discussion grew into a violent argument. It ended abruptly with Gina slamming the car door and screaming.

"Get out of my life you bastard! Have someone come by and pick up your stuff. I never want to lay eyes on you again. You piece of dirt, you worthless piece of dirt."

Gina ran crying to the house never looking back. Tony sat in the car sobbing. He couldn't stop crying. He's said some stupid things in his life. But he just took the cake with this last one. He told Gina that if she would have kept an eye on their daughter that horrible day maybe she would still be alive.

In Gina's eyes she had just been accused of killing her daughter and for that she would never, ever, forgive Tony. Never.

When Tony recognized what he had just said, reality set in. He just lost his wife. His daughter was dead. And, his business was about to go under. He started towards Joe's house but he never made it. He took another path, a path that would lead Tony to a place he never thought he'd see. The gutter! Tony headed for Braden's and it started.

Gina was devastated, her life had just taken a 180-degree turn, and she was frightened. She had decided before their conversation, that they needed a break from one another and she was prepared for it. She just wasn't prepared for what happened. His words were ringing in her ears, when her mother walked in to the room.

"Gina, honey, are you alright? Tell me what happened."

"Mother, I don't want to talk about it right now," she said as she wiped the tears from her eyes.

"Please, baby, let me help you," came the response from her mother.

"You can't help Mom. Only God could have helped."

"What are you talking about Gina? What just happened between you and Tony?"

"I'm not talking about tonight Mom, I'm talking about the fire. God could have taken me instead of Molly!"

"Baby, God acts in mysterious ways. He had his reasons for taking Molly to heaven with him, and he had his reasons for leaving you here. No one knows why things happen. They just do. All we can do is muddle our way through them until it's our turn to face judgment day. The one thing I do know is that my granddaughter is with God, right now, and that is the only thing I need to know." Regina held her sobbing daughter. "Now, tonight is not about Molly. Tonight is about you and your husband. What happened and where is he?"

"Tony and I are done," Gina said, as matter of fact.

"What do you mean? What happened? What did he say?"

"Mom, I can't remember exactly what happened when the fire broke out. All I remember is hearing an explosion and waking up on the floor next to the refrigerator in a room full of smoke. It took me a second or two to realize where I was and another second to remember that Molly was downstairs. I crawled over to the basement stairs. I had to crawl; the smoke was so thick I couldn't breathe. I grabbed the door handle, it was so hot my hand stuck to it," Gina said as she looked down at the scars that had formed on her hand. "I got the door open but flames had engulfed the stairwell. It seemed like the whole basement was aflame. I screamed for Molly, but she didn't answer. I remember grabbing at the railing, I was going to try and pull myself over the top stair thinking I would fall down the stairs and somehow get to the bottom."

Gina had to stop there; welling up with emotion and busting out in an uncontrollable sob. "Oh God. Why? Why?"

After gathering herself she continued. "When I grabbed the railing there was indescribable pain. I couldn't hold on for even a second. I couldn't pull myself. I couldn't do anything but push myself back away from the flames. The next thing I knew I was in the ambulance," she said her body shaking with every word. She sat on the couch and cried.

"You did all anyone could have done, Gina. No one could have saved your daughter. No one," was her mother's response.

"I could have just dived into the flames. I should have done something else," was Gina's reply.

"Then you would have died too. That's the only thing that could have happened," said Regina as she hugged her child and cried along with her.

"Maybe it would have been better if I had," said Gina as she looked into her mother's face.

"Is that what you think Molly would have wanted? Do you think that she is looking down on us from heaven right now and wished that you would have died too? I don't think so and I don't think you do either."

"I think Tony thinks so," said Gina.

"Did he say that to you?"

"Not in so many words, but he said that if I would have been keeping my eye on her maybe she wouldn't be dead. Do you think that Mom?"

"That is the most ridiculous statement I've ever heard. Of course not dear don't you ever think that. Your husband needs help, honey. He needs a lot of help."

"Well he's not getting it from me. I won't live another minute with his problem. My Tony died with our daughter. I don't know who this man is but he is not my husband. I can't and I won't be around him. We're done. Mother, starting right now, I'm a new woman. I'm going up stairs, taking a shower, and going to bed. Tomorrow is the first day of the rest of my life and I'm going to be ready for it."

Chapter 8

Tony spent the next two days with his nose in a bottle of scotch. He never even came up for air. As far as Tony was concerned, no one knew what he was going through and nobody cared. He was too blind to see that everyone he knew felt sorry for what happened. They tried everything they could think of to convey that to him. Their efforts were all in vain. Tony was too far gone for anyone to help. He was so caught up in self-pity that nothing short of a resurrection was going to stop Tony from the path he had chosen. The last person in the world that Tony should have alienated was his brother, Joe. Apparently he couldn't stop himself.

Joe was in an out of a number of Tony's haunts unsuccessfully searching for his brother. Gina had called the family and explained what had transpired and begged for their forgiveness. She hoped they wouldn't hate her for what she was doing but it was the only way she could survive. No one blamed Gina. They knew Tony was off the deep end. They hoped it would end before it was too late.

Joe was looking for Tony to try and stop the insanity. He finally found his brother in an obscure little bar where the city turned to country. It's the country tavern where Joe and Tony often stopped after a great day of one of their two favorite past times, fishing or hunting. The Last Resort Bar and Grille. Ironically, Joe went there as a last resort and was glad when he spotted Tony sitting in a booth by the cigarette machine.

"Where have you been? I've been looking for you all week," asked a frustrated Joe as he slid into the booth.

"I'm staying out on my buddy George's place in Warrenton. You remember his deer hunting trailer. We've been there before."

"Does he know you're staying out there?"

"Yeah, I bumped into him at Braden's Sunday night right after my wife threw me out."

"Well, we'll talk about that after you tell me what you've been doing all week."

"Drinking and thinking," responded Tony. "You want to join me?"

"NO, Tony. NO I don't. Don't you give a damn that you have the whole family half out of our minds with worry?"

"Don't start Joe, I had a bad week," slurred Tony as he took a long pull on his drink.

"Don't start! Are you kidding? I've combed the city all week looking for you! Hell, you could have been dead for all we knew!" said a frustrated Joe.

"I am dead!" exclaimed Tony.

"SNAP OUT OF IT. You're not dead, but if you keep doing this to yourself, you will be," yelled Joe.

"Yeah, yeah, yeah."

Paul Tripi

"Yeah, yeah, yeah, my ass," shouted Joe. "Don't you care what you're doing to yourself?"

"No! Don't you get it? I don't care! I don't care about me! I don't care about my job! I don't care that Gina doesn't love me anymore! I just don't care about anything!" answered Tony.

"When I do care about anything it just gets taken away from me. I'm a loser! Can't you see that? I'm a loser!"

"I see," said Joe "You went from Mr. Middle-class America, with everything a man could possibly want to, I'm a loser, in a handful of months."

"You just don't get it, do you Joe. I didn't lose everything in a handful of months; I lost everything in a handful of seconds."

"Tony, if Molly were alive today do you think that she would want to see you like this?"

"I only wish she was here."

"I do too brother, but she is gone, and all the drinking in the world won't bring her back, but," said Joe.

"But what?" answered Tony.

"But if you stop with this drinking bull you might have a chance at healing your marriage."

Tony smirked and said, "Joe thanks for your opinion but . . . "

"But what, Tony?"

"But as much as I will always respect your opinion, it is still only your opinion and the only opinion that counts is mine. My opinion, and for that matter my decision is, to drink and think. So either join me or get the hell out of here."

"Fine, fine. *Good luck,* Tony. Give me a call if and when you ever decide to be human again. 'Cause quite honestly I'm sick and tired of your self-pity and so is everybody else. If you ever want to see me again you'll have to come looking for me, 'cause this is the last time I'll ever

70

come looking for you."

"Ciao Mr. Pitiful!"

Joe stood up and walked out of the bar.

Tony saluted his brother's back and commenced to drink himself into a stupor. He woke up the next morning hunched over the steering wheel of his car barely remembering the conversation he had with his brother. He had to wait for the bar to open to even leave because they had taken his keys away, like they did most nights. It was a pitiful situation and it was only getting worse.

Time passed like it was standing still. Tony was running out of money so he did the only thing he could to keep his expenses down. He switched from scotch to beer.

He was a living bar rag, a fixture at the Last Resort, a total waste of humanity, and then a priest walked into the saloon. He sat down at the bar, a few stools over from the stool commonly referred to as "the Tony stool," ordered a hamburger and a beer, asked the bartender where the men's room was, and got up to use it. As he passed Tony he nodded a hello and went on his way. Returning from the men's room the priest had the time to take a better look at the stranger in the next seat and couldn't help but feel like he knew this man from somewhere. He just couldn't place him.

"Excuse me," said the priest. "But you sure look familiar to me. Do we know each other?"

"I don't know. Do you drink in this place a lot?" answered Tony.

"No, I've actually never been in here before. I just stopped in for lunch. I'm on my way back to St. Louis from Kansas City," responded the priest in a friendly tone.

"Well then I don't know you," answered Tony in a not so friendly tone.

With that Tony got up and took his own trip to the restroom. The bartender brought the priest a cold beer and put it down on the bar.

"Thank you," said the priest and followed by asking, "Excuse me, would you happen to know the name of the gentleman that is sitting there?"

"What gentleman? You mean, Tony? Yeah, sure Father, his name is Tony Russo."

"Oh my God in heaven!" said the priest not believing what he just heard.

Tony slid back on his stool and reached for his beer. As he was taking a long drink the priest said. "Tony, Tony Russo!"

"Yes, how did you know that?" asked Tony.

"Tom Sutton, you know, Father Tom from handball a hundred years ago."

"You got to be kidding me!" exclaimed Tony. "Father Tom. I thought you'd be the Pope by now," he joked as he reached over to shake the priest's hand.

"Man it's been a long time."

"How you doing Tom?"

Tony and Tom sat for the next half an hour reminiscing about how they met.

It was about fifteen years ago when Tony was a newlywed. Back then Tony played handball every Tuesday and Thursday night with his usual group, Matra, Ticco, and Bacato but sometimes he would just show up at the club to see if he could find a game. This was one of those times. Tony was walking along the observation aisle at the Racquetball Club, looking for an opening, when he spotted a threesome down in court two. He asked if they needed a forth and they were more than happy to oblige him. Doubles is a much better game than three man cut throat.

After the introductions, Tony paired up with Tom and the game was on. It was a very even game with the lead changing hands a number of times. Tom went for a kill shot from the back wall and missed, putting it into the floor. Shit! He yelled as the other team took the lead. This was not a big deal; it was like foul language was just a part of the sport. Tony didn't pay any attention to it at all. They played the best out of three, the other team won. "Damn!" said Tom as the final point was rung up to close Tony and him out. They walked off the court and into the locker room for a shower. While they were showering Tom invited Tony to join them at the Village Bar for a beer. Tony accepted and as they were drying up Tony asked Tom what he did for a living.

"I'm a Catholic priest," said Tom

Tony laughed remembering Tom's language in the court.

"Small world, me too!" he said jokingly with a smile as he walked to his locker to get dressed.

Tony's jaw dropped a foot when he saw Tom put on his Roman collar.

"Oh my God, Father! I'm so sorry about that wisecrack. I thought you were kidding me. I mean you were swearing and everything in the court and I never thought in a million years that you were serious. Wait a minute, you were swearing in the court. Are you allowed to do that?" asked a confused Tony.

"Well, let me explain something to you, Tony. I am just a man, a man like you. I eat what you eat, I drink what you drink, I exercise, and I play handball. My job is to be a priest. I am a servant of the Lord and for that privilege I have given up some of the things that a non-priest can do, including the big one, celibacy. I didn't give up being a man. I'm still just a man, a man who can get frustrated and mad and sometimes lets an inappropriate word go, but I never take the Lord's name in vain."

"Now that you explain it like that, I do understand, Tom, I mean Father, I mean Tom. What do I call you?" asked Tony

"My name is Tom so you can call me Tom but I am a priest and if you prefer to call me father then call me father. It's sort of like being a doctor, if you had a friend who became a doctor would you stop calling him by his name and start calling him Doctor Whatever. I doubt it."

"Well, I guess I'd call him by his name like I always have except maybe if he was treating me as my doctor, I might call him doctor, then," answered Tony.

"Then that settles that. Call me Tom except when you see me in church, then you can call me father. How's that?"

"You know now that I think of it, you sure do sound like a priest, Tom. Where is your parish?"

"St. Mark's over on Hollowly," replied Father Tom. "Are you Catholic?"

"Yeah, well sort of, I'm a C-E," answered Tony.

"What's a C-E?" asked Tom.

"You know, I go to mass on Christmas and Easter," said Tony.

Tom laughed and said, "I usually celebrate the 9:00 a.m. and noon masses on Sunday. Why don't you break your tradition and come see me say mass sometime?"

"Call it done, father."

That's how they met. Tony attended mass almost every Sunday after that. Which really worked out good because Gina was always on him for not going, anyway. Tony had to admit Father Tom was a very easy man to understand and listen to. After talking with him numerous times after handball matches, or listening to him at his church masses on Sundays, Tom made Tony feel like he had a closer relationship with God. It made Tony feel good. Tom got a promotion or whatever it is that a priest gets and was transferred to Los Angeles a year later. This was the first time the two of them had seen each other since.

"Are you stationed or whatever you call it back in St. Louis?"

asked Tony.

"As a matter of fact I'm at St. Ambrose, your old stomping grounds on the Hill."

"My life with God has been completely fulfilling. I couldn't have asked for anything more. Now that I'm home, I'm really a happy camper."

"What have you been doing with your life, Ton?" he asked.

"Well, mostly I've been drinking and thinking," responded Tony.

"The drinking part is written all over your face. Tell me about the thinking part."

"Tom, I'm really glad to see you. You look great, even without hair," laughed Tony.

"You should talk. I remember you with the thickest head of hair in the world, and now."

"Yeah, I'm so mad at my barber, I told him to thin it out a little on top and look what he did." Tony and Tom just sat there and laughed.

"I'm serious, what happened to you, man?" asked Father Tom.

"Well, life was good. Do you remember my wife Gina?"

"Yes of course, Rancuso, the furniture guy's daughter, right?"

"Yeah, well as of right now we're still married but I'm just waiting for the axe to fall."

"OK, so you're telling me you're having some marital problems, so you turned yourself into a bar rag. I don't mean to slam you buddy but I do have eyes."

"That's just the tip of the iceberg, Tom. We had a great life. Had a beautiful little daughter, a wonderful home in Ballwin, just a great life. Then your boss took it all away, in one fell swoop." Tony said as the constant sadness that haunted him reared its ugly head again.

"What happened, Tony?" asked the sympathetic priest.

"A little less than a year ago, my daughter died. Some freak accident in the house. Something blew up, the water heater or something like that caught the house on fire. My baby never got out."

"Oh my sweet Lord." Said Tom "I'm so sorry."

Tony looked up at his old friend and said, "So you know that thinking part. Tom, I haven't said this out loud, but I've been thinking about killing myself. I've been trying with booze but it won't kill me. And I'm too much of a coward to just kill myself outright. I don't know what to do. I've lost everything," he said trying not to cry but losing the battle.

"What happened between you and Gina?" asked Tom.

"I'm an idiot. I drove her away with my drinking. Then to make matters worse I said something so unbelievably stupid."

"What did you say to her that was so stupid?"

"I made it sound like she could have prevented what happened."

"You blamed her? What were you thinking?"

"That's just it, I wasn't. The minute I said it, I was sorry. But, it was too late. She was done with me! She walked out of my life. And, I fell deeper into the bottle."

"Tony you said earlier that my boss took everything from you. God doesn't do things to his children. He does things for his children, and I think he sent me here for you I want to help, Tony. Will you let me?"

"Father, I don't think I can be helped."

"Tony, I think God has a plan for you. I don't think it is just a coincidence that we met again in this hole in the wall, in the middle of nowhere. To be honest with you, even though I was a little hungry the only reason I stopped in this place was because I had to pee. There's no doubt in my mind; God wanted me to find you. Come with me Tony. I really think God wants you to."

"Tom, I swore I was through with God but I'm finding myself

listening to you like I always have. I don't know where you want to take me but it has to be better than this. I'll go with you. Take me out of here. I want some kind of life back."

Chapter 9

Tony wasn't sure what was going to happen to him. He was just sure that whatever it was would be better than the life he was living. Father Tom Sutton didn't realize it but he truly was saving Tony's life.

Father Tom followed Tony to George's trailer, picked up Tony's few possessions, and without a word drove Tony directly to City Hospital. They had a drug and alcohol ward and Tom wanted Tony to admit himself, he was quite aware that he needed to dry out. When they pulled up to the hospital Tony said in a clear voice.

"No way Tom. I'm not going in there. What are you doing to me?"

"Tony. Let's just have them checked you out. I promise I will stay with you while they're doing it. If everything checks out alright, we'll be on our way," said the priest

"I'm not staying here! I mean it!"

"Tony, the road back can be a long one. If you want, I'll take you right back to that hole I found you in, but it might be simpler to just throw yourself in front of a bus. Now, if you want me to help you, you've got to do what I say. Capisce?"

"Yes, Father I understand," Tony said laughing.

"I don't think you've taken a good look at yourself lately. If you would have you wouldn't be questioning what we're doing here," Father Tom said firmly.

"I'm sorry. Let's go see how screwed up I really am," said Tony with a smile he hadn't used in quite some time.

Tony had to be admitted. He had to go through detoxification and true to his word Father Tom stayed with Tony through the whole ordeal. He did leave a couple of times so he could set up some living accommodations for Tony, along with a little job to help him get back on his feet.

When Tony walked out of the hospital, he was a different man. He didn't know whom or what kind, just that he was a different man from the waste of a man that walked in there.

"Tony, I set it up so you could live in the unoccupied maintenance man's quarters at the Rectory at St. Ambrose. He moved into a bigger place off the church's campus so as luck would have it his old quarters are empty and available. If you want to do a few chores we'll even feed you.

"I don't know if you want to contact your family, or what. You might even want me to take you home. I don't know what you want. All I know is that you've got some decisions to make."

"Father, I'm not a fool. Two nights puking, shivering, and sweating hasn't changed me, but at least I'm starting to realize what I've done to the people I love. I can't face them and I can't change things, till I can face myself. Father, I would be happy to take you up on your generous offer. In fact, I don't know how to thank you. I promise you this;

you won't have to hide the church wine. As God as my witness, this world will never see Tony Russo drunk again."

They left the hospital and headed straight to St. Ambrose. Father Tom showed Tony his new quarters. A semi-large room with a nice bed, a reclining chair, a kitchen table with two chairs, and a small television set. It wasn't spacious but it looked comfortable. Against one of the walls were a sink, a small refrigerator, and a hot plate. There was a small bathroom attached with a toilet and a shower. Compared to the hunting trailer, this was the Taj Mahal.

Tony put his bag down, turned to Father Tom, and said, "Father, I might be in the one place on this earth that could restore my faith. Not just my faith in the Lord but my faith in myself. I won't let you down."

"Tony, I wish you could see the difference in yourself in just these two days. I swear to you, buddy. I didn't just turn up in that tavern by luck. God has a plan for you. I don't know what it is, but God has a plan for you. I'm just a pawn doing the Lord's work, but I do have to admit, this particular task makes my heart feel good. Now get some rest. I'll come by in a few hours and we'll get something to eat." He turned, lifted his hand and blessed Tony. "God bless you in the name of the Father, the Son, and the Holy Spirit, Amen."

Tony made the sign of the cross as the priest blessed him and responded "God be with you Father, thank you. I hope you can appreciate just how much I mean that."

"Well you better save your thanks till you taste the cooking around here, and the chores we have in store for you. You might want to take that thanks back."

Tony looked Father Tom Sutton straight in the eyes and said. "I won't forget this as long as I live Father. As long as I live, thanks Tom."

Tony sat on the edge of the bed trying to figure out what happened, and what he was really going to do about it. A couple of days ago, even the mention of the word religion, church, or especially of God, would have set him off. Now Tony couldn't help but think that God really must have a plan for him. Even though he didn't want to believe it, he had to admit Father Tom did show up in the middle of nowhere, in the nick of time, when he was contemplating ending it all.

Is what Father Tom saying about God having a plan for me possible? What would God want with me? Why would he take my life from me and then save it? What am I doing here?

All these thoughts were racing through Tony's mind. There were no clear answers to his questions. He decided to stay awhile and find out some of these answers. When he first met Father Tom many years ago, Tony went from a sometime Catholic to a frequent churchgoer and remembered that made him feel good.

"Maybe if I stay off the booze, and that's a given, and do what Father Tom says, I've got a real chance to get my life back or at least start a new one."

Father Tom knocked on Tony's door at noon.

"Are you ready to eat something?" he yelled through the door.

"Come on in, the door's open." responded Tony. "I can't believe this but I'm starving."

"Well in that case let's skip the church food and go around the corner to Mario's. I think they have the best lunch in town," said the priest. "It's on me. By the way Tony, how are you fixed for money?"

"I've got a few dollars left. But, I did manage to drink up almost everything I've worked for. How's that for stupidity."

"I kind of figured that. So after we eat I'd like you to walk with me. I've got a friend I want you to meet. I talked to him about you and he said he'd give you a job."

"Doing what?"

"Does it matter?"

81

"Not really."

"It's not much of a job, but I've got a feeling you'll like the surroundings."

After a wonderful lunch, Tony and the priest went on their walk. They past the bocce club, a place Tony spent hours in his youth watching the old men play the Italian bowling game. They passed Father Baker's, an orphanage that brought fear to every kid growing up on the Hill. If any of them ever did anything wrong they would all hear the same threat; "If you ever do that again I'll take you right to father Baker's. Although Tony knew the Hill like the back of his hand he still didn't know where the priest was taking him. There were no businesses where they were heading. They stopped and there it was, Dominic's Gym. Many good fighters came out of this gym; it's a landmark in St. Louis.

"What do you think? You feel like working around fighters?" asked Father Tom.

"Perfect," answered Tony. "What's my job here?"

"Well, a mop is definitely going to be one of your tools," joked the priest.

"I figured you could work out a little too, maybe get back into shape."

"I like it!" said Tony.

"Then let's go meet Dominic."

Dominic Michaeloni stuck his hand out to greet his friend Father Tom.

"Is this your buddy?" asked Dominic.

"Yes, Nic this is Tony Russo," replied the priest.

"How ya doin'?" asked Tony as he shook hands with Mr. Michaeloni.

"I'm doing pretty good," he replied. "Father tells me you could use a job. I need a guy to clean up around here. You interested?"

"I could use the work."

"I need someone between 5:00 and 8:00 at night, Monday through Saturday. Just make sure the equipment is put away, the work out rooms and the locker room are kept clean and the towels are picked up and washed. For that I'll give you $150.00 a week, cash. How's that strike ya?"

"Is it OK if I use the equipment?"

"I don't care. Just as long as you don't get in the way of the fighters and you put the crap away when you're through with it. Oh, excuse me Father, I mean the stuff."

"Absolutely. Thank you Mr. Michaeloni."

"Tony, you can call me Dominic, or Nic, or Big Nic, Mr. Michaeloni was my father.

"Thank you Nic. When do you want me to start?"

"I've got a guy till the end of the week, so how's about Monday."

"Great. I'll be here at 5:00 sharp."

"Good. You want to take a look around?"

"Sure, thanks,"

Tony walked off into the big area, where the main ring sits, to get acclimated to the place. While he was doing that Dominic asked Father Tom, "Is Tony an ex-fighter?"

"Not really, he did a little fighting as a youngster but nothing to speak of. He just needs a jump-start. He's been in the doldrums for a while. I can't thank you enough, Nic."

"I'm happy to help you out, Tom."

Tony came back into the office and said, "You got some good boys out there Nic. Anybody you're really high on?"

"Yes sir, I've got two contenders fighting for me right now. Brian Scott's a young middleweight with a lot of promise and of course Paulie

Jay. A heavyweight ranked number five by the WBA. He's in the big ring sparring right now. Did you see him?"

"Yeah, I watched him work a little. He's bad to the bone," said Tony.

"You ever do any sparring?" asked Nic.

"Are you kidding? I stopped shadow boxing 'cause I was scared of my own shadow," answered Tony.

"Well if you ever get the urge, we can always use sparring partners. Keep it in mind."

"Thanks, but there are only two chances of that happening, slim, and none. I would like to work out a bit though if you don't mind. Can I get some stuff and come back?"

"Sure, when you come back there's locker keys in this drawer here, grab a locker for yourself."

"Thanks a lot, Nic. I really appreciate all you're doing for me. You must be a very good friend of the Father here."

"To tell you the truth Tony, Father Tom helped me out when I really needed it. He's a good man. I'm glad he brought you here. Besides, now I'll have someone around here I can talk to. I can't understand what the hell these kids are talking about."

"Thanks, again Nic," said Tony.

"You're welcome, Tony. I'll see ya later."

"Goodbye Father."

"Thank you and God bless you, Dominic," Father Tom said as he and Tony got up to leave.

Tony went out and pick up some work out clothing and a pair of high top shoes. He brought everything back to the gym and got himself a locker. He did a little stretching but he really wasn't feeling well enough to actually work out. He was feeling better than he had in a long time but not that good; he still had a ways to go. He had also picked up a few things he needed for his room. Shaving gear, toiletries, and some snacks. He took them back to the rectory and put them away. After a short rest he went looking for Father Tom. He wanted to find out what chores they had for him. He was anxious to get started. Tony was grateful, it's not like he was on top of the world but from where he started a few days ago it felt like it.

Tony spent the next few weeks acclimating himself to his new life. The living accommodations and the job at the gym where going perfect. He had started working out but he waited till the gym was almost empty. He wasn't feeling like a million bucks, after all, the amount of booze he had drunk over the course of the last year had taken its toll. He thought about calling his family, but wanted to wait till he felt better mentally and physically. The working out was helping with the physical aspect and Father Tom's religious outlook was sinking in and going straight to Tony's heart. Tom helped to make changes in Tony's attitudes almost daily. He started attending church on a regular basis. Not just on Sundays. He found enlightenment in the words of the gospel and in the values they represent. He didn't have a formal plan or a schedule on how long he would stay at St. Ambrose. He would love to go back to his old life but he knew he had caused irreparable damage and wasn't sure that was possible. For now he was content to simply rehab through the opportunities he had at hand. Most importantly he was now starting to believe what Father Tom kept repeating over and over. God had a plan for him. Two questions keep creeping into his mind. What was it, and why?

Chapter 10

Tony just finished cleaning up when Dominic walked into the gym area.

"What's going on in Tony's life?" he said as he watched Tony put away his mop and bucket.

"Not a whole lot. I'm getting by."

"I was getting ready to leave when I saw you finishing up. I wanted to tell you you're doing a damn good job around here."

"It doesn't take a brain surgeon to mop a floor and pick up trash," responded Tony

"That's not what I mean. I'm talking about showing up every day on time and doing your job without complaining about this or that or whatever. I haven't had anyone do that in a long time. I just wanted to tell you that I appreciate that."

"You appreciate me. Are you kidding, I can't begin to thank you for this opportunity."

"Opportunity, you call sweeping up a stinky gym an opportunity?"

"No, Nic, it's more than that. If you know it or not, this job has given me a chance to get my life back together."

"What happened to you, man?" asked Dominic.

Tony wasn't sure he wanted to share anything about his life with Dominic. He thought for a moment and decided, it was a fair question and the man deserved an answer.

"I lost my little girl. When she died, my soul died with her. After that my life is a blur."

"I'm so sorry. I didn't mean to pry. I just thought that maybe it was a money thing. And, if it was, maybe I could help."

"What do you have in mind?"

"Father tells me you did some fighting as a young man. You any good?"

"How's no sound for an answer."

"It sounds like, I'm going to shut my mouth and go home. Have a nice day off, buddy. See you on Monday."

Sunday was a beautiful day. Tony awoke with a smile, showered, and headed over to the church for mass.

St. Ambrose is a beautiful Catholic Church, located smack dab in the middle of the Hill. Its architecture is reminiscent of many of the Catholic churches built in ancient Rome, complete with the most magnificent stain glass windows imaginable. There are three sections of seating, situated in such a position that all the seats have a direct view of the altar. The ceiling is adorned with paintings that can only be described as works of art. As soon as you walk into the church, you can't help but feel the presence of God.

Tony walked past the lingering crowd of parishioners, through the majestic wood doors, blessed himself with holy water from one of the marble vats situated at the head of each aisle, and sat down in about the middle of the church. About fifteen minutes later the church started to fill up. Five minutes later there was standing room only, when Father Tom entered the church from a door at the side of the alter. The parishioners rose, the mass had begun.

Funny how things seem to go full circle in a person's life, thought Tony as he looked around the old church. Here he was again in the same church he was baptized in, made his first holy communion in, was confirmed in, and was married in. To Tony thinking back on all those occasions, it seems like that was a different person, like he was looking at someone else's life and not his own. His thoughts drifted back to his childhood. Playing ball with his brother, long talks with his baby sister, fond memories of his parents, and of course there was Gina. Gina, the one and only love of his life.

As if on cue, Father Tom took the podium.

"God is all forgiving!" he said as he started his sermon for the day. "Shouldn't we follow his lead? Is there someone you need to forgive or someone who needs to forgive you?

"This morning my sermon is about just that, and even more, it's about family."

Tony's ears perked up like a new puppy being called to play. He was just thinking about his family. What was this going to be about? He slid to the edge of the pew as his friend the priest started his talk.

"Today's sermon is The Prodigal Son," said the priest as he broke into the story.

The story of the prodigal son is a simple story based on family, love, and greed. It's a story of a father and two sons. The father, a wealthy landowner, was approached by one of his sons. This son didn't want to wait for his father to die to inherit his portion of his fortune. He asked his father if he could have his share now. He wanted to see the world and increase his status in life.

The other brother was a loyal son, worked the land with his father, and was content. The loving father had no qualms about giving his young son his share of the family fortune and did so. The other son really didn't understand what his younger brother was doing but went along with his father's decision without argument. The young man grabbed his fortune, said goodbye to his father and brother and left his home and his loving family behind. He was going to show both of them what a real success was, and swore he would not return until he accomplished his goal. He was going to show everyone.

Time passed, and all the young man was able to accomplish was to frivolously spend all that he had on good times and bad decisions. He was in terrible shape. He couldn't find work. He had no shelter. And most importantly he had no food. When all else failed he simply begged for food. After all he had, and a wonderful life, he had managed to squander everything and now found himself begging for food just to live.

Believe it or not, it even got worse. He was even unsuccessful at begging and was starving to death. He scavenged through peoples' garbage for scrapes of food and even that was not enough to sustain him. He was at the bottom of life. All he could think of was home. His father and his brother and everything he left behind. He wanted desperately to return but he knew that just couldn't be. He had made his bed and now he had to sleep in it.

Time marched on but not for this poor soul. He was dying. He was malnourished and on his last leg when he decided that the only thing he could do was to swallow his pride, since that was the only thing he had swallowed for a while, and go home. He knew that even the slaves that worked his father's land ate and ate well. He felt like maybe his father and his brother would let him work as a slave just so he could live.

It was a bittersweet feeling the young man had when he set eyes on his old home. All he could do was hope that his father and brother would take pity on him. This was not the way he had planned his return, but he had no other option. He was about to turn around when his father spotted him. He didn't know what to do and he just froze in his tracks.

The next thing the young man saw was his father running towards him with outstretched arms and screaming, "Thank you Lord, my son has come home." The father yelled for one of his servants to bring his son a warm robe to wear and to bring some food immediately.

With tears of joy the father hugged his son. Thanking God the whole time for the safe return of his lost son. His brother too was running towards the reunion. So happy to see his brother that he could burst.

No questions were asked. It didn't matter to either of them what had happened. All that mattered was that the family was together again.

"Forgiveness and family," said the priest. "Do unto others as you would have them do unto you, sayeth the Lord.

"That is the message I hope you got out of today's sermon.

"The Lord puts forgiveness in everyone's heart, but it's up to each and every one of us to use this gift. Is there someone in your life that seeks your forgiveness, or is there someone in your life you need forgiveness from? Think about that!

"Let us pray."

Tony sat dumbfounded by the message. He thought about his family incessantly but felt that with all the hurt he had inflicted on them, not to mention what he had said to Gina, he had no business in their lives.

"What should I do?" thought Tony as he walked towards the back of the church to leave. "Should I call my brother and at least tell him I'm alive? Maybe call my sister instead? If I call mom and dad they could tell everybody. No, dumb idea. I don't know what to do.

"Maybe I should have a talk with Father Tom? I can tell him what this morning's sermon had done to my thinking process and get his advice. No, what is wrong with me, you know what he's going to say. Make up your own mind, you idiot!" Tony's mind worked at a thousand miles a minute as he exited the church.

Tony stood on the top of the stairs starring into thin air when he felt a hand rest on his shoulder.

"*Minga*, Tony Russo, I thought that was you. How the hell are you?" said Mike Matra, one of Tony's oldest friends and handball partner from back in the good old days, when they all met Father Tom.

"Mike, you old reprobate. Why aren't you in prison where you belong?" asked Tony as the two men hugged each other on the steps of the church.

"I would be if I could only find the courage to shoot that old hag I'm married to."

"How is Phyllis? Tell her hi for me."

"She's doing great, Tony. She looks like a million bucks, the old hag. To tell you the truth, she looks the same now as she did the first day I married her. You probably don't remember but you saw us both at the service for your daughter. God rest her soul. We only said a passing hello. I couldn't bear to talk to you just then. I don't even want to talk to you about it right now. There's no reason for the two of us to stand here and cry in front of all these people. I just want you to know that, that day was one of the saddest days in our lives. Philly and I have you and Gina in our prayers. Tony, I don't know what to say."

"Thank you Mike. You just did.

"What brings you to the old stomping grounds, anyway," asked

91

Tony.

"I heard that Tom was back in town over here at Ambrose so I thought I'd catch a mass and say hello. You doing the same thing?"

"Not really Mike," and Tony broke into the whole story.

"Oh Lord, Anthony! What can I do? Is there something I can do? You know I'll do anything for you, just ask. Please let me help."

"There is nothing you can do right now Mike. I have to do it on my own. When the time is right, you'll hear from me."

"I'll kill you if I don't," Mike said as a spry look came over his face. "I'll tell you one thing I am going to do, or should I say you're going to do, and that is you are definitely coming home with me for Sunday sauce. Wait before you answer, and be prepared to fight me if you say no." Without even pausing for Tony's answer, Mike said, "Come on, let's go say hi to Father Tom. We'll get him to join us. Matter of fact, why don't I call all the guys, Tony Ticco, Big George, Steve Hull, and maybe Frank Bacato and we'll have a little handball reunion? What do you say?"

"I'm not up for a party but it would be nice to talk to all the guys. I did see you all that day, but I—I. . . .

"Shut the hell up. I'll call the dragon lady and tell her what's going on. This is going to make her very happy. You know why? Cause it gives her a chance to go shopping. That's why. The woman loves to shop and she cannot, under any circumstances pass up a deal. You know one time she tried to by an escalator cause it was marked down."

The plan was made. Everyone Mike called dropped what they were doing and the reunion was on. The food, the company, and the friendship were exactly what Tony needed. Like they say in that beer commercial, it doesn't get any better than this. It was obvious that everyone stayed away from any questioning when it came to Tony's plight.

Mike had informed them all about Tony's situation, and although there wasn't a guy there who wouldn't tear the shirt right off their backs for him, they respected him enough not to.

When it ended, everyone hugged and made statements to the effect that they should do this a lot more often. You know take turns having everyone over, the same kind of stuff old friends say to each other every time they get together. The only thing different about this parting was that even though all the guys said they wouldn't say anything to Tony about his current situation. They all did. Each and everyone of them took Tony off to the side so the others couldn't hear and begged Tony to let them help. Money, a job, they even offered to let him live with them, anything, anything. Frank, then Tony T., then George, Steve and finally Mike gave it another try. You may as well have made a recording of the conversation and played it five times because they all said the same thing. It was hard for Tony in some ways but the bottom line was plain. You're a rich man when you have truly good friends. Tony felt like Bill Gates.

As Tony got into Father Tom's car to drive back to St. Ambrose only one thing, or should I say one person was on his mind, Gina. All this reminiscing coupled with this morning sermon had Tony locked on the one thought.

"What great people," said Father Tom as he pulled out of the Matra's driveway. "I've forgotten just how great," continued the priest. "You're a lucky man Mr. Russo, if you know it or not."

"They are truly great friends Tom. It's always the same way with them. They're more then friends, they're family. Tom, speaking about family, that Prodigal Son thing this morning and now seeing the guys, their wives and children has got me a little screwed up."

"What do you mean screwed up? Screwed up how? Would you mind expounding on that statement?"

93

"It's just that forgiveness thing. I'm no fool. I know Gina and there is no way it could ever be the same between us. I heard what you said this morning about forgiveness and family and God and all that stuff but nowhere in that story did the Prodigal Son tell his family and everyone else to go blank themselves, over and over again. What I said to Gina rings in my ears night after night. My brother Joe is one of the greatest guys in the whole world. I love him so much that if he needed a heart transplant I'd die just so he could have mine. And what do I do? How do I treat him and everyone who loved me?"

Tony paused for a second. "Never mind Tom I guess I really don't want to talk about it."

"Bull," retorted Tom. "It's not Gina's, or Joe's, or even God's forgiveness you need Tony. You need to forgive yourself, for what I don't know. But you've got a lot of guilt built up inside and that has got to be dealt with. I can't speak for your family but I've got a feeling that your family doesn't hate you as much as you think. Tony, if you would like, I'll drive you over to Joe's right now."

"Thanks Tom, but no. I can't face them yet."

"Well, what about a phone call?"

"Yeah, that's the ticket. I can tell them all about my job as a floor scrubber. That will impress them."

"Impress them. What are you talking about? Impress them! This I guarantee you, just call them and tell them you dried out and you'll be able to see their smiles right over the telephone. Family, Tony, think about what I'm saying, family."

"You're right as usual Tom. I'm going to call Joe. I'm just not sure when. I need to feel a little better about myself first. I'm going to call, pretty soon, pretty soon."

Chapter 11

Tony was feeling down as he walked into his barren room. He was wrestling with the decision to call his family and felt anxiety concerning Gina. For the first time since arriving at St. Ambrose, Tony was thinking about having a drink. With that thought in mind, he sprang from his chair, grabbed his key to the gym, and headed over for a workout instead.

Dum dum dum, dum dum dum went the punching bag as he hit it for all it was worth. Bang, he finished off his speed bag work out with a right hand cross that would have definitely done some damage had it landed on someone's jaw instead of that small leather bag. Tony sweated profusely as he ended a fairly strenuous work out with a jump rope set. He wiped the sweat from his brow as he headed for the showers. No doubt, he was in the best shape he had been in for a very long time.

He looked up at the big clock hanging on the locker room wall above the large scale the fighters use to make sure they make weight. It was 7:30; still plenty of time left to call his brother Joe. So as he contemplated the call, he thought, there's no time like the present. He shoved his gear in his locker, locked up, and headed to the rectory to use the phone. He didn't know what he was going to say but it didn't matter. He just wanted to hear his brother's voice, even if it was screaming at him.

"Hello, Sally, it's Tony."

"Oh my God Tony, where are you? How are you? Are you all right?" she didn't wait for an answer.

All Tony could hear even though his sister-in-law was trying to cover up the speaker end of the phone was, "Joseph, Joseph, come quick."

"What's wrong, what happened," Joe yelled as he rushed to the kitchen where his wife stood.

"It's your brother," said Sally as she handed her out of breath husband the phone.

"Oh my God Tony, where are you? Are you all right? God, where have you been?"

"I'm alright. I'm staying with Father Tom at St. Ambrose right now. I haven't had a drink in a while and I'm trying to get my life back together."

"Thank God!" said Joe. "Where at St. Ambrose. I'll be there in half an hour."

"I'm at the rectory, but you don't have to do that."

"I don't have to do that, my ass," was Joe's response. "The only reason I haven't gone to the police and filed a missing person report is because I knew in my heart that you were all right. I knew it in my heart. I'll be there in half an hour. Don't move."

Tony was sitting on the rectory steps, head down, when Joe's car pulled up. He was too ashamed to look his brother in the face. Joe too wasn't sure what to do. Run to his brother and hug him or run over and punch him in the face. He opted to slowly walk over, looking around acting real cool. That worked real well until they looked into each other's face. Tony stood up, the two men moved towards each other, tears welled up in their eyes and they hugged.

"I'm so sorry, Joe," said Tony as he hugged his brother, like Joe had just returned from the grave."Please forgive me."

"I should have never left you alone at that bar. I didn't know what to do." He continued with, "I just didn't know what to do. I'm the one who's sorry, Anthony. I should be begging you for your forgiveness. I'll never leave you alone again."

"You didn't leave me Joe, I threw you out. I'm the ass here!" said Tony.

"I don't care who did what to who or for what. I'm just so happy to see you. I love you, Anthony."

"I love you too, Joe. More than you'll ever know."

Tony explained the chance meeting with Father Tom and told Joe what Tom had done for him. Joe remembered the priest but really didn't know him. Tony invited Joe in to the rectory to meet the Father but Joe declined. He wanted to talk to his brother in private. Tony took Joe to his room and put on some coffee.

"Well, what do you think?" Tony said proudly, recognizing all along what he was showing his brother.

"Very nice," answered Joe. "Very nice. Now get your stuff, we're going home."

"What are you talking about?"

"I'm talking about you getting your stuff and coming home. To my house, I mean our house. You live there now. I'm not taking no for an answer and that's It," he said matter-of-factly. "Now get your stuff."

"Now wait just one minute Joe. I don't think I've explained my situation or my feeling, exactly."

"Well, what exactly are you talking about? Because I'll tell you exactly what I'm talking about, I'm talking about me having this big beautiful home, filled up with people who love and miss you so much I had a tough time leaving them home, when they heard where I was going. I'm talking about a wife that was shouting 'bring him home with you' as I was walking out the door. I'm talking about a brother who is living in a place that's smaller than my office for crying out loud. That's exactly what I'm talking about. Now get your stuff, period."

"Joey, calm down for just a minute. We'll have some coffee and I'll explain. But first I want to know about Gina. Have you seen her? Is she O.K.? Is she staying in touch with the family? Tell me, do you talk to her?"

"I don't know anything. I am not talking about Gina right now. I really don't know anything."

"You don't know anything or you're not saying anything?"

"Tony, let's not talk about Gina right now, let's get this living thing settled first."

"No, I want to know about my wife."

"I'm telling you Tony, don't make me take the Fifth. I'm not talking about Gina. I'm like Schultz in *Hogan's Heroes* I know nothing."

"She's got somebody, doesn't she?"

"I know nothing, now get your stuff."

"O.K., O.K., let's get this settled," Tony said staring into his brother's face, I know you want me to come home with you, I know your wife loves me, and I love her too. I know I'm welcome in her home probably for as long as I want. You know how much I love Sarah, Sandra, and Anthony. That's not the question here. The question is, am I ready to leave this place, and the answer is no. I don't care about the size of the place or that I do menial chores around here for food or even that I clean up over at Dominic's Gym for spending money."

"What, you're a broom pusher?"

"Let me finish. What's important is that I'm not ready to leave. I'm redefining myself right now and if you laugh at what I'm about to say I'll slap you, I mean it. The thing is, I'm rediscovering my life through God."

"I don't understand what you're saying. Are you telling me you want to be a priest?"

"No, not that, I don't know what I'm saying. I guess what I mean is that I'm sort of convinced that this chance meeting with Father Tom was a wake-up call for me and Tom seems to think, and so do I, that there was a reason for that meeting. Tom thinks that God has some kind of plan for me. I was pretty far gone, bro. I don't want to worry you, and I probably shouldn't even tell you this but if Father Tom hadn't shown up in my life just then, I probably would have killed myself. I was close; I just didn't have the guts to do it."

"That's it, get your stuff, I'm not leaving you alone for another minute."

"Joe, you think I would tell you this if I had any intentions of doing anything like that. No, I wouldn't, so just let me finish. Tom showed up at that hole in the wall bar out of thin air, he only stopped 'cause he had to piss for Heaven's sake. Because of that I'm here. God does have a plan for me. What his plan is I have no idea but man I really do believe there is one."

"I don't know Tony, I just don't know what to do and now I don't know what to say but I just don't feel good about not taking you with me. This God stuff is over my head but if you are off of the booze and you're starting to get back on your feet, I'm happy. Just tell me what you want me to do and what you want me to tell everybody."

"Tell everyone that I'm sorry first of all. Then tell them all that I love them and that I'll see them real soon. Tell them I'm in a good place in my mind and in my heart and that with the grace of God things are going to be real good for me in the future. I just don't know what that's going to be but right now. What used to be important to me has changed. Material stuff is not important anymore. It's who you are not what you own."

"Tony, I really can't just sit here and do nothing."

"Are you kidding me? Just seeing you has lifted my spirits beyond belief. I was so afraid that I had ruined everything."

A loud silence came over the room as both men just sat there not knowing what to say or what to do.

"You hungry, Tony? You want to go out and grab something to eat? Maybe go back to the house for something."

"No thanks Joe, I'm not really ready to face the family right now. Give me a little time. I'll tell you what, if you don't mind having me for sauce on Sunday, I'll come by and see everybody then. Don't make a big deal out of it though."

"Don't make a big deal out of it! It is a big deal! This is great Tony, just great. If you'd like to get together sooner, just give me a call, but for sure you're coming Sunday, right?

"Yes, Joey, for sure. Tell Sally and the kids I love them and I'll see them then. Tell Betty, Sam and their kids, I'll see them all on Sunday too, right?"

"Are you kidding me, I guarantee you that Betty and Sally are talking on the phone right now, the whole family will be eager to see you Tony, and that's an understatement."

Joe realized that the conversation was at an end and he didn't want to press any more issues with his brother. He got up from his chair, took one more look around, walked over to Tony, and kissed him.

"I want to see you. Don't pull another Houdini on us, you hear."

"Don't worry Joe, I'm back, I'm just different that's all."

"O.K., call me, call me for sure."

"I'll call, and I'm coming on Sunday. I promise."

"See you later Anthony."

"Count on it Joseph."

Tony felt that the weight of a hundred horses had been lifted from his back. Just the fact that he had seen his brother and nothing really seemed different from the past, gave him the strength to follow through with the family reunion on Sunday. He just wanted to get that part over with. Not that he wasn't anxious to see everyone, he just wasn't looking forward to explaining everything, and he was really not sure what he was going to tell them about his new life and his inexplicable feelings about God.

He knew they were all going to think that the booze ate away part of his brain, but it didn't matter. It didn't matter because the more he thought about everything that had happed to him since the priest walked into that bar, the more he was convinced that God really did have something in mind for him. He still just didn't know what it was. He didn't know what it was but it was about to start.

Chapter 12

The week flew by. It was Sunday morning before Tony knew it and he was worried sick about facing his family. He hadn't contacted Joe since their meeting, and he was actually contemplating skipping out on the dinner. Although he was thinking about it he knew he couldn't. He knew this was his chance to get back into the family's graces and he wasn't about to blow it. It's just that he was so embarrassed and regretful of what had transpired over the course of the last year, it was going to be hard to face them all.

"I guess I'll have to suck it up and be a man," Tony said aloud as he stared into the small mirror over the sink in his bathroom. He was combing his hair, getting ready for church. He put the comb down, took a step backward, and took a long look at himself. Mentally, spiritually, and financially, he was searching for answers, but physically he looked good, very good. His arms and chest muscles bulged as he flexed them in front of that little foot square mirror. "Not bad for an old guy," he thought. He then put on his shirt and headed to the church for mass.

He approached the steps of the church with his mind running a hundred miles an hour. What was Tom's sermon going to be today? Would it be something that might help him deal with his family later?

That's the thing, he never knew what he was about to hear or how it would fit into his life, but he walked up the stairs of the church full of hope.

"Today my sermon is not a sermon. It's a story. It's a story about me and a story about God. I'll bet I've got your interested," said Father Tom as he addressed his congregation.

"The most frequent question that I'm asked is, *what made you become a priest?* I answer the same way each time. I always say, 'It seemed like a good idea at the time.' That answer usually brings a smile to the questioners face and I leave it at that.

"The real answer is a little more involved and it leads me to my story. You see God has a plan for each and every one of us. For some it is as simple as trust in the Lord and he shall provide. For others it's more specific. You see God needs certain people to perform special tasks here on earth. These people are his soldiers, soldiers of Christ. God contacts each of these people in all kinds of ways. Maybe through Scripture or through some revelation that these people might have had, or through a thought that may just pop up into their heads, but God contacts them. Maybe it's just to help the needy or volunteer some time to the sick or the old. Maybe it's to help through contributions, their time or their money. I'm not pretending to know what he needs or wants, or how he passes his message on to us. I just know that God has a plan. And for me, well that brings me to my story. What happened to me was magnificent. I can't prove it. I can't even be 100% sure it really happened. All I know is what I heard and what I heard changed my life. I was eleven years old. I was coming home from boy scouts. We had just visited a nursing home and passed out some gifts to the old timers. They were just boxes of Kleenex that we wrapped up as Christmas gifts but those people just loved them. Actually I thought it was going to be a terrible experience but it turned out to be really special. The people were so happy it made me feel good inside. Well anyway, I was walking across the field where the old rubber company used to be before it burned down. I sat down on a big rock to tie my shoe. It was an overcast day and cold, when all of a sudden the clouds in the sky seemed to open up, a beam of sunlight shined right down on me and I felt warm, and then, and then, it happened. I heard a voice, it was a man's voice, it was soothing, not scary at all, and he said, "**TOM, YOU'RE A GOOD BOY, YOU'LL BE A GOOD MAN, PREACH THE WORD OF THE LORD.**" I looked around for all I was worth but there was no one in sight. Could it be, I thought? Is it possible that I was just contacted by God? I walked the rest of the way home in a daze. I wasn't sure what just happened. I didn't know if I should tell anyone or not. When I got home, I didn't say anything. I didn't want my parents to think I was crazy.

"Was that something that happened in my mind or did God really speak to me? I still don't really know, but I do know one thing, here I am. I'm telling you this for a reason. We are all servants of the Lord. We can all be a soldier for God. Maybe it's just that we should love one another and pass that love on. Maybe we should take the time to help those less fortunate than us. But most importantly, believe in the Lord and follow his preaching and you shall be saved. Belief is a powerful word. Belief. Let us pray."

Tony listened to what Father Tom said but it wasn't what he'd hoped it was going to be. He was hoping for a message that would help him cope with the day facing him. After a few moments of contemplation Tony realized he apparently hadn't listened at all because if he had he would have recognized that what was being said was as unselfish as you can get and what he was looking for was exactly the opposite. He sat in the pew awhile as the others filed out of the church. He wanted to digest Tom's story. Wow, he thought as it sank in. "No wonder Tom feels the way he does. God truly has touched him. I guess if I'm to be a soldier of the Lord he'll let me know, until then I'm going to go with that belief thing. Belief, I get it Tom."

Tony walked to end of the isle towards the marble holy water vat. He dipped in his fingers and what happened next was staggering. A shiver, a shiver like he'd never felt before, ran up Tony's right arm, numbing it. His whole body shook. For a moment he thought he was having a heart attack. He stood there motionless trying to figure out what was going on. He turned towards the altar and waited. He was actually waiting to hear the voice of God. He stood there for a few moments, smiled and thought, "Man, this belief thing is powerful. Here I am waiting for God to talk to me. I guess I got carried away with Tom's sermon." He laughed out loud and walked out of the church.

Tony was shaking his head and smiling thinking about this morning's unusual happenstance as he pulled up to Joe's. A feeling of guilt overcame him as he stared at the big house in front of him. "What am I going to say?" He thought as he approached the door. "I can't believe I'm afraid to face my own family."

"Yo bro." Is what he heard when his brother opened the door. "He's here," Joe yelled back to the family room where the family was anxiously awaiting. The family flocked to the front door. Tony's head was down as he felt the arms of his sister squeeze around him and heard the voices of his nieces and nephews shouting, Uncle Tony, Uncle Tony.

105

He hugged all the kids at once, kind of a group hug, kissed his sister Betty and sister-in-law Sally, and shook the hands of his brother and brother-in-law Sam. What he feared for all this time was nothing but his own guilt. He was welcomed like a soldier returning home from the war. Tony's heart was bursting with love for his family and the realism of just how much he missed them.

"How are you?" said Betty and Sally simultaneously.

"I'm fine," replied Tony with a sheepish smile.

"Come on in. Let's go into the kitchen and have some coffee. You hungry Anthony?" asked Joe.

"I'm not hungry, but a cup of coffee would certainly hit the spot." Tony looked into the faces of his family and made a brief statement. "I know you guys gave Joe a taste of his own medicine and grilled him like he was a witness at the O.J. trial the minute he got back from our little get together, so I think it would be a good idea for me to fill you in on all that happened and is happening."

He finished his story with "I don't know how to apologize to all of you. I made a situation that was already unbearable, impossible. For that I am truly sorry. I shunned the only people who cared. When we needed each other the most, I bolted like a scared rabbit. Believe me when I tell you, I never stopped loving you for a single second. It wasn't about you; it was all about me. Me, me, me. What a sad thing it must have been for all of you. First to deal with the tragedy and then to deal with a brother who wasn't.

'The whole ordeal has changed me, I'm certain of that. How, I'm not sure. I touched on the church and Father Tom and such but God has taken a big role in my life. Father Tom says everything happens for a reason. Maybe, God does have a plan for me. Maybe this is his plan, for all of us to be together again. I don't know. All I know is that I'm different and that I want to make a difference. Life is short, of that I have no doubt, so if God has a plan for me, or for you, or for all of us together, I'm ready."

"That sounds great Tony, but DO you have a plan? Where are you going to live? What are you going to do? What are we supposed to do?" asked Betty.

"Right now, I just want to keep doing what I'm doing. I'm building a new me, and the church and the people around me right now are forging that life. I don't want to sound like a Holy Roller but I feel comfort in the Lord's word. I feel strength in His message, and if called I will serve."

"What do you mean?" asked Sam. "You talking about being a priest?"

"No, if God had that plan for me I think I'd of known that by now. I told Joe and now I'm telling all of you I don't want to inflict my beliefs on anybody. I just want you to know where my heads at. I'm alive, well, and searching. For what, I'm not sure. But I'll know when I find it. Until then I'm just happy to be with all of you again. I hope you all understand because I don't want to hurt any of you again. I've hurt you all enough for one life time."

No more questions were asked. They all just sat around talking about food, politics, and sports, and were enjoying each other's company. The past was not brought up. No one wanted to upset Tony so the conversation was mostly small talk. Until.

"Have any of you seen or talked to Gina? Is she OK?"

"We talk to her but we really don't see too much of her. She's sort of pulled away from the family Tony," answered Betty.

"You know if she's seeing anyone?"

"We really don't know a thing. She's gotten pretty hard to talk to. You know Tony everyone deals with tragedy in their own way. Gina has withdrawn and we simply don't know what's going on with her," was

Sally's response.

"I called Babe Rancuso a couple of times, checking up on her and I can tell you this, that family is not too enamored with you right now," added Joe.

"I can't blame them, after all, I did run out on everybody. Do you know if she's filed for a divorce yet?" Tony asked Joe sadly.

"I don't think so. If she had I'm sure I would have been contacted."

"If you want I could try and call her, you know, tell her where you are?" said Betty.

"Na, I'll call her myself when the time is right. I don't have anything to tell her right now. No matter what happens, I brought everything on myself. I'll deal with it. If I thought I could make things better for her with a call, I'd call her as we speak but I don't think hearing from me is going to help her right now. I hate to keep saying this 'cause I don't want you guys to think I traded the bottle for a bible, but God will show her the way. I know I don't have to tell you guys this, but I still love her. I hope someday she can forgive me."

One of the things that separate Italians from the rest of the world is that most people eat to live. Italians live to eat. With that said, Tony was really living. He ate more pasta and meatballs than maybe ever. He was so full he was forced to unbuckle his belt. That, however, did not stop him from eating dessert.

The afternoon came to a close and Tony got up to leave. "My house next week," shouted Betty.

"Sis, this has been one of the best days of my life, but I'm not ready to fall back into the regular routine. I'm not withdrawing or running away from you. On the contrary, I still just need some more time to find myself. I know you get together on Sundays and I hope I'm always invited but would you mind if it takes a little time before I can always accept?"

"We just want to be there for you Tony," said Betty. "We love you!"

"I know that Sis and I love all of you. That's got to be enough for right now. I'm fine, and everything is going to be fine. Just give me some more time. I need to start believing in myself again and start respecting myself again. I'm working on it. Trust me. You have my number and I have all of yours so we will definitely talk and I promise we'll get together for dinner soon. Is that alright with everybody?"

The family nodded their heads in unison. Everyone hugged one another and Tony left.

Tony had mixed emotions as he drove back to his retreat at the church. He was so happy to see his family that he felt a warm glow inside, but seeing all of them made him feel such loss for his wife and child. Tony made a conscious effort not to rehash the past but when your love for people is that deep it's impossible.

Tony was heading back to his room but when he looked up he was parked in front of Dominic's. A physical effort sometimes eased his tension and was a good way for him to avoid the always-present desire for a drink. He slowly got into his work out gear, still thinking about Gina, wondering if there was the slightest possibility of them getting back together. He started his work out with some light calisthenics and then broke into an easy jog around the small track that circled the main gym. After he had broken into a pretty good sweat he walked over to the speed bag. He put on his punching bag gloves, and started on the bag. Dum, dum, dum—dum, dum, dum went the bag at a steady pace.

Then it happened. Tony threw the patented right cross he used to finish off the speed bag work out. The small leather bag exploded at the seams. The inside rubber bladder burst like a balloon being pricked by a needle, and the leather outer shell was split at every seam.

"Holy mother of God," yelled Dominic. He had just walked into the place, heard the bag, saw it was Tony, and was just walking over to say hello, when he saw the most powerful punch he had ever seen thrown in his life, and believe you me he had seen a lot of punches thrown in the twenty-eight years of owning that establishment.

"Sorry Nic. The bag must have been defective or something. I'll be happy to pay for it. I didn't mean to hit it so hard."

"You kidding me? I have never seen anything like that in my entire life. Can you do that again?"

"No man, of course not, that bag was rotted. No one can punch that hard. You think I'm superman or something."

"I didn't say you were superman. I just wanna see you throw a couple more punches. Come over here. Let's see you hit this heavy bag. I'll hold it. Give it a few shots."

Dominic stood alongside the heavy sand filled canvas bag hanging from the rafters.

"Come on, let's see what you got. Give it a good lick."

Tony shook his head, walked over to the bag and threw a quick left jab into it.

"How's that," he said dropping his hands to his side.

"Come on, I'm not an old man, I can hold this thing, now hit the damn thing."

Dominic put his shoulder behind the big bag and braced himself. Tony threw a couple of more left jabs and then a solid right directly into the middle of the bag. The next thing you know, Dominic was sitting on the seat of his pants with a giant smile on his face.

"You have got to be kidding me," he said as Tony helped him up from the floor.

"Never in my life," he said again. "Look at that," he said pointing to the ground beneath the heavy bag. Sand was pouring out of the bag and was hitting the ground in a steady stream.

"I don't know what to say," said Tony. "I'm sorry. I don't know what else to say."

"Tony, I don't give a damn about the bags. I can't believe what I'm seeing here. You got the biggest punch I've ever seen. Ever. By anybody, anywhere, at anytime. Tell me again, just how old are you?"

"I'm forty, but what does that have to do with the price of bananas?"

"George Foreman was heavyweight champion of the world older than that."

"What are you, nuts? What just happened here was a freak accident. You think just because I broke a couple of bags, which by the way were probably defective, that I'm a fighter. You're way off. If you had seen the few fights I had as a kid, you would have peed your pants from laughing. I'm no fighter, so don't be getting any thoughts in that head of yours."

"I don't know about when you were a kid but I can see for myself right now. You hit somebody with that right hand and they ain't gonna hear the man count ten."

"Nic, I'm old, I ain't got nothing in the tank. I couldn't last a round with one of these young lions. They'd kill me for crying out loud. What are you thinking, really, get real man?"

"I'm thinking you won't have to go a whole round. You land one of those rights and its Katie bar the door, man. I'm thinking we need to talk about this, Tony."

"Talk about what. Nic, I promised myself a long time ago that I'd never step foot in a ring again, and for sure it's not going to be at this age."

"Tony, whatta ya got to lose?"

"My life. You think I want my brains spread all over a ring somewhere?"

"I hear what you're saying, but I don't get it. How could you waste

111

a punch like that, man?"

"To be honest with you Nic, I didn't know I could punch so hard. You see last time I was in a ring the only thing I hit hard was my back on the canvas. Now, really Nic, no more foolish talk about the fight game. Thanks for the compliment but I'm outta here."

"I understand what you're saying but this ain't quite done yet. You hear me Mr. Russo. Not quite yet. I'll let it go this time but you're making a big mistake. A big mistake."

Tony just smiled, picked up his towel, and headed for the showers. The water beat hard on his shoulders as he contemplated what just happened. He knew he had never hit that hard before and wondered why and how he just did. Things just kept getting more and more confusing for Tony. He let it go at, he must be getting stronger from all the working out. Either that or maybe it has something to do with the holy water episode he had this morning. His arm was numbed. Why? Could that have something to do with what just happened? Could God have something to do with this evening's happenings?

No, he thought. Father Tom is really screwing with my mind. But there is no denying what just happened. Something's going on. Tony just didn't know what.

Chapter 13

Tony had a restless night. The punching bag thing was eating away at him. He wanted to talk to Tom about it but found himself hesitant. He felt like Tom did when he was eleven years old, you know, about people thinking he's crazy, so he decided to just keep his mouth shut and see what happens. He got up and started in on his chores around the church.

Later at dinner he did mention to Tom that he was feeling strong and he asked him if he thought that working out like he was could make him feel stronger than he ever felt before.

"I don't know how you feel but you sure look good!" answered the priest. "It sounds like you have something on your mind buddy?"

"Not really. It's just that, oh never mind. I'm finding that I've been over analyzing everything lately. It must be old age setting in."

"I know what you mean. These old bones of mine are getting pretty squeaky themselves. Maybe I should come with you over to Nic's and work out? I could use it."

"Why don't you?"

"If I could find the time I would."

"You'll have to make time."

"Yeah, I think you're right, I just might surprise you and show up over there sometime."

Tony got up, went to his room, watched a little television and then got ready to go over to the gym. A lot had happened over the course of the last thirty-six hours but one thing was the same: if he wanted money he had to go to work. He was picking up towels in the locker room when Big Nic walked in.

"Tony, you got a minute?" asked Nic in an inquisitive tone.

"Sure Nic, What do you need?"

"Nothing much, I was just thinking. What do I pay you, 150 bucks a week?"

"Yeah, what's up, you finally giving me a raise?"

"Something like that. How'd you like to make another $150.00 for ten minutes work?"

"I'm not liking the sound of this," Tony replied.

"Just listen to what I've got to say here. I can't get last night out of my mind. I know you said you didn't want to fight but I got this idea. Give me three rounds as a sparring partner. I'll pay you fifty bucks a round. That's five times more than I pay anybody for that. You can't tell me you didn't think about those shots you threw last night. Aren't you the least bit interested in how you'd do in the ring? I know I am, and this is a good way to really see what you've got. Come on, you're in good shape. I got a real good feeling about this. What da ya say?"

"Look Nic, I'm not in the mood to take a beating right now. Don't let a couple of lucky shots fool you. I'm no fighter."

114

"I know what I saw and that wasn't luck. You've got real power Tony. I'll tell you what I'll put you in with a middleweight. You outweigh the guy by sixty pounds; you're not going to get hurt. I just want to see how you move. I already know you can punch. I'll give you the 150 for two rounds. How can you refuse that?"

"Hell, you're not going to give up are you? Two rounds and that's it. OK, you got it. I could really use the extra money anyway."

"Great, grab some head gear and I'll tape your hands up myself. I'm looking forward to this."

"Well, I'm not. Let's just get this over with."

Tony walked out of the locker room and over to the main ring. Standing in the middle of the canvas was Brian Scott, Nic's ranked middleweight.

"Wait a minute Nic," bellowed Tony as he saw his opponent. "Give me a break here. I ain't gonna fight the kid here, he'll kill me."

"I told you, you out weigh him by sixty pounds or so. You'll be fine. Show a little backbone."

"I've got plenty of backbone; the problem is I have even more brains. Fighting Brian is not a very smart thing regardless of the weight difference."

"Warm up. A deal's a deal," responded the big promoter.

The next thing you know Tony was strapping on the headgear and climbing into the ring. The bell rang and Tony started dancing. The kid was quick and fast and Tony covered up and took quite a few shots although he was doing a very unexpected thing by blocking a lot of them with his arms. Bang, Tony threw out a stiff left and Scott winced. Scott looked over to Nic and gave him a look that said, this guy can punch. Big Nic smiled. after all it was nothing but a left jab. Bang, bang Tony threw out two more lefts and to his surprise the kid was backing up. Tony got aggressive and started moving in. He faked a left and threw the right. It landed on Brian Scott's left shoulder and knocked the kid clear off his feet.

"Time," yelled Dominic from the side of the ring, even though they were only half way through the round. "Tony, come over here!" he yelled.

"What did I do?" Tony asked as he pulled his head gear off.

"Are you kidding me? I don't want the kid hurt. Get out of the ring and sit here for a minute, I want to talk to you."

"Is the kid all right Andy?" yelled Nic, in the direction of Andy Carlo, Brian's trainer.

"Yeah, boss, what are you doing putting the kid in with that big guy. He's got way too much power to be fighting a middleweight."

"Yeah, I know. Sorry, give the kid a rub down and send him to the showers. That's enough for today."

Dominic Michaeloni turned to Tony and shook his head. "Who are you?" he said with a look of fear in his eyes. "Are you hiding out from something or you on the lam or what, 'cause there is no way you're not a fighter. Who are you?"

"Nic, I'm nobody. I'm not a fighter never have been. I had a few fights as a kid but when it came to the nut cutting I simply wasn't good. I'm just a guy down on his luck and apparently a guy with a good right hand. I'm not lying to you. I swear I really didn't even know I could hit this hard. Honest."

"Well, stay right there. You still owe me a round." He looked around the gym and yelled to the big fighter working out on the heavy bag. "Hey, Paulie, Paulie Jay, I want you to get in the ring for a round of sparring."

"Come on Nic," said Tony "I can't get in there with Paulie. Come on man cut me a little slack. He'll kill me. Getting in there with the kid is one thing but this has stopped being funny. I don't need the friggin' money that bad."

"Tony, I can't believe I'm saying this but I'm more worried about my contender than I am about you. I just don't know what to say. Scott's a fighter; a damn good fighter and he can take a punch. You knocked him three feet in the air with an arm punch. I have never, never seen a punch like yours. Just get in there and I don't know, keep away from him as much as you can and see if you can land that bomb you throw." Nic shook his head and waited for the sparring to begin.

By this time the whole gym was quiet and every guy in the place was focused on the center ring. Tony was scared. Paulie Jay was a contender who is ranked number five by the WBA. One or two more wins and this guy's got a legitimate chance at the title. Paulie Jay was laughing when he stepped into the ring. He saw it was the clean up man with the headgear on and thought that Nic was playing a practical joke on him. He knew what just happened with Brian Scott and figured that it was all a set up but he figured he'd play along with the joke.

"Hey, towel boy, you ready for this?" he blurted out from his corner.

"I guess this is Nic's idea of fun," Tony answered.

Nic yelled, "Time."

Paulie came out slow and cautious but his two guns were cocked and loaded. He wasn't going to let this joke go too far. He'd bide his time and finish off the cleaning man with one shot. Tony on the other hand was thinking "What if I could land this right hand maybe I can get out of this with my life." and he moved towards the well-muscled fighter.

Like a bolt of lightning Tony threw out the right hand and caught Paulie Jay square on the jaw. The contender left the ground and landed four feet from where he was standing. Out cold.

Dominic slapped his hand on his forehead. He looked at Tony with amazement. The whole place was buzzing. What is going on?

thought every fighter in the building. Nic was dumbfounded. He gathered his thoughts and called Tony over to the side of the ring again.

He said shaking his head. "We've got to talk right now."

Tony's mind raced. He was no fool. He knew that something was going on. He was as dumbfounded as everyone else, but now he was now putting two and two together. "God did this," he thought. God has done something to him. "Why? Why?" he thought as he stepped out of the ring.

He walked over to Nic put his hand on his shoulder and said, "I don't want to talk just now Nic, O.K. You're going to ask me a bunch of questions and I don't have any answers for you, so let me take a shower and I'll come into your office when I'm done." Tony bit the ends of the laces on his gloves to untie them, pulled them off and headed to the showers.

Thirty minutes later he stood in the doorway of Big Nic's office. "I don't know what happened out there. I'm not a fighter," he said almost pleading for Nic to understand.

"Tony, I've never seen nothing like this. That was Paulie Jay, man. That wasn't some two-bit punk I pulled out of the gutter to stand there and take a beating. You knocked out Paulie Jay with one punch. Hell you knock him flying and out cold. You're a fighter all right. You're the most powerful fighter I've ever seen."

"Look, keep your money. I was wondering myself what I got going here and to tell you the truth I still don't know. I do know what you're thinking Nic, and I'm too old to be a fighter. I'm forty years old, man. I know you're thinking I can really dish it out but at this age I don't think I can take the beating a fighter takes. Thank you for the thrill. I have to admit I didn't think I'd make it through a single round, no less what happened. It was exciting, but that's it. I'm no fighter."

"Tony, here's your money. You've earned every cent but even you have to recognize what you have in those fists. You have lightning speed and enough power to knock out an elephant. I've been sitting here waiting for you and honestly I don't know what to say. Just don't count anything out. Go home. Forget about cleaning up right now. Go home and think about this. In a year I can make you a rich man, a very rich man. Don't say no. Don't say anything. Just come back tomorrow about 5:00 and we'll have dinner and we can talk. I'm going to make a few phone calls in the morning and then we can talk. Promise me you'll have an open mind about this. I'm telling you Tony, riches upon riches. I'm not lying. I know what I've seen. Let's just talk tomorrow."

"O.K. Nic. I'll have dinner with you tomorrow, but . . ."

"Hold it right there Tony. No buts. Dinner tomorrow."

"I'll see you tomorrow Nic."

Tony left the gym with his mind in a state of confusion. But one thing was pretty obvious to him. That shiver, that unbelievable shiver was "God". It had to be, but why, and for what. He picked up his pace as he headed for the rectory, Father Tom was the only person on his mind right then and Tony was hoping for answers. The only problem was he didn't even know the questions.

Chapter 14

Tony was flat out running when he hit the stairs of the rectory. He found Father Tom in the library working on next week's sermon. Tom looked up at Tony and immediately knew something was wrong.

"What happened? What's wrong?" asked the priest instinctively.

"Father, I don't know what to say. I, I, something is happening to me. Something that just can't be explained. I know what you've been saying all this time but I just couldn't and didn't believe it."

"Slow down. What are you talking about?"

"You know from the first time you said it I thought you were right but I really never, I had no idea. I'm not even sure if—"

"Tony, what in the Sam Hill are you talking about?"

"Tom, you know how you told me when we met up about God must have a plan for me? You said you know that he must have sent you there to find me. You said that you think I'm supposed to go with you, that its God's will."

"Tony, get to the point."

"Well, Tom something has happened, and I can't explain it, and I don't even know what it is. I don't have a clue of what I'm supposed to do. Not even to mention if it's going to last."

"For crying out loud Tony would you mind telling me what you're talking about?"

"O.K., I'll start from yesterday morning. I was sitting in the church listening to your story about when you got the calling. I'll be honest I wasn't absolutely convinced that the Lord actually spoke to you. I was thinking maybe that happened in your mind. But now I am. Tom, the thing is, I'm supposed to do something for the Lord. I've been contacted I guess. I say I guess 'cause I wasn't told anything. I didn't hear a voice. There was no message. I'm not even sure what happened. All I know is that I waited until almost everyone was out of the church before I got up to leave. You know I had all that family stuff on my mind and all. Well, anyway as I was blessing myself to leave I stuck my fingers, these two fingers here (Tony held up his index and forefinger of his right hand) and when I put them in the holy water I got this indescribable shiver that ran up my right arm kind of numbing it and then the shiver went through my entire body. I thought that I was having a stroke or something. Then I thought that God was going to talk to me and I actually waited a few seconds to listen. I started laughing when I realized what I was doing, and I blamed the whole thing on your sermon about being a soldier for God."

The priest stood there in the library with a look of astonishment on his face and waited with bated breath for Tony to continue.

"Anyway, I didn't think anymore about it until last night." Tony continued and told the priest everything from the punching bag part, to the fights, all the way through until his final conversation with Dominic

121

Michaeloni a few minutes ago. "What is going on? Please Father, you've got to help me. I have no idea what is going on!"

"Tony, I don't know what to tell you. I don't know. This is not an everyday thing here. Let's sit down and analyze what has happened and try and put some options to this whole thing."

Tony and Tom sat down in the two easy chairs in the corner of the room. "First of all Tony, I don't think it would be a good idea to be broadcasting this to anybody. I'm not sure people will believe you. Secondly, are you sure you're not just stronger from all this working out you've been doing?"

"Tom, if you would have seen the power in the punches I've been throwing, you wouldn't be asking me that. I'm telling you Tom, I'm carrying the right hand of God here. I'm not kidding you." Tony stuck out his right fist and reiterated.

"The Right Hand of the Father, Tom!"

"O.K., let's say that I believe you, and I do believe you, it's just that what you're proposing is extremely hard to believe. I guess the question is, *why*."

"What the blazes do you think I've been asking you since I got here?"

"I know Tony, but I really don't know. That's what we're going to have to figure out."

"Well I'm all ears Tom, come up with something."

"Let me see. I can hardly get a handle on this, buddy, but assuming that he gave you this power to be a fighter, to gain fame. What could you do for God's cause if you were a famous person?"

"Then you think I'm supposed to start fighting. That doesn't seem like a thing God would want one of his soldiers to do. Do you think?"

"I am not now nor have I ever thought that I could figure out what God has in mind for anyone for any reason. I'm just looking at the options. You know not everyone who spreads the Lord's word is a priest, a minister, a pastor, or for that matter a rabbi. The Lord moves in mysterious ways and spreads the word through a multitude of different sources. This could be one way."

"I don't know Tom. Who says that I'll still have this punch tomorrow. This could be a freak thing or something. I don't think I can just get into the fight game at this stage in my life. I'm just way too old for this."

"You're not that old and besides, that just doesn't matter. If God chose you and he wants you to spread his word through this medium it wouldn't matter if you were 100, so let's not delve into the reasons or the methods, let's just try and figure out the what you are supposed to do with it question."

"Well, I guess it would be something if an old guy started fighting. It would probably get some attention and I guess if I were any good I'd get the ear of a few people. I guess if I could get somebody to write something about me I could try and preach the word. But Tom I don't know what the word is. I'm no priest."

"All we try to do as priests is let the people know that God is there for us. That he is all forgiving and there will always be a place by his side for anyone who follows. We are all children of God. If I were in a position to pass on a message to the multitudes it would be a simple one. It would be that God exists and that he loves us."

"Amen," said Tony. "I hope I'm not blowing this out of proportion. I hope I'm not reading something into this that's not there. But I'm telling you Tom if I can stay away from getting my brains knock out and I land this punch, I could win some fights. I know how crazy that sounds but it's not me who's doing it. This arm here is attached to my body but Tom, I said it earlier and I mean it, this isn't my right hand and the power it holds isn't mine. I'm supposed to meet Dominic tomorrow night for dinner. He wants to talk to me about fighting. I guess I'd better listen to what he has to say. If I'm supposed to spread the word of the Lord by boxing then I'd better get started. I'm no spring chicken. The thing is, how is Nic going to get anybody to put a forty-year-old rookie on a fight card. I don't know, this whole thing is way over my head, but I'm going with the God must know what he's doing thing. Let's face it, who am I to argue."

Tony got up to leave. The men looked at one another and simply shook their heads. The Lord works in mysterious ways all right, but this was beyond belief.

"One thing, Father. I think you're right. I won't be telling a living soul about what happened in the church. Let's just keep this between us. Besides you and me, who else would believe a story like this anyway?"

The next thing you know Tony was sitting at Tom and Jay's, a cozy restaurant owned by the Brocconi brothers, close friends of Dominic's.

"Listen Tony, you've got talent but at your age it's gonna be kinda hard for me to get you a fight. I called a couple of promoter friends of mine and I couldn't get you anything. If I can put something together at my place, something in the line of an exhibition fight, would you go through with it? I don't want to push and I realize that I am, but I've been thinking about nothing else for the last couple of days. I just can't get this out of my head and feel like you'd be wasting an unbelievable amount of talent if you don't get into the ring. And I mean now. Are you or are you not interested in exploring the possibilities?"

"Look Nic, I don't know how to go about it. I do know this though, I feel like if I could land a few shots I could hold my own in the ring. I'm just not sure I have the speed to fight these young guys. It takes a lot more than a good punch to win a fight. You tell me that you can train me and not get me killed. I think I could do all right. I've been doing a lot of thinking myself. I don't want to get religious on you, buddy, but I talked to Father Tom a little about this and he thinks why not give it a try. Maybe I could let a few folks know that I'm a believer and sort of pass on that thought. Like I've said before I'm not a holy roller but I've been helped here in my life by my faith and if I can help others, why not."

"I don't care what you pass on, Tony. All I want is to see what you can do in the ring. You trust in God, I'll trust in my talent as a judge of boxers, and man you are a born fighter. That punch of yours is out of this world and I just want to see where it can take us. I'll train you all right, and I'll manage you. All I want is twenty-five percent of your action."

"Is that a normal number?"

"Normal is a funny word. What happens in the fight game is that the purse is split up between the fighters according to contract or in the beginning there is a purse you fight for and the winner gets a bigger share. Then everyone gets a piece of the pie. The promoter, the manager, the trainer, the cut man, hell, in the beginning you have to pay for your locker for crying out loud. At the end of all the pieces the fighter usually ends up with less than half that's for sure. But in your case I'll take care of everybody and everything from my twenty-five percent and you can have the rest. Trust me I don't give deals like this but I want to see you fight. I want to see you fight real bad."

"O.K., I'll do it but when I say it's over, it's over. I know damn well you're going to hand me some kind of a contract and I want to make sure you don't hang me out to dry with it."

"Tony, this is no regular thing that's happening here. This is not a money thing for me. Well, maybe a little. Why not make some money if we can. But man I wish you could understand what I've seen you do. Man, I want to make money but that's not why we're talking right now. Don't laugh but you've got more talent than any fighter I've ever seen.

You're not young, you're a total unknown, but people are going to follow you my man, this is going to be fun. Bottom line, the fight game stopped being fun for me a long time ago Tony, and you can bring some life back into it for me. I've already got enough money to quit this game so it's not for the money. This is going to be fun, man, fun and exciting. I'm not wrong buddy. This is flat going to be fun."

The two men shook hands and a smile came over Dominic Michaeloni's face like a Cheshire cat's. They had their dinner, then talked about what they would have to do to get the ball rolling, and before you knew it, it was done. Tony Russo was back in the fight business. Not like he really ever was, but he was back just the same.

"I'll take care of everything Tony, and as far as a contract that hand shake was good enough for me. I'll get something down in writing but it's not going to be too much, just enough to explain some things and say that we already shook hands and it's a deal. If you don't like what's on there let me know and we'll change it. You ain't no kid, and I'm not trying to pull anything, it's just good business to have something in writing.

"By the way we'll work out something as far you having a little money. You're going to make something for this exhibition fight but as of right now, you're fired from clean up duty. I don't want the next heavy weight champion of the world doubling as a clean-up man." Dominic laughed as he said it but in his heart it wasn't all that funny. "Starting tomorrow you're in training. Come to the gym around noon and we'll get started."

Tony was mystified by the last few days' happenings. He lay in his bed non-stop thinking about what happened and what was about to happen. He wasn't sure about either. The only thing that he was sure of was that everything in his life was about to change. How and what was going to happen he didn't know. He just hoped he'd live through it.

The Right Fist of the Father

Chapter 15

Every eye in the place was on Tony as he walked out of the locker room all taped up and ready to train. The word spread thru the gym, like wild fire, that Tony was getting into the game. This would have been funny if not for the fights they saw. These fighters know what it means to get in the ring with the caliber of fighters the likes of a Brian Scott and Paulie Jay. Just to come out whole is a feat but to knock them both out, and both in the first round. This was someone these fighters wanted to see. An old mop man, and now they're all standing around and watching him like he was **Muhammad Ali.**

"Hey Tony, come here a minute," said Dominic walking out from his office. "This is Andy Carlo, I think you know him, he trains some of the boys around here. He's Brian Scott's trainer and the best trainer I know. I want him to work with you. You have any objections?"

"No, Nic, great. Did you tell him that I don't know my ass from my elbow about fighting?"

Andy held out his hand to shake Tony's and said, "If I had your punch Tony I wouldn't worry about knowing the ins and outs of the game. I'd just try and figure out how I can land more than I take, and from what I seen when you fight there's only two sounds: you hitting them and them hitting the floor."

"Did I hurt your boy?" said Tony inquisitively.

"Only his pride." Andy answered. "But we're not here to talk about Brian, we're here to get you ready for a fight and we don't have much time."

"What's up? Did Nic put something together already?"

Nic stepped between the two men and said, "A week from Friday a four fight card, you're fighting the second fight against a kid from East St. Louis, Jackson Lannie. This guy's had ten fights and is seven and three with five knockouts. He's big. 265. But that means slow. He'll have a hard time hitting you if you move around a lot and if you land that bomb. Well, let's see how it goes. The purse is $2500.00. The split is two grand to the winner. It's being held at the Casino on the river so there should be a nice crowd. Scott's on the card as the main event, and that will help. How's that sound?"

"Hell, I haven't even broken a sweat yet as a pro and I'm fighting in a week and a half. You don't fool around, Nic. We'd better get started. Andy, I don't want to look like a fool, number one, wait a minute, I take that back. Number one I don't want to be killed. Two grand ah, well $500.00 don't sound that bad. How many rounds?"

"Oh, just four, but I'm not worried about that with that punch of yours it will be lucky to go two."

"Nic, you've got a lot more confidence in me than me. I'm just wanting to survive."

"Don't worry about a thing. This is just the beginning. I've got a good feeling Tony. I've been saying this but I mean it. I've got a real good feeling. Now Andy, see what kind of shape this guy's in. I wouldn't want him embarrassing himself by puking in front of all those people." Nic laughed and walked away.

Tony went through his normal routine with Andy tweaking it slightly. He didn't want to change too much. Tony worked out on both the heavy and speed bag, he ran, not roadwork, but running; he jumped rope, did sit-ups and other stretching exercises. In general it was a decent work out. Andy felt that it was enough to get him through till this first fight and then Tony would find out what a pro boxer's workout was really going to be. But for right now Andy was satisfied with Tony's workout and his shape.

The week went well. Tony was starting to feel like a boxer. The only thing that he wasn't sure of, and how could he be, was the power in his punch. He knew that he couldn't punch the bags with any authority without breaking them so that was his guide to tell him that it was still there. He was as ready as he was going to be. What he was going to do after was still way up in the air. He wasn't going to be able to preach or anything like that. After all it was an under card fight with an unknown. Who cared what he had to say about anything, so Tony really wasn't sure what was going to happen. If the opportunity doesn't happen the way he and Father Tom wanted as far as promoting the word of the Lord, what is he supposed to do? What purpose is all this?

Tony sat in the dressing room at the Riverboat Casino, listening to the crowd cheering during the first fight. He was nervous of course but not scared. He was ready. Nic and Andy were in the dressing room giving Tony his final instructions. They heard the decision for the fight that just ended, Tony said a prayer, and the three men got up to go to the ring. Tony hadn't said anything to his family or friends about this. He wasn't sure how it would be accepted. He may have known someone in the crowd but he wasn't about to look around. He was focused on the corner of the ring as he came down the aisle. He climbed into the ring, powdered the bottom of his shoes in the rosin box, and danced to get warmed up. His opponent, Jackson Lannie, was already in the ring and was ready to go. Their names were announced, to no great amount of applause. The bulk of the crowd was there to see Brian Scott so these under card fights were considered just warm ups. The referee gave the men the rules, they touched gloves, and went back to their respective corners to wait for the bell.

The bell sounded, signifying round one. Tony came out cautiously, and watched Jackson intently. Jackson threw caution to the wind and rushed Tony. Jackson landed two very fast left jabs, surprising Tony with the speed of his hands. For a big man he could zip them out. Tony danced to his left trying to nullify the big man's right hand but as he did he got caught with a big left hook. It staggered Tony for a second. He hadn't been hit that hard since he was a kid fighting in the Golden Gloves and he was stunned.

Lannie saw an opening and kept on coming. "Get the hell out of there," yelled Andy from the corner. But Tony couldn't move. It seemed like his feet were made of cement. All he could do was cover up because he was pretty sure Jackson wasn't finished with his barrage. Tony threw out a solid left jab himself hoping to stay off the charge. He caught Jackson on the top of his head and stopped the big man's forward progress like he ran into a wall. Tony got his composure, danced away and survived the first round.

"You've got to throw some gloves out there Tony. What you have is a punch but it doesn't do you any good just sitting there. Go out there and hit him like you're working out on the heavy bag. This guy cannot stand your power. I promise you he'll fall like a turd from a tall horse. Don't give him a chance to get away. Just pound him." Andy threw a sponge full of water into Tony's face, smeared some Vaseline on his eyebrows got him up and sent him in to do battle.

Tony came out of the corner like a bull in a china shop. Left, left, left, left, and Jackson was covering up. Two more lefts and Tony had his man backing up all the way to the ropes. Jackson bent down to duck the battering ram left jabs and Tony unleashed a right upper cut.

BOOM was the sound his glove made as it caught his opponent square on the chin. The force of the punch lifted him up and clear over the ropes. He landed in the first row out like a light. The crowd was totally silent as the referee signaled the fight over immediately.

No one uttered a sound for what seemed to Tony an eternity then a roar rose from the stunned fight fans that was deafening. Lannie was helped to his feet by his corner men and Tony swore he heard Jackson say "Somebody answer the phone."

The crowd was wild. They cheered as Tony's hand was raised. "What a punch," and "Oh my God," along with a vast array of expletives could be heard throughout the arena. Tony was mauled by the fans, who had just been treated to a once in a lifetime knockout, as he exited the ring. Many men have been knocked through the ropes but never had a fighter been knocked over them. This was special, and these fans knew it.

"Holy crap Tony!" shouted Nic. "I knew it! I knew it! I knew it!" screamed Nic.

Tony looked down at his glove and held it up to the ceiling and thanked God for not being hurt. He looked over at Nic standing over in the corner and said, "I caught him a good one, buddy."

"Are you kidding? What an understatement! You have no idea! This couldn't have worked out better. They'll be talking about that punch forever." Nic laughed and laughed.

"I won't have a lick of trouble getting you booked for another fight. Every promoter in town will be calling. I couldn't have scripted it better if I tried. I knew it. Damn, I knew it."

Within minutes there was a knock at the dressing room door.

Nic got up to answer it. He smiled when he saw who was standing on the other side of the door. This doesn't happen. Not at this level. Reporters, reporters were standing there asking Nic if they could talk to his fighter.

"Come on in fellows," responded Nic.

"Tony Russo, hell of a fight, fella. Are you aware of the size of the guy you just knock over the ropes?" asked Pat Dryjal the fight desk sports reporter from the St. Louis Star.

"First I'd like to thank my Lord and Savior Jesus Christ, and thank him that no one was hurt. And the answer to your question is I don't know exactly how big he was but I do know that he sure hit like a big man. I can barely hold up my arms from the punches he hit them with."

"Well I've got to tell you, I have never seen a punch like that. Never. You must have eaten all your Wheaties this morning, fella. Man, what a hitter."

"Thank you, but it's not the Wheaties. I fight for God." Nic rolled his eyes as the reporter said, "Excuse me."

"I fight in the name of God. I'm not crazy or some religious fanatic. I chose to fight at a later time in life because I thought that I could let the people know out there through my fighting that God loves them and that He'll always be there for them. Trust in the Lord and he shall provide."

Pat turned to Nic and asked, "Is this some kind of a joke?"

Nic responded, "All I know is that I believe the guy. He's over forty and he hits like nothing I've ever seen before. But why ask me, my fighter's right in front of you. If you have any questions just ask him."

"O.K. Tony. How long have you been fighting and how old are you? What's your record? They said out there that this was your first

133

professional fight. What's with that? Where are you from and what have you been doing until now? How did you get into the fight game?"

"Hold it guys. I'm not dodging your questions. I just don't want to answer every one of them right now. I'll just give you this statement. Then you can go out there where the real fighters are putting on a show and forget about this fluke punch I just landed. My name is Anthony Russo (Tony). I'm forty years old. I fought years ago as a kid but haven't taken the sport back up till now. I'm from right here in St. Louis. I'm born and raised on the Hill. I got hooked up with Mr. Michaeloni and he convinced me to fight, he liked my style. He thinks I hit hard. I'm a guy who just rediscovered the Lord and would like to let others out there know His message. I'm no priest and I'm not a holy roller. I'm just a guy who wants to spread the word. If you guys write this you'll be helping God too. I've got to tell you it makes you feel pretty darn good."

They asked him some more questions concerning the fight. He answered and gave a lot of credit to Nic and Andy. He also mentioned the gym and a bunch of fighters in it. They listened intently but it was obvious that the punch was the news item and they did single in on that. After the questions they all shook hands and they left to cover the next fight. Nic closed the door behind them.

"I know you said you wanted to pass the word but man Tony you're not the Pope. I'm not complaining but these guys want to hear that you're an animal or something that they can sell papers with. They want to really hype up that shot they saw and they come in here and you give them Sunday service."

"Nic, I told you. I'm just glad they even talked to us. I did a little advertising for the gym. What did I do wrong?"

"You didn't do anything wrong. We'll just have to wait to see what they write if they write anything at all. Trust me, they'll write something about that knockout and that's all that we need to move up. I thought

that it was going to take something special for us to be noticed but I had
no idea that this would happen. You really turned some heads. By
tomorrow morning people in this town will know who Tony Russo is.
Mark my words. Nice fight Tony. Nice fight."

Tony showered up and headed home. He was anxious to tell
Father Tom. Funny he wasn't as excited about winning the fight as he
was about talking to the reporters and preaching the word. "God works
in mysterious ways!" thought Tony as he pulled up to the rectory. He
was excited about talking to Tom but he knew he'd better call his
brother first. He didn't want him hearing about this from somebody else
or even worse reading about it in the paper. So as he walked into the
rectory he picked up the phone and called.

"Hey, Tony. Where you been? We thought we'd hear from you
sooner than this. Is everything alright?"

"Yeah Joe, in fact I've got something to tell you." Tony told Joe
about the fight. He told him about preaching and all but he didn't tell
him about the power. Well he told him about having this real good
right hand but he didn't tell him where it came from.

"You have got to be kidding me. Jesus, Tony you're forty years
old. I don't mean to sound pessimistic but you're going to get killed. What
came over you?"

"Joe, trust me. I'll know when to stop but it's not right now. I'm
pretty good bro. I'll let you know when my next fight is and maybe you
can come and watch."

"You know, I'll bet there is no other guy in the world that has a
brother like you. I mean it. I never know what's going to come out of
your mouth but this takes the cake. Look I don't understand. I don't
understand at all. But if there were ever anybody who could pull off
anything like this it would be you. I swear, so what can I say except let
me know when and where. I'll be there. Now what's this about reading

the Star in the morning?"

"You'll find out. You'll find out."

Tony hung up and immediately went looking for Father Tom. He was eating a sandwich in the kitchen when Tony came in.

"All I can say is, you should have come," Tony said with a big smile. "You missed it."

"Are you saying you won?"

"Everybody won Tom. Just read the paper tomorrow. Everybody won."

Chapter 16

The next morning there it was at the bottom of the second page of the sports section in Pat Dryjal column. *"Local fighter records knock out.* The story went on to say *Tony Russo a forty year old home town fighter from the Hill, in his debut fight, knocked his opponent out alright, he knocked him clean out of the ring, and more than that he knocked him over the top rope."* Dryjal went on to say *"It was the most powerful punch I have ever witnessed. When asked why he waited so long to start fighting especially since he packed such a wallop. Russo responded that for many reasons, he fights for the Lord. He said he thought that if he was good, he could get a little media coverage, and that would be a good way to pass on the message that God exists and that he loves us. I don't know about you out there but if you could have seen this fight you too would be inclined to listen to what this guy says. I'm looking forward to his next fight."*

Tony was sitting at the table in his room drinking a cup of coffee when there was a knock and the door opened. There was his brother Joe standing there with the morning paper in his hand.

"What is going on?" he said with a look of amazement on his face. "Dryjal is making out like you're some kind of superman, some kind of Holy Roller superman. What the hell is going on here Tony?"

"Joe, I told you I've been working out and I developed a pretty good punch."

"A pretty good punch, Tony you knocked the guy over the ropes. A pretty good punch, Dryjal says it's the best shot he's ever seen. Are you kidding me?"

"Joe, a lots going on right now. I told you I'm a new man when it comes to my beliefs and coupled with fighting I can do some good, so I'm going for it."

"I don't know what to say. I don't understand any of this. From this place you're living in, to all of a sudden you're a professional boxer. I don't get it. I simply just don't get it."

"There's nothing to get. I was working out. Dominic saw me and was impressed, put me in with a couple of his fighters and he liked what he saw. The next thing you know he entered me into this fight and I won. What can I tell you, it's a good way for me to make money and at the same time pass on the word of God, so here we are. If I get to a place I don't belong I'll quit, but Joe, I can fight. Don't be worried for me. I can fight. I'm not planning a long career here. I know how old I am but there are a lot of guys out there that are fighting later on in life then me. I'm really not that much of an oddity."

"Tony the old guys out there are finishing off their long careers. They're just hanging around for a few more paychecks. They're not just getting started."

"Joe, trust me. I know what I'm doing. What do I have to lose especially if some good can come out of all this? I'm telling you I'm not

138

a holy roller but I'm alive today because of God and if I can help his cause in any way I'm going to try and do it. I had one fight. One lousy fight and already I've been able to pass on a little of his message. Plus I made few bucks. What's wrong with that? As long as I can stay away from being hurt everybody wins."

"Yeah, but that's a pretty big if."

"Joe, I'm all right. Thank you for worrying but trust me I'm going to be fine. I know it. Don't ask me why but I know it. Now I was just going to go out and get some breakfast you want to join me?"

"Sounds good. I've got a little time before I need to be in the office. I guess you can fill me in on what you have to do for this fighting thing. Do you have any idea when and where your next fights going to be."

"Yeah, now you're interested. The answer to your question is no but if I know Dominic, it won't be too long. Let's go eat, I'm hungry."

Tony walked into the gym around 11:00. As soon as he hit the door Dominic called him over.

"Nice fight Tony. I'm already working on a second."

"Have any idea when, where, and who?"

"Just give me until tomorrow and we'll have something. You've got to strike while the fire's hot and that little ditty Dryjal wrote is just the ticket. By the way I've got your money here from the fight. Let's see the winners' share was $2,000.00. I took my share $500.00 that leaves you with $1,500. Here you go buddy. This is just the start."

Tony grabbed the money and was somewhat surprised about it. It's not that he couldn't use it but he felt like he didn't deserve it. He stood there looking at it and wondering.

"You said you were going to take care of Andy and expenses from you end, right?"

"That's right, no big deal, I told you this isn't about money for me.

139

When the big fights start happening, I'll do alright."

"Thanks Nic. Thanks for everything. Without you I'd be cleaning toilets right now."

"No thanks needed Tony. This is going to be some ride. I feel it. I knew it when I saw that bag blow and now I'm sure. We're going a long way together. You just wait and see."

Tony walked out of Nic's office and went directly into the locker room to get taped up and changed. This was no longer just some exercise—he's better get in the best shape of his life or pay the consequences. Andy called him over and they got started.

Tony was lost in thought as he showered and got dressed after the workout. He wanted to talk to Father Tom about something. He was hoping Tom was in his quarters as he walked into the rectory.

Tony found him where he usually was, in the library, working. "Father," said Tony.

"Hey Tony, what's up?"

"I got paid for the fight today. 1500 big ones."

"Nice, it looks like you could be on your feet in no time at this rate."

"Yeah, but Tom I've been thinking. You think this is what God had in mind. You know me making money off of this whole thing. I don't think so. I'm thinking about doing something nice with this money. Something that can help others."

"Like what Tony?"

"Well Tom just the other day you said something about that nursing home over on Shaw Ave. You said something about them having a dinky little TV that had a terrible picture and you felt sorry for the oldsters sitting around trying to watch it. I've got 1500 hogs here; let's go buy those poor people a big screen. That's what I want to do with this money."

"Tony Russo, God sure picked the right guy to do whatever it is he wants you to do. You're a good man Anthony."

Off they went to Brewer Brothers appliances to buy the TV. They went there because they guarantee next day delivery and Tony wanted to make sure he was there when it was delivered. He wanted to see the smiles on their faces.

Tony and Tom had smiles from ear to ear as they left the nursing home the next day. Tony's heart was bursting from happiness as he got in the car.

"I think this is what it's all about. Not just talking about God's gift but actually giving. I think I'm supposed to give the money I win away. I'm supposed to help others with it. What do you think Tom? Doesn't that make sense?"

"Tony, I don't know. You keep asking me questions about what God wants from you and I don't know. I think what you just did was great. I'm so happy for those people and for you. I know that it is far greater to give than to receive. But, you just spent about a grand. If I was a betting man I think God wouldn't mind if you took the rest of the money and bought some stuff you might need. Maybe buy some sorely needed clothes and stuff like that. If you think that you should share in your good fortune with those less fortunate, I think that's great. But I also think that you should better yourself if you can. I love having you at the rectory but you deserve better living quarters than that."

"Yeah, maybe Tom. Let's see if I end up with any more money. I could get my head caved in the next fight and not win a dime. If I still have the punch that's enough sign for me. I'll at least share whatever I win with the needy. I feel pretty good right now and it's a feeling I want to keep around. That's my decision."

"God bless you Tony. God bless you."

"Thank you Father. I think he already has."

141

The next couple of weeks went by without a hitch. Tony worked out as hard as he could and he got into better and better shape every workout. He was strong, he was getting more and more stamina, and his hands were getting fast. That's an unlucky combination for his next opponent. It's bad enough that when he hit you, you went flying. Now he actually was getting the speed in his hands so he can land that big punch. He was starting to think he could live through this. He knew he had the punch but he wasn't sure he could deliver it. He was starting to get some confidence when Nic called him into the office. He had just signed him for another fight.

"One month from tomorrow, the Savis Center, Willie Allen, ten rounds, $10,000 purse, $7500.00 to the winner. How's that for a second professional fight?" Nic said laughingly. "I just knocked a year off of our schedule."

"Hold it. What schedule?" responded Tony

"Madison Square Garden. That's where we're going. I don't know when or against who but that's where we're going."

"Slow down Nic. I'm not worried about Madison Square Garden. I'm worried about Allen. Plus man, I can't go ten. I'll be dead tired in the fourth."

"Then knock him out before the fourth!"

"You know Nic, you're starting to worry me. I'm a novice and you've got me ready to fight the champ. You'd better slow down your thinking here pal or you're going to have a dead older Italian on your hands."

"You didn't say anything about the money. How's that for a second fight purse?" boasted Nic.

"You are good Nic. Either that or you snowed someone."

"It's that over the top rope thing buddy. People want to see if that was a fluke or if you're for real. You need to win this fight, and you need to win it big."

"How good is Willie Allen and what kind of a chance do I have against him? What's his record? What's his style? What's his knock out ratio? Can he put me out with one shot? You've got me winning big and I don't know if I can last a minute with this guy. Nic, you're going to get me killed. I'm not ready for the Savis. Man, I'm a little scared."

"Scared, scared, the way you punch the only people who should be scared are Allen and all the people in the first two rows. I wish you'd realize your potential Tony. I don't give a damn about how many fights you've had. You are one tough man. I wouldn't want to step in the ring with you, and that's a fact.

"Now as far as Allen, he's a good fighter. He doesn't have the big punch but he punches in combination very well. It takes a good combo for him to knock a guy out so I'm not worried about him landing a lucky one and ending the fight. Andy will school you on this guy and we'll have you sparring with a couple of guys with his style. We'll have you ready. Don't get your panties in a bunch. We'll have you ready, alright."

Tony walked out of Nic's office with a strange look on his face. This was all happening too fast and he didn't know how to control it. He was worried he was way over his head. Fighting at the Savis, the arena where the St. Louis Blues Hockey Team played, was exciting but very scary. The Savis Center seats 20,000, that's an awful lot of people for a second timer to be fighting in front of, but it's also a whole lot of publicity. Maybe if he can win again, his voice will be even louder. Giving him a better chance to pass on the message.

These were some of the thoughts running through Tony's head along with the big question which was what are the chances this guy could kill him or split his head open and leave him for dead. Tony was aware that he could punch, after all he was pretty sure where that came from, but he still wasn't convinced that he could keep from getting hit, getting hit hard and often. It's a chance he's just going to have to take. No one said that what he was trying to accomplish was easy. Tony was still wondering about the whole thing when he called his brother.

"Joe, I've got another fight. It's on Saturday April 7th at the Savis. I'm fighting a guy by the name of Willie Allen. You think you can make it?"

"This is wild. Of course I'll be there. I'm already getting a load of calls from everyone we know about you and your fighting. I guarantee you there will be a bunch of people we know at this next one. I'm not really telling them anything, because I'm still not sure I know anything. This is wild."

"I wish I knew what to tell you, brother. All I can say is I'm being told I'm good by everyone around me. I guess all you can tell people is better late than never and let them speculate about the whys and whens."

"What about Sally and Betty? What are they saying about this whole thing?"

"I don't know bro. I'm pretty sure they are not going to watch you fight anybody for any reason. Boxing is a brutal sport. I'm not sure they would like seeing that. Especially if you're getting the snot kicked out of you. I'd say leave it up to them. I'll tell you what. Why don't we talk about it at dinner on Sunday? You available?"

"I don't know. I don't really have any plans."

"I guess this means you're coming. How about 2:00?"

"Yeah, I think it's time for another what the hell is going on with Tony talk. I'll fill in the family with the parts you leave out. I wish everyone would just accept this for what it is. I'm trying to make a little money and if I can, pass on a little religion. Is that all bad? I really don't think so."

"When you put it like that, it doesn't sound so weird. I guess if you

144

were twenty years younger this would make more sense. All I can say is good luck brother. I'm with you all the way."

"Thanks Joe. I've got to get going. I'll see you on Sunday."

Tony hung up. He desperately wanted to ask Joe if there was any chance that Gina might be coming but he was afraid that it was a dumb question. He figured if Gina were interested in seeing or talking to him she would have tried. He rationalized the situation but that didn't help. He was still sad. He loved Gina and he always would. He was aware that he made his own bed and he had to sleep in it. If only, he thought. If only I wasn't such an idiot I'd have a chance. He thought about it for awhile and then said out loud, "What the hell" and he called his brother back. "Joe, Tony again."

"What's the matter?"

"Nothing, I was wondering if maybe Gina might want to come on Sunday. I know she wouldn't if I called but maybe if you called. What do you think?"

"Look Tony, Gina's in another place right now. She's moved on and to be honest with you bro, you didn't move with her. I hate to tell you this. Gina's got somebody. Don't ask me a lot of questions about him 'cause I don't know anything. All I know is she's been seeing someone for a while. Gina's a done deal, bro. I'm sorry."

"O.K. Joe thanks. I just thought it was worth a try. I'll see you Sunday. Bye."

Tony hung up the phone. He sat back and memories of his wife and daughter danced into his head. His heart felt heavy. He tried not to cry; after all it had been a long time since they broke up. He fought off the tears, but that was one fight he was bound to lose. He sat in a small chair, situated in a tiny little room in the rear of the rectory of St. Ambrose church, and sobbed. Some things are just not meant to be.

Chapter 17

Dinner was perfect. Joe put braciole in the sauce. Braciole is an Italian meat roll made by taking a piece of round steak and pounding it as flat as you can. Then you take cut up hard-boiled eggs and place them in a line along the top of the meat with celery and onions and season to taste. Next you roll up everything in the meat and tie it with a string and place it in the sauce to simmer for three to four hours. It was one of Tony favorite dishes. You still put meatballs and pork in the sauce but the braciole makes it that much more special.

The conversation went as expected. Tony explained his position as best he could. His sister Betty was the most vocal and was absolutely against Tony taking on such an unhealthy career this late in his life. She was trying not to nag but she felt that her brother had been through enough and this was too much.

"Tony, I still don't understand why," Betty said almost pleadingly.

"Betty, I'm trying to tell you. Number one, I'm pretty good. Number two; I can make a lot of money. And number three I'm trying to pass a little of what was passed on to me through faith and kindness. If that sounds bad, then I'm sorry."

"I didn't say that it sounded bad, Tony. I said that it sounded dangerous, and I'm afraid for you. We all love you Tony and we don't want anything to happen to you."

"Thank you, Honey, don't you think I know that. I'll be absolutely fine. I promise. Now let's talk about something else."

"Wait," said Sam. "I want to talk about it. I read that you had a punch that could stop a train. I can't wait for the fight. Can you get us good seats?"

"That's what I love about you Sammy, you always just go with the flow. Of course I'll get you good seats. How many you need?"

"What do you think Joe, twenty?"

"With everybody we know calling, that might not even be enough," replied Joe.

"Who's been calling?" asked Tony.

"Are you kidding, everybody you know plus everybody I know. You had one fight and you're a damn celebrity."

"Yeah, sure. They're probably calling to see if I've lost my marbles. Well whatever. I'll ask Dominic to get you as many as he can. I hope it's enough."

"Just make sure you get me and Sam good seats, we're related to one of the fighters," Joe said laughingly.

"You're nuts Joe."

"What about 'em," Joe answered.

Tony laughed out loud and said, "You're sick, you know that?"

"Thank you, now pass the cream."

Tony desperately wanted to talk to either Betty or Sally concerning

Gina. Since they both had such a close relationship with her, they just might know what's going on, but he didn't want to put them in such an uncomfortable position. He let it rest.

Tony had a wonderful time with his family. Father Tom was right; things were starting to get back to the way they were before. His future was pretty well decided with the holy water experience but what was in his future only God knows, no pun intended. All he could do now was trust in the Lord. Tony wanted to stuff himself with desert but he had to watch what he was eating; after all he had a fight in less than a month. He finished his coffee, kissed everyone good-bye and headed home to the rectory.

Tony trained exceptionally hard the next few weeks and Andy was happy with his progress. His footwork was improving and he was starting to move enough to dodge a few punches. This comes in quite handy when a 235-pound man is trying to punch you in your face. His defense was improving along with his foot speed, another asset Tony was adding to his arsenal. His fighting skills were becoming more and more formidable day by day.

Andy kept Dominic up to date with progress reports and both men were getting more and more optimistic. Nic was aware that the competition was starting to push Tony's fighting skills but still felt that Tony's power could make up for his inexperience. Andy's analysis of Tony's progresses had Nic looking past Willie Allen. It's great to be confident but there is a fine line between confidence and cockiness. Nic was starting to push the envelope.

April 7th came quickly. Tony spent the morning at the gym getting warm, a few light calisthenics, and a rub down. He was getting dressed when he looked up to see his brother Joe standing in the doorway of the locker room.

"Just thought I'd check in and see how you were feeling."

"I'm as ready as I'm going to be."

"I'm proud of you Tony. You're superman. You know that?"

"Joe, a man's got to do what a man's got to do."

"Can I quote you on that," Joe said jokingly. "I just want to tell you there is going to be a bunch of our friends there tonight. Everyone's asking if they can come and see you back stage or whatever you call it?"

"Not before the fight, Joe. If I'm not too beaten up during the fight you can bring whoever you want back to the dressing room after. I'll tell the guards to expect you and Sammy. If you've got more guys with you make sure they're good friends. I can't let you bring a big crew with you. It might be best, as long as I'm up for it to meet at a restaurant or someplace after. I just don't want it to be any big deal. Is everybody interrogating you? Does everyone think I'm crazy?"

"It don't matter what anyone thinks. Like I just said the whole family is proud of you Tony. Just that you have come back is enough for us to be proud but this, I have to tell you, this is something else."

"Thanks Joe. You want to go with me for my pre-fight meal?"

"Sure, now?"

"Yeah, let me get Andy and Nic and we'll head out."

There was a great crowd at the Savis that night. Tony was anxious to get his fight underway. His was the first fight on the card. He sat in the dressing room with Nic and Andy while Andy walked him through the fight. He wanted Tony to use his newly acquired footwork, bob and weave and shoot out his left, wait for the opening and land the bomb. It's kind of the same fight ritual they've been talking about since day one. Nic was putting the finishing touches on Tony's gloves; a strip of tape applied around the wrist portion of the glove holding the laces in place, as fight time neared.

"You ready Tony?"

"Yeah, I'm ready."

"There's a nice crowd out there. If you can win impressively it sure would help our cause."

"Nic, I think we have different causes, but I know what you mean. Don't worry, I won't let you down."

Tony danced in the corner while the announcer sang out "In the red corner, weighing in at 219 pounds, with a record of one fight, one win, one knock out, St. Louis's own, Tony Russo."

Tony felt a sense of pride rush through his body as the crowd gave him a big hand. He knew he had a lot of friends out there and could see Joe, Sammy, Father Tom, Mike, Tony Ticco, George, Jim, Mark, and Frank sitting just a few rows back of his corner. Nic must have pulled some strings for them to have such good seats and Tony was grateful. The guys were cheering like mad men when they announced Tony's name. Tony was lost in thought and didn't even pay any attention when the ring announcer was barking out Allen's stats. He was just waiting for the bell.

Ding, the bell sounded and Tony came out of the corner watching Allen's every move. Willie bounced around very light on his feet and threw out a left jab that Tony picked off with his right glove. Tony threw a couple lefts of his own but neither one got through Willie's defenses. The first minute of the fight not much had landed by either fighter; until Allen landed a hard left hook to Tony's head. Bang was the sound in Tony's head as the punch landed. It was a good punch and shook Tony up a little. He danced back to avoid a combination but he was too slow. Willie landed a good right, left, right, and Tony was forced to hold on. The referee broke up the clinch and Allen kept coming. Tony hadn't landed a thing, when he got hit with another flurry. A cut was opened under Tony's right eye. He wiped the blood from his face with his glove and tried to get out of the way of Allen's punches. He danced away again, this time punching as he backed up but again not landing a thing. The bell rang ending round one and it was a good thing for Tony. He lost the round badly and he needed the rest.

"What the hell are you doing out there," screamed Andy as he wiped the blood from Tony's face. "How many times do I have to tell you, if you don't punch, this guy will eat your lunch? You've got to land something or Allen will not stop attacking. Get your gloves up and stick him. If you can't land a jab there's no way you're going to land the haymaker. Now stick and move and throw that bomb whenever you can. You hear me? You're getting killed out there."

The cut wasn't very bad and they were able to stop the bleeding before the bell rang to start round two. Tony came out aggressively to start the second but he was met with two solid right hand leads for his trouble. Tony was being out classed badly and quite honestly this guy wasn't really that good. Tony was just getting beat to the punch. The entire second round found Tony on the run. He took quite a few more shots and his face was starting to puff. The crowd was booing Tony as round two came to a close.

"Alright, listen," said Andy as he gave Tony the water bottle. "You've forgotten all we worked on this past month. You're slow and this guy is not one bit afraid of your power. Hell he hasn't seen it yet. So right off the bat, throw the right and keep throwing it till you land it. You've got to slow this guy down and if he feels any of your power that could get him off the offensive. Just throw that big right. You got that? You got that Tony? Throw the bomb."

Ding, the bell sounded for round three. Tony rushed out to the middle of the ring. He cocked his right arm and let it fly. Kaboom, it landed and Allen went spinning in thin air. He made two full revolutions before he hit the ground, out cold. The crowd went wild; what they just

Paul Tripi

saw couldn't be done. Even Dominic was stupefied by the unbelievable show of power. This shot made knocking the first guy over the ropes look like it was nothing. There was no hesitation on the referee's part. He along with both trainers was out to look at Willie Allen the second he hit the canvas. He was out for a few moments but recovered quickly and after a few seconds was up and on his feet. He had no idea what just happened; he just knew he was knocked out. The crowd was even crazier when the referee raised Tony's arm in victory. Tony turned to go to his corner and couldn't help but smile when he saw what fools his brother, brother-in-law, and friends were making of themselves. They were hopping around and jumping and cheering like never before. Joe was screaming like a twelve-year-old boy, "That's my brother, that's my brother!"

Tony went back to his corner. Andy and Nic were standing there just starring at Tony. This was not real to them. Nobody could hit like that. Absolutely nobody. Tony looked a lot more like the loser than the winner. His face was swollen and without doubt he was going to have two black eyes. Especially the right eye; it was already starting to close. Andy put the cold metal to the lumps to help stop the swelling but it wasn't going to help too much. Tony was going to look like a car just hit him no matter what they did.

"Tony, again I'm speechless," said Nic. "You are without doubt the toughest man I've ever seen in my life. Bar none! Are you alright?"

"I'm fine Nic, thanks. Is Willie alright? I seen him walking around but when I went over there to shake his hand he looked pretty shaky. Go make sure he's O.K., will ya?"

"The doctor's over there right now, I'll talk to him when he's finished. Unbelievable Tony, simply unbelievable."

"Calm down Nic. For crying out loud the guy almost killed me. I should have lost the fight, man. If I wouldn't have caught him I was a

152

goner. I'm feeling happy to come out of here with my life. I don't know if I can fight another fight, Nic. I'm telling you guy, I can hardly see out of this eye, and I feel like I just got ran over by a Mack truck. Don't let a lucky punch fool you."

"Tony, it might have been a lucky punch the first time but this is four lucky punches in a row counting the guys in the gym. You're not lucky buddy, you're definitely the real deal."

"Well, I'm not feeling like the real deal right at this moment."

They started climbing out of the ring. The fans were going crazy for Tony. Tony just waved as he headed towards the lockers. "Thank you God," Tony said raising his glove up to the ceiling as he made his way back to the dressing room. Tony waved to his brother and friends to follow him and he left the arena with the crowd still cheering.

Tony asked Andy if it would be OK if a few of his family and friends could come in.

"Are you kidding? I wouldn't say no to you for all the tea in China. Man, I'm a fan too, and I've been around fighters all my life. You have got the best right hand in the business. I don't care who you want to bring in here. It doesn't matter to me at all. I've got to tell you pal, I'm excited. The fact that you've only had a couple of fights that doesn't mean a thing! Tony, the shots I've seen you throw are indescribable, in deeescribable. I'm amazed. If you're up for 'em to come in, have at it."

Tony signaled the guard to let everybody in. Joe led the way.

"Tony are you alright? I'm telling you bro I had a hard time even watching the damn fight. I thought you were going to be killed, but what a punch. I still can't believe it. Did you see the guy spinning? Did you see it? He spun like a top."

"Yeah Joe, I was pretty close at the time. I saw it. I landed a good one, didn't I?"

All the guys piped in then. It seemed like they were all talking at the same time. Sam was beaming he was smiling so much.

"Look, I can't answer everybody at once. Just hold it. Let me talk," said Tony. "First Hi Joe, Sam, Mike, Frank, Tony, George, Mark and hello Father. Thank you guys for coming. It was great seeing you out there in the crowd. Secondly, did you notice how many times I smashed the guy in the hands with my face? He won't be able to make a fist for a week," Tony said laughing.

Frank spoke first. "You are a wonder, buddy. An absolute wonder. What, how, why, I don't even know what to ask you?

"Guys, I have no answers for you. This fighting thing just happened. Right now, the way my face and body feels, I wish it wouldn't have. But I'm making a little *zorde*—some money—and I'm spreading the word. I told all you guys, and Father here not only can verify this because he's the main reason but my life was saved and turned around when God came into it. Please don't make me explain myself. I can't. I just want to live my life with God in it and I hope I can help others do the same. I've said this too many times already but I am not a holy roller. I just want to repay the Lord's kindness with anything I can do to help. It seems like fighting is what I'm supposed to do, so here I am."

"Can I write that?" said Pat Dryjal who was standing and listening at the door.

"Hello Pat," replied Tony. "You can write anything you want if it helps the Lord's cause. Guys give me a minute here. I think I'm about to have my fifteen seconds of fame. This is Pat Dryjal from the star. He's probably here to ask me how I survived out there. It's pretty obvious that Allen knocked the poop out of me."

"Tony Russo, what did your mother feed you when you were young? It's like watching a Popeye cartoon when you fight. Does spinach have anything to do with it, because what I see, I don't believe?

"Do you have a story here? If so, I can't wait to hear it."

"Pat, thanks for asking, but I really don't. I told you this already; I had a normal life, with its normal ups and downs. When I was down, this guy right here," Tony pointed to Father Tom, "Father Tom Sutton was there for me. He, along with a lot of help from God, turned my life around. I fought when I was a kid, I always liked the work out I got from fight training, I was working out at Dominic's Boxing Gym, Big Nic saw me, thought I had a big punch, gave me a look see, here I am.

"Bottom line, I don't know how to fight very well, Andy here is trying to teach me, but I can hit pretty hard so I've got lucky and landed a few blows and they were enough to win these fights. The fights are important but not the number one thing to me. The big thing is, you, if you'll write what I have to say about the Lord, people will listen. So here goes. Again I want to thank my Lord and savior Jesus Christ for not letting Willie or me get hurt out there. I want to thank Nic and Andy for their help and support. I want to thank my family and friends for showing up. That's my brother Joe and my brother-in law Sam right there, and these other guys are lifelong friends.

"But most of all I want to thank God for being there for me and last but not least I want your readers and anyone who will listen to realize that God will be there for them too. Whenever they need him, he will listen. His answer is not always yes, but he will listen. God loves us all, and all he wants is for us to love each other. Do unto others as you would have them do unto you. Is that so hard for us to do? You got all that Pat?"

"I got it, I understand, and I'll write some of it but Tony, what my readers want to read about is this punch you have. Last month you knocked Jackson Lannie over the top rope with a punch I never thought I'd ever forget. Tonight you almost make me forget that punch with, I don't know what it was, but Allen spun around in mid air before he hit

Paul Tripi

the canvas from that right hand of yours. He spun around a couple of times. There has got to be some secret or some kind of special training or something here 'cause this is not human, man. It's just not human. Where do you get all this power?"

"I told you last time. I fight for God. It must come from my faith 'cause I don't do anything different from any other fighter when it comes to training. You know some fighters can hit harder than others. I'm one that can hit hard. I don't know what else to tell you."

"These knockouts have to be witnessed to be described, so you're testing my skill here Tony. I've been following this fight game for a lot of years and I have never seen anyone like you. One more question. You took a lot of shots out there, were you ever in any trouble?"

"Are you kidding, *yes*, I was in trouble the moment I stepped into the ring. Willie Allen is a great fighter. I was lucky to beat him. It's a good thing I landed that punch because if I had missed I would have been in all kinds of trouble. You see what I mean about God. He shall provide. And apparently in this case he has, because if he hadn't you'd be in Allen's dressing room and not in mine."

"Thanks Tony. Maybe we can sit down some time and you can tell me your life story?"

"No, thank you Pat. You were kind with the first story you wrote. I trust you. As far as my life story. Let's just say my life just started and leave it at that. O.K."

"I'm no fool, I'm not about to contradict anything you say. Not while you still have those hands attached to your body." Pat laughed, waved to the guys standing over in the corner, and left.

"*Minga*, you're famous," said Tony Ticco as the guys all crowded around Tony again. You feel good enough to go out for a little something."

"Guys, I'm hurting a little. We'll get together but how about some

156

other time. I need to soak and I'm shot. We'll get together soon. I promise, just not tonight. Is that O.K.?"

"Sure Tony," everyone sounded in unison, and they headed to the door.

Joe and Sam stayed a few extra seconds. "Are you sure you're not hurt?" asked Joe.

"I'm fine Joe. It just stings when someone beats the piss out of you."

"O.K., we get it, we're going to head out then." Joe walked over to his brother, kissed him, and he and Sam left.

Tony looked over to Nic and Andy and said, "Well boys, now what?"

Chapter 18

"The total comes to $4,058.00 Mr. Russo," said the salesperson at Noels, the best playground equipment company in St. Louis.

"That's expensive Tony, are you sure about this?" interjected Father Tom.

"Tom, I got six grand from the Allen fight and those kids over at Father Bakers Orphanage sure will love this stuff. I told you before; this is what I'm supposed to do with this money. I know it is. Plus how good does it feel? Admit it."

"Tony, it's wonderful, and God bless you for your generosity. "That's all I can say."

"I'll tell you something else and I sure hope it's alright but, you know Rusty, the Down syndrome kid that's been helping me with the chores around the church? I gave his mother 500 bucks for him and he's going to take over my chores at the church. That way I won't feel like a free loader staying in my room. You think that'll be O.K.?"

"Tony, that is truly fine and Rusty is a very good boy. We all love him. There is no problem with that. The only problem is, and don't think we want you to leave, we all don't, it's just that you are definitely improving you're stature in life, so don't you want to improve your living condition. That's a very small space you're living in."

"Father, with all that's happening, I wouldn't want to change a thing. I'm comfortable and the atmosphere is exactly what I need. As long as no one minds, I'd like to stay for awhile longer."

"Done, but we should talk about this some more soon. It's not the accommodations that are affecting your life buddy. I'm sure that God can find you pretty much anywhere. Don't put so much credence on that room at the rectory. It's just a room."

Over the course of the next handful of months, Nic was busy and Tony was fighting. The fighters were getting better and the purses were getting bigger. The results were all about the same. Tony Russo was gaining a name in the fight game, and not just in St. Louis.

In fight number three Tony had to go five rounds with Jolly Jack Reggie. Jolly Jack danced and stayed as far away from Tony's right hand as he could. He did a fairly good job too, but at two minutes and fifteen seconds of the fifth round he jigged when he should have jagged and he found himself on the canvas for the ten count.

Gilbert G. Gilbert, Tony's fourth opponent, took a completely different tack and rushed at Tony from the opening bell. That was definitely a mistake. Tony threw one punch and he was four and zero with four knockouts.

Pat Dryjal had taken quite a liking to Tony and he definitely was cooperating with publicity for Tony's punching skills along with a small message about God that Tony would ask him to print. Messages like, strength comes from within, and trust in the Lord he shall provide.

These were unusual comments to be written in a boxing column but Dryjal knew it was part of Tony's being and just wanted to report the facts. Tony was also putting some very big smiles on the faces of some needy folks in the St. Louis area.

It wasn't until just after Tony's fifth fight, a knockout win over southpaw, Bomber Zouglas, that Dryjal got wind of Tony's generosity. Tony had just purchased a van for St. Ambrose to use for their meals on wheels program, the program that delivered hot meals to elderly people who lived alone and were unable to prepare their own meals. No one knew where the information came from and Dryjal wasn't about to tell but Father Tom had an unusually big smile on his face when he and Tony were sitting at the breakfast table discussing the article they had just read.

It was a full column article about Tony. The headline read, "There's a new saint in town and his name is Tony Russo." The article told of the generosity that this fighter displayed to the homeless and needy people of the town. Dryjal held back nothing when he stated that he wasn't a mathematician but if you were to add up all the things, and he listed many of them, St. Tony, a new handle dubbed by Dryjal, had been donating and added up the money he had been winning as a fighter, you'd find that Tony Russo was barely keeping any money for himself, this from a guy who lives in the maintenance man's quarters in the back of a rectory.

Dryjal said that Tony had been telling him after every fight that he fought for God and for God's causes. Dryjal admitted in the article, that he had heard that song and dance from a number of other athletes in his years as a sports reporter but never had he witnessed anyone taking it to this degree. Dryjal went on to say that St. Tony is a very special person and that he felt honored and privileged to know him. He said he wished him all the luck in the world and that even though he was supposed to stay neutral when it came to sports he was going to admit to the whole world that when St. Tony fights I root for him. There is something special about this guy. He has made his hometown, St. Louis a better place to live.

"Well," said Tom as he sipped his coffee.

"This is not what I wanted," answered Tony. "Now he's got the focus of what's being accomplished by me instead of where it really belongs."

"Tony, God does not want publicity. Trust me on this. Aren't you spreading the word? Aren't you passing on a message? Don't you think that people are watching and listening? Tony when I speak, my message only goes as far as this parish. I envy you, when you speak it goes to the masses. If you don't see that now, I don't know what to tell you."

"You're right Father. I guess I didn't want people to know too much about the giving part. It sounds so hokey."

"The last thing it sounds like is hokey Tony. It sounds like you are for real, to these people, and it makes your message that much more real too. Man, when you came to me with the holy water thing even I had a tough time believing. But I believe now. This must be why that whole episode happened. This must be why."

"Uh-oh," said Tony as his brother Joe walked through the door with a rolled up paper in his hand.

"Hello Joe," said Father Tom. "You want some coffee?"

"Thank you Father, that's sounds good." He paused and said, "Hello Robin Hood. How are you doing this morning?"

"Joe, I told you about this, now, don't start."

"Tony, I'm not saying not to give stuff, I think it's great but come on bro, you're getting your brains half knocked out of your head and you're giving everything away. Christ, sorry Father, for crying out loud Tony there's such a thing as overdoing something."

"Joe, I'm keeping some of the money. I just bought a whole new wardrobe and I'm putting a little away for a rainy day. I got a fight coming up the end of this month and if I win I'm up for a nice piece of change. I won't give it all away, I promise. One thing though, there is a homeless shelter over on Kings Highway that needs beds, and I plan on donating some. There are people sleeping on the floor over there, Joe. Some of them are kids. God wants me to help. He wants everyone to help but in my case I can feel that a little more than others."

"You know, every time we have any conversation about all of this, I come here loaded for bear, thinking I'm going to convince you how wrong you are. Every time I end up having to agree with you. I know what you're saying and you're right but couldn't you do some kind of percentage kind of deal with yourself. A guy has to live, Tony, and at your age, especially earning money the way you are, it can all come to an end in the blink of an eye.

"You're living in a tiny little box, no disrespect intended Father, and your livelihood could end with one punch, then what."

"I don't know right now. I think about it but I'd rather focus on what I'm doing than what I'm going to do when all this comes to an end. Believe me Joe, I'm well aware of my longevity and I will soon start to save some. Right now there's people who need it more than me. The percentage thing sounds realistic. O.K., I'll do that. Does that make you happy?"

"Yes." Joe said as he opened the rolled up paper he was holding in his hand. "Now that I've done my duty as your brother I think it's time I do my duty as a proud brother. This article is fantastic. Sally was crying her eyes out all the while she was reading it. The kids even read it and were saying nice things about you. They were saying how much they loved their Uncle Tony. I'm proud of you Tony, I always have been but right now," Joe paused a moment, "I'm just proud to be your brother."

"Sit down and shut your face, you're embarrassing me in front of the Father here. Thank you, I love you too, now you got something else on your mind, I know that look."

"Well, I do have the seats for today's game and I have no intention of going into the office. What do you say?"

"All right!" answered Tony. "The only thing is I'm supposed to do some sparring this morning. How about we go over to the gym for an hour or so then from there it's Russo brothers' time."

The brothers had a great time. The Cards had on their hitting shoes and outscored the Dodgers eleven to two. The only thing different than the norm was that Tony was approached by a whole lot of people they didn't know and, believe it or not, he was asked to sign some autographs.

Tony was near blushing when asked but of course he did accommodate any and all. Joe stood back in disbelief. A year and a half ago he wasn't even sure if his brother was going to survive. He was so low he had to look up to see the ground, and now people were asking him for his autograph. Even Joe had to admit the Lord works in mysterious ways. They left the ballpark and headed home.

Joe dropped Tony off and said, "You coming Sunday?"

"Yeah, what time?"

"People are coming around two but come whenever, and invite Father Tom, will ya."

"O.K. bro but he's kind of busy Sundays, we'll see."

"I think I'd better make an extra big pot. I've got a feeling we may get some drop-ins. You know, now that you're some kind of a star, who knows who will show up."

"Don't start with that malarkey."

"People would have asked you for your autograph too, if they had any idea who you were. Who are you anyway?"

"With that, I'm leaving. See you Sunday."

"Thanks bro, I had a great time, I'll see ya."

Tony's nephew Anthony had a bunch of friends over when Tony arrived at the house. Tony hugged and kissed little Tony and shook the hands of all of his friends. Sarah and Sally were just behind and gave their uncle a big hug and kiss. It made Tony feel very warm inside. He loved these kids and he was so glad that they never swayed from loving him too.

He went inside and Sally greeted him with a hug and kiss of her own. She told Tony how proud everyone was of him. Not just the boxing part of which she could care less but for the humanitarian acts he was beings so praised for. She asked if she could help. Tony said yes, it's something that he'd like to see the whole family get involved with. Not right now but I was thinking about something we could do as a family at Thanksgiving. He said he'd fill her in on the details when it got closer but that he was counting her in. He told her she wouldn't believe how great it felt to watch the faces of people when they receive the gift of kindness. "You'll see," he said "You'll see."

"What do you want to drink?" Joe said almost holding his breath after phrasing the question that way. He saved it by saying, "Soda, water, lemonade, or ice tea."

"Give me a lemonade, and don't think I didn't catch that, oh hell thing. I don't drink, Joe, and I'm not going to drink either. You can relax."

Joe came back with the drinks put them down on the coffee table and asked. "You didn't say who you were fighting next."

"You ready for this, Wild Bill Dalton."

"The ex-champion of the world Wild Bill Dalton."

"You are correct sir." Tony responded with his best Ed McMahon imitation." He's trying one more comeback and Nic got the deal. I just found out that it's not a purse fight it's a straight contract deal and my end is thirty big ones. You hear me my brother $30,000.00 cash, win or lose."

"*Minga* Tony, I can't believe this. The only thing is how do you expect to spend the money when you're dead? This guy could kill you Anthony. We're talking about Wild Bill Dalton here."

"Come on Joe, he's older than me. I could live. It's possible."

"That ain't funny Tony. I think Nic's off his rocker. He's moving you up too fast. I don't like this. I don't like this one bit."

"Nic said this fight would give us national exposure. Joe, national exposure for a guy in his sixth fight, you can't buy that. Nic's said if I win this fight I'll move up in the pecking order. Maybe after a few more, I can get a fight with a ranked guy. That's when things happen."

"Yeah, I hear what you're saying but I also know who you are. I know you can hit, brother, but now you're talking about fighting guys who can hit back. I'm mean hit back just as hard. You sure you're up for this?"

"Joe, I feel like Martin Luther King. *"I have a dream."* I'm getting better and better. My stamina is growing stronger each day; I'm ready to go ten. That's all it takes. Now understand, I'm not so dumb as to think that there will ever be a day when I'll be going fifteen. That's a championship bout. But when you're fighting ten-rounders you get national exposure. Maybe even a shot on some cable fight station. If I can even once just get fifteen seconds of interview time I can accomplish my goal. You know how I feel about getting the word out. Wouldn't that just be the best? I know I'm getting ahead of myself but I'm starting to see some true possibilities here."

"O.K. Rocky, but if I'm not mistaken Wild Bill will probably not just fall down from fear when you guys get in the ring. You better worry about that before you crown yourself champion."

"I didn't say anything about being champion and you better shut your pie hole before I shut it for you."

"I ain't afraid of you. Bring it on old man."

Sally walked in and as usual had to break up what was just about going to be another brothers wrestling match. "You two better grow up. The kids are going to see you and then what?"

"Bring them on too." said Tony "They don't scare me."

"You two are absolutely crazy. I swear. As for you Joseph Russo, you better go and stir the sauce before it starts sticking to the bottom of the pot. Tony would you like something to eat now? We won't be eating till about four. Betty's running late."

"Yeah, Sally but I'll get it. Are the meat balls ready yet?"

"Close, I'd say in about a half hour."

"I can wait. Hey, what time are Sam and Betty coming?"

"You never know with him, you can call him if you want."

"No, I just wondered. Who else is coming for dinner?"

Sally waited a moment before answering and said, "Tony, I hope you don't mind but we invited Gina."

Chapter 19

Sam, Betty, and the kids came about 3:30. Although Tony was very glad to see them, he was really anxious to see Gina. It was about 5:00 and the family had finished dinner and was just about to have coffee when the doorbell rang. Tony's heart stopped for a moment as he watched Sally walk towards the door. It was Gina. She looked fantastic. Everyone was so glad to see her; it had been awhile. Tony, who was never at a loss for words, was speechless as Gina came to the table. The kids all gathered around her like she was old Mother Goose. Aunt Gina, Aunt Gina, the kids were so happy to see her. So were Betty and Sally. This breakup was hard on the whole family and there wasn't a person there who wasn't thrilled that she showed. Especially Tony.

"Hi everybody," Gina said with a smile that could melt butter.

"Gina," replied the family in unison.

"Hello Gina," said Tony uncomfortably.

"Hi Tony, How have you been?"

"Good and bad, good and bad. How 'bout yourself?"

"I'm doing pretty well," she answered. "How's your family? Everyone doing O.K."

"Dad's been having a lot of trouble with his back but Mom couldn't be doing better."

"Sit down and I'll make you a dish of pasta," said Sally.

"No thanks Sal, I had a late lunch and I'm not hungry at all, but I'll have some coffee."

The next half hour was spent filling each other in on what's been happening since they've seen each other. Tony didn't say a word. He just listened, never taking his eyes off of Gina. Finally Joe started talking about all the stuff that Tony was doing. Really bragging up his big brother.

"I've been reading about you in the paper Tony. I'm so happy for you. And what you've been doing in the community is the talk around here. Congratulation."

"Thanks Gina, it kind of all fell in my lap."

"Gina, you look like a million bucks," said Sam.

"Well, whose ever idea it was to join the Y, I owe. I've been working out well over a year now and I'm not kidding you guys. I feel ten years younger."

"I've been working out a lot too," joked Tony. "But I don't look anything like you, Gina. You look like a young girl. What are you doing with yourself?"

"I'm with Dad at the store. Kind of in charge of human resources, you know payroll and benefits and such. I love being out in the working world, and Dad, well, you all know my dad. He's just the best. I love being around him."

Tony desperately wanted to ask Gina some personal questions but was aware this was neither the time nor the place. He just sat there and listened to the small talk. The rest of the family did the same. There was no way that anyone was going to ask Gina anything private, all it would do would make her stay away and that's not at all what they wanted.

Gina broke first and asked "Tony I don't mean to pry but how in the world did you end up being a prize fighter. I don't mean anything by that but you of all people. I've been asked that question by dozens of our, I mean my, friends and I don't know how to answer them."

"Gina, neither do I. All I can tell you is that I took a job at Dominic's Boxing gym and the next thing I know I'm fighting. I know I'm old but they think I'm pretty good. The rest you probably know."

"Well, sort of, but, and please don't take this the wrong way, what I've been reading sure doesn't sound like you. You've changed."

"Gina, you can't imagine. I will tell you that God has come into my life just when I needed him most and I guess that's the major change. My whole life is so different. I really can't explain it."

Tony was about to get into the, without you, I'm sorry, forgive me, I love you, kind of thing but he caught himself in time. He just simply said, "It's really great to see you Gina."

There was an uncomfortable silence for a few seconds and Joe filed it immediately with "Who wants pie? We've got apple and cherry. Sam no reason to ask you if you want any so which one do you want?"

"Joe, I can't make up my mind so why don't you just give me a real big piece of both."

"Sam, you never cease to amaze me with your consistency. Coming up. Who else?"

After dessert Gina got up. "Guys it has been great to see you all. I'd love to stay but I've got a previous engagement and I have to leave." She stood up, kissed everyone, and headed for the door.

169

Paul Tripi

"Gina," said Tony getting up and walking towards the door, "Can I have a quick word with you."

Uh-oh, was the collective thought of the rest of the family as Tony approached Gina.

"Gina, I've never received any papers or anything and I, I, I don't know what to ask. I guess I'm asking, what am I suppose to do?"

"Tony, please don't ruin everything right now. We can have a talk someplace another time. Just leave everything alone right now. I almost didn't come because I was afraid of this."

"O.K., O.K., I'm sorry. I didn't even ask you where you live or what your number is."

"I live in Manchester and you can find me at the store anytime during the day. I did want to see you Tony. I'm glad you're all right. We'll have a talk but I'm not ready to deal with anything. I'm just living my life and I don't want anybody or anything to change it right now. We will have a talk but not for a while, O.K."

"You hate me, don't you?"

"Tony, I lost the ability to hate, along with the ability to feel anything a while ago. I don't hate you. I'm numb. I've been numb, and all I want out of life right now is peace. I just need peace."

"Alright Gina but I've just got to tell you this."

"Don't Tony. Don't say anything. I have to go. I have to go."

"Is it O.K. for me to say that this was the best day I've had in I can't remember?"

Gina walked out the door without answering. Tony watched as she got into her car and left. He watched as she drove off and didn't stop till she turned the corner. He stood there a few seconds. He didn't want to go back to the table but he knew he couldn't just leave. He felt alone. Really alone.

You know it's true, a man really doesn't know what he has until

170

it's gone. A dark sadness engulfed Tony. He loved Gina with all his being. She was his soul mate. He fell in love with her the first time they met and he would love her till the day he died. He would die for her. As he turned to go back to his family a feeling of hatred came over him. He tried to shake it off but he couldn't. Tony hated, Tony hated himself for what he had done. He didn't blame Gina for a second. She deserved no blame. In the few seconds it took for him to get from the front door to the dining room Tony made a decision. He was going to make it up to Gina. He was going to make up for the way he treated her. Not just the unforgivable thing he said, that he can't take back, it was said and it would never be forgotten but for all the things before that. For being such a domineering man, for stifling her growth as a woman, for not listening, and the most important thing of all, for taking her for granted.

Italian men, maybe all men, have selective hearing. They don't listen. The most important opinion in a persons' life is their spouse's opinion and Italian men don't listen to it. Not all of them, but most. It seems that Italian men are patriarchal. They run their homes like they're king. Not true. If you really look deep into an Italian family, it just seems like the man is running things but in truth, it's the woman of the house who really runs things. Tony felt like he didn't share. He felt like he didn't listen to the important things. Hindsight is 20/20, and Tony now had the best vision in the world. If he could only have another chance it would be different.

All this ran through Tony's mind as he sat down and picked up his coffee. He didn't say a word and neither did anyone else. They just drank their coffee in silence.

The next two weeks were bad for Tony. He couldn't get Gina out of his mind and he couldn't shake the feeling of guilt that was taking over. He trained intently for his upcoming fight he knew he had to. Wild Bill had to be licking his chops. Bill was trying to position himself for one

more big payday and some newcomer with a heavy punch by the name
of Tony Russo was standing in his way. ProbablyWild Bill planned on
ending this fight early and not using much of his reserves on a rookie.
Tony worked hard physically but mentally he just wasn't there. His mind
was in a furniture store in Manchester. After his shower he was sitting in
the locker room staring at nothing when he decided. He had to talk to
Gina and he had to talk to her now. He hopped in his car and headed
over to Rancuso's.

"Hello Babe," said Tony as he walked into the back offices of the
store. Babe Rancuso turned slowly and smiled when he saw who was
standing at the door.

"Hello Tony, it's good to see you. How are you doing?"

"I'm doing all right. You know some days are better than others
but I'm getting by."

"Well, according to what I've been reading you're a lot better than
fine. I read things that have me feeling very proud of you, boy. Very
proud. I never had even an inkling that you were a fighter. I'm happy for
you, son, happy and proud."

"Thanks Dad that means a lot to me. I wasn't sure how the
family felt about me after what I've put you through. I want to thank
you for everything you've done for me all my life. You've treated me
like I was a son, not a son-in-law, and I repaid your love and kindness
with disrespect. For that I am truly sorry. I have no defense but I hope
you can forgive me."

Babe walked over and hugged Tony. "Tony, that was a time in all of
our lives that we need to put behind us. There's nothing to say here."

"Babe, I don't know if you know this but I'm fighting Wild Bill
Dalton on the 30th at the Savis. Here's some tickets if you'd like to come.
I was thinking maybe Tommy might even want to come down."

"Tony, I can't believe all of this. People are saying you're the hardest hitter they've ever seen. I'm excited, confused, and elated for you. We'll be there. We'll be there with bells on."

"God works in mysterious ways, Babe. I can't believe all this myself but I guess this was my destiny. Better late than never. Hey, Dad, is Gina around?"

"She's around Tony, but I'm not sure she's going to want to talk to you right now. She told us about your dinner and she's had a rough time ever since. Let me go back and see. I'm sorry that it has to be this way, but . . ."

"You don't have to apologize, and neither does she. I understand. Will you ask her if we can talk a minute?"

Babe went into the warehouse and a few minutes later Gina came walking out.

"Hello Tony, what brings you here?"

"Gina, I was wondering if maybe we could have dinner or lunch, or even coffee sometime?"

"Why? What good could come of that? I don't want to dredge up the past Tony, I moved on."

"I don't either. Will you at least think about it?"

"I don't know Tony, I just don't know."

"I understand Gina, I didn't come here thinking you would but I had to try. Here's my number at the church and here's my number at the gym. I'll meet you any time, any place, just call. I know you don't want to hear this but I never stopped loving you, and I never will. I don't expect a response I just had to say it out loud.

"I'm sorry for everything. I'm so sorry. I'm not asking you to take me back. All I want is to have you to at least consider the possibility of forgiving me. Please don't hate me. But if you do I understand. I have a tough enough time trying not to hate myself. You don't have to say a word. Just think about it and call me."

"I don't know what you want me to say. I can't do this, Tony. It's too hard for me. I—I—I've got to get back to work." She turned to walk away but turned back and kissed Tony on the cheek. "I do wish you all the luck in the world. What you're doing with your life is great, I'm proud of you. Good luck in your next fight. If it helps you to know, I do worry about you. I have to go now. Goodbye Tony."

Tony turned and walked away. He didn't expect much coming into this but he was leaving with even less than expected. He was hoping that they could at least talk but it was obvious that Gina flat didn't want to. He loved her so much. As he got in the car one thought ran through his head. Why did all this have to happen? Why?

Chapter 20

Wild Bill Dalton peered into the Tony's corner. The gloating expression on his face seemed to say he was thinking thank you Michaeloni for this easy fight, I should get out of this fight without even breaking a sweat.

The bell rang and out came the combatants. Dalton played with Tony the first round, moving in and out, throwing a bunch of left jabs and scoring but not really hurting Tony at all. Tony was doing about the same, all the time hoping for an opening to land the right. The bell rang signifying that round one was over.

Round two was much different. Wild Bill threw everything but the kitchen sink at Tony, landing in bunches and doing some damage. Tony was hurt. After a small beating he walked slowly back to his corner for a much-needed rest.

Andy removed Tony's mouthpiece, threw a sponge full of water on his fighter's face and said. "Tony, can you hear me? Are you all right?"

"Man, this guy is good. I can't hit him Andy. He's moving all over the place."

"You've got to work him towards the corner. Keep him out of the middle of the ring. Once you get him in the corner, work the body. You've got to slow him down. Make sure you keep your guard up. He's working the weave on you. (The weave is a punch combination using lefts and rights systematically) he's setting you up for a right upper cut. When he throws the double left, don't duck down, that's what he wants. Keep moving sideways. He wants you to duck down so he can land that upper cut. Do you understand me?"

"I got it. Don't duck down. I got it. How do I counter?"

"When he throws the double left, he's going to follow with a right upper cut, understand? That will leave the right side of his head open, throw a big left hook. You got it? Throw a big left hook as soon as he lets the double left go."

Ding, round three. Wild Bill was fairly fresh. He hadn't been hit too often. Tony was the opposite. His face was red and puffy but he wasn't cut. Both fighters still had a lot of leg left and they both danced on the balls of their feet.

Andy was right. Dalton tried the double left right hand upper cut move and Tony countered flawlessly landing the biggest punch of the night, a perfectly thrown left hook to Wild Bill's jaw. The punch would have stopped many a fighter but this guy wasn't just any fighter. He shook off the effects of the punch and was able to stay away from Tony the rest of the round, by sure skill. He was out on his feet for a good minute but he wouldn't fall.

"That was it, you had him Tony. Damn it if you had thrown the right you would have finished him. Why didn't you?"

"I tried, I couldn't land it. He's too elusive. He's too good, Andy.

176

Man, is he good."

"Well, you just changed the whole game. He's coming after you this round buddy, count on that. You hurt him and he's not going to take any chances. He's coming out fast so cover up and try and get inside. You might be taking some punches but if he's willing to trade with you, you can knock him out. Go get him. You can do this Tony. Knock this guy out!"

Ding, round four. Andy was right on again. Wild Bill came out fast and furious. He landed two solid rights before Tony even knew it. The fighters then stood in the middle of the ring and just hammered each other. Tony was in trouble. Dalton landed a left cross that opened a small cut over the bridge of Tony's nose. Wild Bill followed up with two more lefts that had Tony reeling. Pow, a right hand from Wild Bill Dalton and Tony went flying into the ropes. Tony was staggered, he tried to push himself from the ropes but Bill would not let him right himself. The ex-champ was relentless. Blood ran down Tony's face and he frantically tried to wipe some of it with his glove. Pow, another right hand and Tony went down.

A small figure stood up amongst the screaming crowd and headed for the exit. She was crying and couldn't take another second. Gina turned as she got to the end of the aisle just in time to see Tony struggling to his feet. He didn't have a clue where he was, but he was tough enough to get to his feet. The referee came over to check Tony's eyes, when ding, the sound of the bell ended round four. The bell saved him because if it wasn't for the timing of it Tony was a goner.

Andy jumped through the ring ropes and grabbed Tony directing him to his corner. Tony was in no man's land. Andy threw water in his face and put an iced towel behind his neck. "Tony, do you know who I am? Tony, do you know who I am?"

"Is that a trick question?" replied Tony who was just starting to

177

clear the cobwebs. "Yes, Andy, I know who you are. Is the fight over?"

"It will be if you give me the word. You want me to throw in the towel?"

"Don't you dare, Andy, I got him just where I want him. This round he's going down. You hear me. He's going down."

"I believe you, man. I believe you." What a battler, Andy thought as Tony left the corner to start fighting again. He was near killed two minutes ago and now he's going out for more. Not only that, he's going out to try and win. What a man. What a man.

Dalton came across the ring like a man on a mission. He knew he had Tony in trouble and he wasn't about to let him out of it. He came across with full intentions on ending the thing. Pow, a right hand that was so hard it knock the mouthpiece right out of Tony's mouth. Tony hung on.

He held on to Wild Bill with all his might. The referee came in to break them up, took a look into Tony's eyes, and signaled the fight to continue. Bill threw a roundhouse right attempting to put an end to it right then. He missed and for the first time Tony landed a right of his own. Not all he had but enough, Dalton looked like a bird that just flew into a window. He was stopped dead in his tracks. Tony let loose two hard lefts and landed both of them. This guy was tough, he just took three good shots from Tony and he was still standing there. They stayed away from each other for the rest of the round, each of them trying to gather some composure. The bell rang signifying the end of round five and both men limped to their corners. The fans where definitely getting their money's worth.

Round six, a place Tony had never been before, started out slow. Both men knew they were in a war. Tony shot out two lefts and landed both jabs. Even the jabs were taking a toll now. Dalton landed a lead right hand right in the middle of Tony's face reopening the cut that his

178

corner had continually stopped. Tony than landed and Bill returned. It was ugly.

Both fighters were covered with Tony's blood when Tony brought a right hand up over the top and caught Wild Bill Dalton on the forehead. And what a right, it looked like Dalton just decided to sit down except that there was no chair. His ass hit the canvas first then the back of his head slammed down. He was out. The referee stopped counting at three and waved the fight over.

The ring filled with people immediately and for a few seconds Tony was scared for Bill. Then Dalton rolled over on his side and was pushing himself up when a bunch of corner men grabbed him and helped him up. The two combatants stood face to face again in the middle of the ring. This time to admire each other's courage. The respect for one another was shining through like a search beacon when they touched gloves.

The referee held up Tony's arm in victory and the crowd cheered. What a fight. Tony looked more like the loser than he did the winner as he climbed out of the ring.

Tony sat on a bench in the dressing room as the doctor looked into his already closed right eye. His left was just about closed too.

"Get him to St. Paul Medical Center. I want to keep him there over night," said Doc Ash, the fight doctor.

"Is something wrong?" asked Nic worriedly.

"Take a look for yourself Nic, this guys taken quite a beating. I just want to make sure. I'm having a tough time getting a good look at the retina in that right eye and I want to keep him quiet for the night."

"O.K. Doc, whatever you say."

There was no fanfare or reporters or even guests in the dressing room but outside the door stood a crowd of Tony's friends. Joe was at the lead; standing next to him was Sam, Babe and Tom Rancuso, Father Tom, and a myriad of Tony's closest friends.

Tony was being helped out of the room when he heard his brother's voice. Tony tried to look up but quite frankly he couldn't see.

"Joe, they're taking me to the hospital. Will you come?"

Tears were sliding down Joe's face as he looked at the painful mess that use to be his brother's face and said, "Someone would have to kill me to stop me Anthony."

Joe was sitting in the waiting room of the hospital when in through the door walked Babe and Tommy, and Sammy.

"He's only in here for observation guys. He's alright," said Joe sticking out his hand to shake each of their hands.

The men stood around talking about the fight and about Tony for a while when Doctor Ash came out of the E.R. Joe walked up to him immediately and started questioning him on Tony condition. The doctor answered assuring all that Tony was fine. He just wanted to keep him there till he was sure that there wasn't anything he missed. What with the eye closed shut like that it's hard to see. Joe thanked him and turned to report.

"There's no reason for us to stay. It sounds like he's fine. I'll stay with him tonight or at least for a little while. I'll tell you what Babe, why don't you bring your family to my house tomorrow for sauce. About 4:00? We didn't get a chance to talk at all. I'll make sure Tony comes and we can all visit then. How's that sound?"

"Joe, just call us in the morning. If everything is O.K. with Tony that would be nice."

"O.K., but count on coming Babe, you too Tommy."

"I'm staying too Joe," said Sam.

"Alright Sammy, if you want."

They stayed about an hour. They got a chance to talk to Tony and felt relieved by the conversation. Just as they were getting ready to leave Joe looked up and saw Gina standing at the nursing station.

"Joe," said Gina, when she spotted him. "How is Tony?"

"He's fine, Gina, they just brought him here for observation. That's a normal thing."

"Thanks Joe, then I'll be leaving. Oh, Joe, please don't tell Tony I was here, O.K."

"O.K. Gina. If that's what you want," said Joe softly. "Hey, Gina, I invited your family for dinner tomorrow. Can you make it?"

"Joe, I'd love to see everybody but I can't. I just can't. I wish I could. I hope you understand." She kissed Joe on the cheek and left.

Joe was at the hospital bright and early Sunday morning. Tony was discharged with a clean bill of health and they left. Joe insisted on taking Tony home for dinner and begged him to stay a few days or at least until he looked semi-human again. Tony felt fine. Yes his eyes were nearly closed and completely black and his entire face was swollen but other than that he felt fine. He thanked Joe for the invitation but said that he was looking forward to having a nice dinner, seeing the family, but wanted to go back to his place just to rest.

The Rancusos showed up minus Gina. It was a tad uncomfortable for a minute or two but after that it was back to usual. The Russos considered the Rancusos family and there was no mistaking that, at all.

Tommy questioned Tony about the fight game, how he got in it, and how long he planned on staying in it. He answered, but ever so vaguely. Tony was very happy seeing his in-laws again. He truly did love these people. It was hard not asking about Gina but he restrained himself. It turned out to be a very pleasant day and all there had a good time. After a wonderful dessert, brought by the Rancusos was devoured, they left.

Paul Tripi

"I wish Gina would have come," said Tony sadly. "I guess it really is over isn't it Joe."

"I'm not so sure. Maybe if you can get Gina to go with you for some counseling you can rekindle the flame," answered Joe.

"A flame, Joe? I've got a bonfire going here. It's her. I'm afraid the fire has gone out for her. I don't blame her; after all I may as well have thrown a bucket of water on it. I wish I knew what to do. I still love her so much."

"Call her Anthony. Call her and tell her."

"Joe, I've tried. She's just not interested."

"I think you're wrong. I think she still has deep feelings for you but she's just afraid of getting hurt. Maybe if you could get her to talk to your priest friend. Maybe he could help. But the first thing is to open the lines of communication. If I were you I'd call her until she meets with you. If it's over Tony, it's over. You'll have to live with that. But it's not over till it's over. Give her a call. What do you have to lose?"

"I wish we could talk. It wouldn't matter to me what was said, to be honest with you bro just talking to her warms my heart. I'll keep trying. You're right, I'll keep trying."

Tony said his goodbyes to the family and headed home. His heart was sad but his body wasn't capable of any sort of a workout at all so he would forgo his usual I feel terrible trip to the gym and simply go home for a much-needed rest.

Father Tom awakened him the next morning. Tom told him Dominic had called and he wanted Tony to wear something presentable and be at the gym at 11:00 o'clock. He said Kevin James from channel 4 sports was going to be there. He was real excited and must have said the words TV coverage ten times. Father Tom was excited too. He was excited for Tony.

"Tony, this is unbelievable. You know that? This whole thing is

182

unbelievable."

"I know Tom. I just wish I knew what I was doing. God works in mysterious ways we all know that. I just wish it wasn't such a mystery to me. I know he gave me this power," he said holding up his swollen right hand, "but to this day I don't know if I'm using it right. Father I have no idea if I'm doing the right thing."

"Tony, all that we talked about is coming true. Aren't you helping as many people as you can with the money you've been making? Aren't you spreading the word? Aren't you about to have the entire city as your audience in just a few hours? Yes, Tony. If you ask me, this must be what he had in mind. I've told you before, no one knows what God is thinking, but in this instant this all feels right."

"I guess you're right Father. I'd just like to know how it's going to end," said a beaten up Anthony Russo. "I'd just like to know how, and when, it's going to end."

Chapter 21

Tony arrived at the gym right on time. He was dressed in a stylish pair of slacks and a golf shirt. It didn't really matter though because the only thing you noticed on the man was his swollen, bruised face. He walked into Nic's office sat down and said nonchalantly, "What's going on?"

"Kevin James is on his way here. He wants an up close and personal on you. I know he'll ask who you're planning on fighting next. If he does, tell him it's someone pretty big but the who, the where, and the when is all under negotiation and we're not ready to disclose that information as of yet. You got that. It's important," answered Nic.

"Yes, I understand but you got something going already? I can't even wash my face without pain how the hell do you think a punch would feel!"

"You'll be fine in a couple of days. Quit your whining and be a man."

"Why don't you let me punch you in the face a couple of hundred times and see how you feel about being a man? Come on big guy," Tony said as he jokingly stood up and got into a fighting position.

"Haven't you had enough fighting for awhile?" said a voice standing at the door.

Kevin James, an ex football star from the University of Missouri, paid his dues working as a sports radio commentator and was now the sports anchor person on CBS channel 4 in St. Louis.

"Hi Nic, hello Tony," said the handsome well-built reporter. "I certainly appreciate the time."

"Come on in," said Nic. "Who's that you have with you?"

"This is Sean Blair, my video man, and Angie Moe, my assistant."

"Come on in everybody, can I get you people something to drink?"

"No thanks Nic. All we need is a few minutes of your fighter's time. Is it alright if we do the interview standing by the ring out here?"

"Sure," said Tony with a sheepish grin. "But is it OK that I look like I just got hit in the face by a car?"

"You look like a fighter who just had a fight," answered Kevin. "And a damn good fight at that," he added. "You ready Tony?"

"Let's do it."

Kevin's people got into position. Sean turned on the blinding lights, and the interview was on.

"We're standing here at Dominic's Boxing Gym in the heart of the Hill with Tony Russo, the hard hitting St. Louisan who has come from nowhere to a place of prominence in the boxing world in a very short time. Yes he's a tough guy, and you can get that verified by his first six victims. He's won every fight he's had by knock out. But he's much more than that. Tony Russo is first and foremost a Christian. His demeanor and his manner do not depict the stereotypical boxer. His generosity in and around the city has piqued the interest of many a St. Louis resident. He's coming off a knockout victory over one-time heavy weight champion Wild Bill Dalton and as you can see the victory didn't come easy.

"Tell me Tony does that feel as bad as it looks?"

"Well first Kevin I have to thank my Lord and Savior Jesus Christ for everything that he's provided for me and mine and for everything still yet to come. With God there is always hope. And no, it looks worse than it feels. It hurt a lot more when I was getting hit than it does now. Wild Bill is a terrific fighter and a gentleman. I was very lucky to come out a winner against a man of his caliber."

"Tony our viewers would really like to know, who is Tony Russo? Where did he come from? How did you get started boxing? And what are your plans for the future?"

"Kevin that's a lot of questions, I'll try and answer some of them for you. I was born in St. Louis right here on the Hill, just about when cars were invented," Tony said jokingly avoiding giving his age. "I was a fighter as a youngster, fighting in the golden gloves, but I wasn't really good enough to take the sport any farther than that. It wasn't until God came into my life that I really started getting interested in boxing again.

"Dominic Michaeloni, the owner of this gym, was the main reason I started fighting again. He saw me fooling around, gave me a shot, and here I am. Nic's the reason I'm fighting, but the reason I'm winning is because of my faith. My belief in God has giving me the strength to compete and I feel His pleasure when I get the chance to pass on his message. Trust in the Lord and he shall provide."

"Is that why you've donated so much of your winnings to so many different causes here in the St. Louis area?"

"Yes Kevin, you know the old adage it's much better to give than to receive, well I'll tell you, you can't believe how good it feels when you see the faces of these underprivileged kids, or the homeless, or the elderly when you give them something they're not expecting. It's heart-warming. I love St. Louis and I love the people in it."

"What's up next for Tony Russo?"

"Well before I do anything I'm going to take some time to heal," Tony took a brief pause and made a quick statement to the youth out there in the television audience. "You kids out there, let this—" he pointed to his face—"be a reminder to stay in school and get a good education. This ain't all it's cracked up to be. So be smart, stay in school, don't make me come after you." Smiling, he held up his fist at the camera.

"Well getting back to what I was saying. Dominic's got a deal in the works right now. He said he'd disclose all the details when all the negotiations are finished. I'm going to get well and get ready. That's all I've got planned. I take fights one at a time. Kevin is it alright if I say something to my wife, my family and my friends out there?" Tony didn't wait for the answer. "I love you guys," he said raising his fist up in victory.

"That's Tony Russo and I'm Kevin James reporting for channel 4 sports, from Dominic's Gym on the Hill. Good night."

The next week was a busy one for Tony. In a fairly short time his face was almost back to normal and he was out meeting and greeting tons of folks. The television spot was a windfall for Tony as far as popularity, and Nic loved it.

Tony bought those beds for the homeless shelter and all in all he was feeling pretty good. He'd heard from quite a few of his friends and his family including the Rancusos thanking him for his message. The only person who didn't contact him was Gina. Tony had mixed feelings about that though. He realized that he said the words my wife on the spot and wondered if he'd be getting any response from her.

He figured no news is good news so when he didn't hear anything he took that as a positive. After all, they were still legally married so he wasn't lying. Still he had hoped for some response. The newspaper articles and the TV spot helped Tony build a wonderful relationship with the city. He wasn't famous but he was definitely on his way. Nic took full advantage of Tony's newfound reputation and turned it into three more high profile fights in a relatively short time span. All three were first round knockouts.

He took Ron Franklin out in forty-five seconds with a right that caught Franklin right on his forehead. He hit the canvas, rolled, and popped up sitting against the ropes. He was sitting there out cold, looking like he was in his living room watching television.

The second fight was with a very big fighter. Randy Dak, a six foot six mountain of a man with unusual speed. They fought in Dak's hometown of Chicago, Illinois. Funny thing is the Chicago crowd seemed as though they were rooting for Tony. Tony's reputation was heating up and it was starting to spread nationally.

The fight started out with Dak coming out hard and fast and in full command. He had landed several combinations and had Tony hanging on within the first minute of the fight. As the round was coming to an end Randy saw an opening and threw a right hand that if landed would have ended Tony unblemished record. Lucky for Tony he saw it coming and made him miss. Unlucky for Dak, Tony's counter right cross didn't. Tony hit Dak so hard that the big man did a chart wheel in the middle of the ring, without putting his hands down. He just spun with his feet completely over his head and hit the canvas out like a light.

The Chicago crowd went crazy. Fight fans outside of St. Louis heard of Tony's punch but most people thought that they were just stories and blown way out of proportion at that, sort of Paul Bunyanlike, but the knock out power of this Italian fighter from St. Louis came into full focus that night in Chicago.

The knock out was shown over and over again on ESPN the nations all sports cable channel. Tony Russo was famous and Nic took advantage immediately by promoting Tony's first fight with a contender. The fight was in Caesars Palace, Las Vegas Nevada, in late August. Denny Lee, the WBC's eighth ranked heavy weight, was Tony next opponent. Denny Lee from Tennessee was one tough hombre. He had an impressive record of thirty-three wins five losses and one tie with twenty-one knockouts. The build up for the fight was nothing short of spectacular as far as Tony was concerned. It was Tony's first televised fight and was shown on ESPN's fight night. It seemed like ESPN ran the advertisement for the show every hour and Tony's fame in his home town was at its peak at fight time.

The sixty-second advertisement was longer than the fight. Tony hit Denny Lee from Tennessee with a round house right thity seconds into the fight and Lee went down. But not before he spun around like a ballet dancer doing a pirouette. It was almost humorous when you think about it. Here is this six foot three, 238 pound man looking like he was performing a ballet move in Swan Lake more than a boxing match and the announcer called it just that way. The fight was over before it started and Tony Russo found himself in front of a national audience.

"Tony, Tony Russo, Tony, can I get you over here for a minute?" said Danny Crystal, ex-middle weight champion of the world and ESPN's fight night announcer. "What a punch you've got pal. It appeared that Lee never saw it coming. Tell us about the punch."

Tony answered the question the way he always did by thanking God. "First I'd like to praise my Lord and Savior Jesus Christ for everything he's done for me and mine. Trust in the Lord and he shall provide." He kissed his glove and raised it to the heavens and continued.

"Danny I faked a left hook and Denny raised his right to block it. When he did he lowered his left and he gave me a clear shot. I took the opening and here I am. It was a solid shot and usually when I land that I've got a pretty good chance of winning."

"A pretty good chance, are you kidding? A horse couldn't take that shot and stay on his feet. You've got just about the best punch I've seen in this game in a long time, maybe ever. What do you attribute this power too? Do you have a special way to train or do you do a lot of weight training? What is your secret?"

"It's no secret, I fight for the Lord, and with God's help all things are possible. When I win I feel His pleasure. I've said this before and I mean it, I'm no holy roller, my life has just been so much better since the Lord has come into it that I try and tell others who could use him that he will be there for them. God loves us all remember that all of you out there. God loves us all."

"That's nice but I was wondering what's on the agenda for you now? This was a big fight. Are you looking for a title match?"

"Every fighter who's ever put on a pair of gloves looks for a title match. So of course, but I leave all that up to my manager Nic Michaeloni. I'm just glad I lived through this fight. Denny Lee is one tough competitor and I was lucky enough to stop him before he got the chance to show me. I watched a bunch of his fights and I don't mind telling you I was a little scared. I'm just glad it turned out like it did."

"Thanks Tony, Nic, Nic, Nic, can I get you for a second? Nic, where did you find this guy? I've never seen anything like him. What's next?"

"You know Danny I've been around Tony so long that his religious stuff is starting to rub off on me. I think God must have sent him to me because what you've seen tonight I've seen him do ever since he stepped into my gym. This is one special fighter Danny and one special man. As far as what's next, we've had some offers but I'm not sure. We'll take a few days to digest what's happening and we'll make a decision."

"Alright, thanks Nic, Nic Michaeloni, O.K. guys, back to you."

Tony sat quietly on the plane ride back from Vegas contemplating all that has happened in his life in the past few years. Joe who was sitting next to his brother glanced over and said, "Penny for your thoughts."

"I was thinking Joe, I just made more money today than some people make in a lifetime. There's a good chance I'm coming out of this fight ranked. I've just had a national audience and spread the word of the Lord. Me. All this and the only thing on my mind is my wife. I don't think about her every minute but I do have Gina attacks and I'm having one right now. I wish I knew what to do. I guess I've got to accept what the Lord has given me and move on but that's easier said than done. What do you think my brother? I need advice. Do you have any idea of what I can do about these feelings? They're killing me Joe!"

"Tony, only you can control how you feel. I can only voice my opinion, so here it is. Gina is a lost soul. She has never come to grips with Molly's death and probably won't. The easiest way for her to punish herself is to keep away from the one person in the world she loved as much. It's you bro. She still loves you. She just can't take you back without feeling guilty.

"Yes, back when no one was able to make sense out of anything, you made a few big mistakes. Maybe unforgivable, but maybe not, time can heal. I do know this: she's been following what you've been doing Tony. She's worried about you. People who don't care don't worry. I think she still loves you. I just don't know what you should or could do about it. I think doing nothing is wrong.

"If it were me, I'd get together with her and let her know exactly how you feel, what you're willing to do about it, and get her feelings on that. See what she's willing to do about it if anything. If she says she doesn't love you anymore. Then that's that. Move on brother. I really don't know what else to tell you, and I certainly realize it's easy for me to say. I don't know what I'd do if Sally left me, but I'm sure begging would be involved. You got to do what you got to do."

"I know this Joe, I love her too much to let her go without a fight. I look back at a lot of things now. I'm sorry for so many, but the past is the past, I can't change that, all I can do is try and let her know I'm a different guy then the one that said those awful things. All I can do is let her know how much I love her. Right now my life is a storybook and I'm having a tough time enjoying it because she's not part of it. I feel like I'm not whole.

"I feel like all of this is meaningless. I feel like, I feel like—"

Joe interrupted with "Don't tell me Anthony, tell her!"

Chapter 22

Tony paced in his small quarters. He had some decisions to make and they weren't coming easy. Should he move out of the rectory? He'd banked $750,000 bucks so far, what should he do with that? Should he call Gina? How long should he keep going on with this fighting stuff? What was he supposed to do with his life? Tony felt the weight of the world on his shoulders and needed help. He needed to talk to God but since he couldn't, he settled for the next best thing.

"Father Tom, I need to talk. You got a minute?" said Tony sticking his head into the library.

"What's up Tony?"

"Too much Tom, it's decision time for me, for a whole lot of things. I need your help."

"Shoot."

"Tom, I love it here but I think it's time for me to move on.

Maybe get a place downtown I don't know, maybe Clayton, someplace where I can hang my hat and it's not in my way. You know what I mean."

"Well, it seems to me that you've already made up your mind about it but for what it's worth I've been telling you that for awhile now. We love you here too but you've outgrown us, Anthony."

"I don't know what to say right now, Father you saved my life. There will never be a time that I won't be there for you. I would lay down my life for you. I know you know that."

"You kidding me? Do you have any idea what it's meant to me and the other priests around here to have you with us? You've made us better men. Don't thank me, Tony, I'm the one who was saved. You've restored my faith in my fellow man. I'm going to miss you pal, I'm going to miss you a lot."

"Whata ya talkin' about. I said I needed some more space. I'm not changing how I live and Tom you're a big part of my life. I'll always be around. I have no idea what's going to happen next. You're the tour guide. I'd be lost without you. So quiet down for a second and let me ask you the important question.

"What do I do about Gina? You know how I feel. I've been telling you that until I'm blue in the face. I just don't want to blow it and I'm scared."

"Call her. Call her and tell her how you feel. Lay all your cards on the table and let nature take its course. If it's meant to be it will be. Don't push, just let her know how you feel. Put the ball in her court."

"That's the most clichés I have ever heard strung together in my life."

"I just don't want you to put all your eggs in one basket."

Tony grabbed the priest and put him in a bear hug. Both men were laughing.

"Tom you are too much. I want to say thanks. Thank you for everything. But most of all, thank you for being my friend."

"The pleasure and I do mean pleasure is all mine."

"You know Father, there is one thing we need to talk about. I've got all of God's money and I think I've got an idea how to spend it."

"Wait Tony, you keep saying the same stuff over and over again and man you're way off base. Let me ask you. Did God actually say to you take all the money you earn and spend it on the poor? I don't think so. That's your idea. That's what you think you should do with the money, but it's not and I repeat not God's money. Your generosity is beyond belief but the bottom line is you buy whatever you want with that money. It's yours and yours alone, if you wish to help others that's your choice. Am I making myself clear?"

"Yes, I got it, now here's my idea. You know the church has been working with the Sisters of St. Paul Health Center trying to help unwed teenage mothers care for their children and still get their high school degrees. The number I heard bantered about was around a half a million bucks to build the thing, set it up, and place the girls. I've got that much and I want to build that home. Can you help me get involved?"

Father Tom stood there dumbfounded and answered, "Yes Tony, I can certainly take care of whatever you want to do with that but don't you listen to a word I say? That's too much. That's way too much to donate. I can't let you do that."

"You have no choice. That's what I want to do. I just don't know how to go about it."

"Tony you amaze me. I swear you amaze me. The Tony Russo home for girls, it has a, excuse the pun, a nice ring to it."

"No Father, I don't want my name on it. But if it's at all possible I would like to honor my daughter's memory."

"Molly Russo's Home for Girls, I'll get the ball rolling and take it from here." Tom stuck out his hand to shake Tony's, when their hands clasped he pulled Tony close and hugged him instead. "God sure made a good choice," he said as he embraced his friend.

Tony left the rectory and headed over to the gym to work out. He walked into Dominic's office and said, "What's up."

"Glad you're here. I got big news. The WBA rankings came out today. Guess who's the sixth rated heavyweight in the world?"

"Get out."

"I'm not kidding man. Madison Square Garden, here we come. The phones have been ringing all morning. I just hung up with Steve Sophy. It happened, you're rich buddy. I told you I was going to make you rich and I did. Here's the deal. October 31st, Halloween night, you and Valerie Minderoff, the Russian Champ, at Madison Square Garden, HBO, the whole nine yards. Your end two million bucks," Nic laughed as he pounded his hand down on the desk. "Two, I repeat two million dollars!"

Tony plopped down in the chair he was standing next to. He had already made a fortune but the numbers now were turning into Monopoly money, simply not real. He looked up to Nic and said, "How is this possible? I don't understand how this is possible."

"Tony, you're the biggest draw going. Hell, you're more popular than the champ, Mark Piper, for crying out loud. The whole country's talking about you and your punch. I had a number of offers but this one leads us to a title fight. They started the deal out at half a million and in one sentence they were up to a mil. It was a piece of cake getting 'em to two. It's as simple as this: you win this one, buddy, and we'll get that title shot. You hear me. A shot at being champion of the world." He pounded his hand down on his desk again. "HA HA HAA, I knew it. I told you, didn't I? I knew it."

Tony sat quietly. Just drinking in what had just been said. "Nic, I don't know what to say."

"I think 'thank you your highness' would be appropriate."

"Thank you Nic. Thank you for believing in me. I won't let you down. I'll take this Russian all right. Count on it. I want that title fight. The truth is, you've got me believing." Tony reached his hand out to shake Nic's and said, "Two million. You know for that kind of money I'd fight the Russian and the champ at the same time."

"One at a time pal, one at a time. This Russian is big and tough, and he hits like a mule. You just concentrate on him. I believe in you, buddy, but we're running with the big dogs now. People ranked in the top ten can take you out with either hand at any time. You make one mistake and you won't hear the man count ten. Let me get Andy in here. We've got a lot to do and not a lot of time to do it in."

Tony left the gym with a stunned look on his face. He got in his car and raced over to his brother's office. Joe was surprised when his brother walked in.

"What's the matter? Something happened. I can see it in your eyes," questioned Joe. "Has something happened?"

"Yes Joe, something's happened alright. I just got ranked by the WBA, I'm the sixth ranked heavyweight in the world and I'm fighting the Russian Champion Valerie Minderoff, on HBO, Halloween night. I can't believe what I'm going to say next but here it is. My end, win or lose, two million."

"Oh my God, Tony. Oh my God. Oh my God. I just can't believe this."

"I want to call everybody I know but I know I don't have to. The whole world will know as soon as Nic starts spreading the word. I'd better call the folks though. I don't want Ma to have a heart attack."

"Where's the fight?'

"Madison Square Garden."

Paul Tripi

"Oh man, this keeps getting better and better. I'll be there, you can count on that."

"Joe, I'm taking the whole family, everybody, kids and all. I'll send tickets to the folks, and hell, I'll send some tickets for a few of their friends too. They'll like that. I still can't believe all this. It's like a dream."

"You better get a hold of your buddies and let them know, and the Rancusos," said Joe.

"I think I'm going to head to the store right after I leave here. I'll tell Babe and I've decided to confront Gina. It's time. What da ya think?"

"It's past time bro, you've let this drag on and on and it's not right for either of you. She's either interested in you or not. I think she loves you, but don't go by me. I think you tell her how you feel, find out how she feels, and that's that."

"You're right, I've just been afraid the answer's not going to be what I want to hear. But you're definitely right. I'm going over there right now. I hope she's there. If I get bad news, I'll call you. I don't want to do anything I might regret."

"You call me either way. Ya hear. Either way! Matter of fact, if it's bad news, we do dinner tonight. Period."

"OK. Man, life, what a yoyo," said Tony shaking his head.

"You can say that again, brother."

Tony walked slowly into the furniture store, like he was sneaking in. Babe was behind the counter, saw Tony, and motioned him over.

"Hello, Tony, what brings you here?"

"I've got some news, Babe."

"Good or bad?"

"Actually, it's great. I just got ranked in the top ten by the WBA and here's the deal, I'm fighting Valerie Minderoff, the Russian

Champion, Halloween night, at the Garden in New York. Madison Square Garden, Babe. I thought you might want to come. It will be on HBO if you can't."

"Are you kidding, I wouldn't miss that for the world. Thank you son, and congratulations."

"Thanks, Babe, hey is Gina back there?"

"Why, yes. I'll call her for you."

"You don't have to, I'll find her. I want to take her out to dinner if she'll go."

"Good luck, with the fight and with my daughter."

As Tony stepped into the back room Gina was turning the corner heading for the showroom.

"Gina."

"Tony, what are you doing here?"

"Gina, I got a lot to tell you and something I want to ask too. But I'd love to talk over dinner. Can you, I mean will you join me?"

"I can't right now Tony. I've got so much to do around here."

"Nonsense," said Babe who just happened to overhear their conversation, by accident of course. "There's nothing that can't wait until tomorrow. You kids go have something to eat. Tony's got good news. Go on, get out of here."

"I guess we can get something quick, Tony. What's your big news?"

"Oh, no. Not until we're sitting in a restaurant. Where do you want to go?"

"It doesn't matter. We can just go across the street to the café. That'll do fine."

"No way. Let's go someplace expensive. I'm in the mood to celebrate."

"Celebrate what. Will you tell me what's going on here?"

199

"I told you, not until we get to a restaurant."

"Then let's just go across the street."

"Gina, Please."

"OK, But I don't want to be out late at all. Dinner and that's it."

"Great, that's great. I promise dinner and I'll take you right home."

Tony turned and shook Babe's hand. He knew without his urging Gina wouldn't have come. "Thanks Babe!"

As Gina and Tony walked away Babe Rancuso whispered to himself, "I liked it so much better when he called me Dad."

Chapter 23

Not much was said in the car, only small talk. Tony didn't want to spoil the big news. He wanted to wait until the ambiance was just right before they had any conversation about the possibility of a future.

This wasn't at all about the money he was about to make for this next fight, the money had nothing to do with what he wanted to discuss. He knew that Gina could care less about his finances, anyway. He was more concerned about the length of time that had passed since they had the chance just to eat a meal alone and talk. Tony was petrified that out of sight out of mind would be the dish served and he didn't think he could stand the finality of what might happen.

Here's a guy who's about to fight a man that could possibly kill him with one blow and the only fear he had on his mind was a simple little word, no. He drove directly to Mario's, the best Italian restaurant outside of the Hill. It was a restaurant that they had spent many a wonderful evening together, Tony was pulling out all the stops. They walked in; it was early so there wasn't much of a chance that they wouldn't get a table. Plus with Tony's reputation it wasn't hard for him to get a table at any restaurant in the city.

They went in and were directed to a lovely table in the covered courtyard overlooking a beautiful waterfall and garden.

"I'm glad we came here," said Gina. "I'd almost forgotten how beautiful this place is."

"Me too. I've almost forgotten how beautiful a lot of things are."

"Tony, don't start."

"I'm sorry Gina, but I can't help it. You are a beautiful woman and that's just simple fact."

"Well, thank you. That's nice of you to say. Now what's this big news?"

"I've got a few things to tell you but first a question."

"Tony I just said not to start."

"Gina, will you let me get this out, believe me this question is not at all what you're thinking. Here's the deal. You know that I've been making a lot of money lately, right?"

"Yes, and I'm glad you brought that up. I want to tell you that never in my life have I been more proud of anyone. Tony, what you've done for this town. There isn't a day goes by that someone doesn't say something about your generosity. You're a good man Tony. That's all that I can tell you."

"Thanks, but you know I've tried to stay anonymous about this stuff. I'm just trying to help. But anyway that brings me to what I want to tell you and ask you. I've made a big decision about the money I've got left. I've been talking to Father Tom and there's this home they're trying to build for teenage girls with babies. These poor unwed girls lose any chance for life if they can't at least get a high school education, and how are they supposed to go to school when they have a baby to take care of. So they want to build this home where the girls can live with their babies. They can help each other out, and there will be a small staff to help too, so these girls can go back to high school.

"I've decided with the money I have left I can afford to build that home, and I'm doing it."

Gina hesitated a moment and replied, "Oh God, Tony!" She bent over the table and kissed him on the cheek. "You simply amaze me."

"Thank you honey but that's not the whole story. Here it is. With your permission it will be called The Molly Russo Home for Girls."

There was dead silence. Gina just sat there until the tears started flowing and then it escalated into a full-fledged cry. Tony slid his chair over and held his estranged wife in his powerful arms. She hugged him back without saying a word. Within moments they were both crying. Their daughter's name hadn't been mentioned between them. It was a subject that neither of them could discuss. Nothing was said for a moment or two until Tony gathered his composure, grabbed a cloth napkin from the table, wiped Gina's tears and then his own. He started to say something but no words came out. They sat for few more seconds and then Gina spoke.

"That is so wonderful I don't know what to say." She reached over and held his hand.

"Do you want to be involved in the project?" he asked.

"Yes Tony, I do."

"OK, I'll get you all the particulars and you can do as much or as little as you want. That's up to you. If you'd like to be in charge of the whole ball of wax, that will be your decision, totally. I'll have Father Tom call you in the morning."

"Something like this is so big, is this going to take all the money you have?"

"Well, yes and no. It's will cost me almost everything I've got now, but."

"But what."

"But, I just found this out. Guess whose fighting, on HBO, in Madison Square Garden on Halloween night."

"Oh my Tony. How did all this happen? I can't believe it."

"God, that's how. God has no bounds, Gina. This is all God's doing. I told you that. I'm just the one he picked."

"Picked to do what?"

"I don't know. All of a sudden I'm this great boxer. I'm way too old. Hell, when I was fighting as a kid I wasn't good. Now I'm fighting on HBO. My thinking is that I'm supposed to do some good through all this. That's why I'm doing the stuff I'm doing. I figure I'm supposed to spread the word of the Lord. And I'm doing that. But I don't know. This home thing, I was thinking maybe that's what it was all about but maybe not. Maybe not Gina, cause I'm getting a whole lot of money for this fight in New York. More than you can imagine. I don't know what I'm supposed to do."

"Who told you all of this?"

"No one told me. I just figured it out for myself. But it didn't take a brain surgeon. How could all this be happening without God's help? How? You know if I were to win this fight I'll probably get a shot at the title. Are you hearing what I'm saying, a shot at being the heavyweight champion of the world. Everyone thinks I'm taking all this in stride, but I'm freaking out. On top of all that Gina, I'm scared. This guy is tough. I know I can punch but a big punch doesn't stop the other guy from punching back, and punching hard. I haven't said this to anybody but I'm scared."

"Wow, wow. Don't think I haven't been thinking about all this. Don't think for a moment that I haven't been scared myself. I came to one of your fights and I had to leave. I couldn't bear to see you hurt like that. I can't tell you what to do but if you ask me, maybe this is a good time to stop. Why take any chances now. You've accomplished so much."

"I can't, Gina. Deals have been made. I can't let everybody down. Plus we are talking about millions here."

"Millions of dollars?"

"Yup, so for that kind of money I'd fight a moving truck. I just hope I'm around to spend the money. Just think of the good I could do with that. Not to mention, it would be nice to move."

"Let's stop talking about that right now. My head is spinning. I had no idea you were talking about that kind of money."

"Well, I'm sorry, I shouldn't have said anything but it'll be in the paper within a day or two so I figured I might as well tell you."

"Wow, when you have big news, you have big news. I am so happy for you."

"Well, is there any way you could be happy for us. Let me rephrase that, Gina, is there still a chance for an us?"

"Tony, please, how much do you think I can take in fifteen minutes? I knew you were heading up to this, and I don't know how to answer you."

"Well, will you at least think about what I'm saying here? Please. I love you Gina. I have never stopped and I never will. You are everything to me. I'm sorry about everything. I'm so sorry, but that was the past. I don't want to talk about the past. I want to talk about the future. I'm a new man. I swear to God I'm a new man. I know that you are a new woman. Why do you think I haven't approached you before with this? I know you're a new woman but why can't the new Tony and the new Gina see if they want to be together. Can we try?"

"Tony, I don't know. I really don't know."

"Maybe counseling, maybe counseling will help."

"Help what. Help what?"

"Help us open our eyes to the possibilities. Gina no one on earth can or will ever love you as much as I do. It's impossible. I would do anything for you anything. I swear, I would die for you. I'm not asking that much. I'm not asking you to come back. I'm just asking for you to think about the possibility. Maybe we can date. Maybe we can just spend some time together. That would be a start. I don't want to bring up the past but I can't live with what I said to you. Please, Gina, please forgive me for that, you know there is no way I meant what I said, absolutely no way! How I handled things, I can't expect you to forgive me for that. For that I can't even forgive myself."

"Tony, this is a little too much for me right now. I really don't know how to answer you. Being with you like this definitely brings back very fond memories and of course I have feelings for you. The thing is I put those feelings away and I'm not sure I can or want to resurrect them. I am different woman, you're right. I'm just not sure who I am right now.

"Why don't we just have dinner right now and we'll see. I'm not promising you a thing other than dinner tonight. After that we'll see. How does that suit you?"

"How does 'thank you Jesus' sound for a response?"

"It sounds a little premature. Dinner tonight and then we'll see. That isn't any reason to be thanking Jesus, Tony."

"Anything that wasn't the word, *no*, is to me Gina. OK, let's stop talking about that and let's just talk about regular stuff like, how's your mother? How's the rest of the family? How's business?"

Tony and Gina sat and talked for hours. As far as Tony was concerned it was the best night he'd had since he really can't remember. Afterwards he drove her back to the store to pick up her car. They kissed good night, not a passionate kiss, but it was on the lips. Tony was in paradise. In the last twenty-four hours his life had gone from unbelievably good to unbelievably great. He didn't know where this was going but he knew that at least it's moving forward. Now all he has to do is live through this upcoming fight.

That was going to be easier said than done. Valerie Minderoff is the toughest man in Russia, maybe the toughest man in the world. Tony was happy now but who knows how he's going to feel the day after Halloween. Only God could say.

Chapter 24

Tony's feet seemed to barely touch the ground as he walked into the library at the rectory. He told Father Tom about his dinner with Gina, filling him in on their conversation concerning the home for unwed mothers. He asked him to contact her and to keep her abreast of the happenings. Tom was elated with the news. He knew how happy his friend was simply by the glow that emanated from him. He was more than thrilled about the situation and was happy to oblige.

After numerous phone calls and a few meetings the project was on its way with Gina Russo at the helm. Tony, Gina, Father Tom, Lisa Damis the president of the SSP Health Center, Vito Tamoli the CEO of 1st Commercial Bank, and Cheryl Kate VP of the Catholic Charities Foundation made up the board of directors. In just a matter of a few weeks the hopes and dreams of a number of young women who thought their lives were over before they started, were about to change. God certainly does work in mysterious ways.

Gina threw herself into the project finding purpose in her life for the first time in a long while. After setting up the board of directors Gina contacted Tony to arrange a meeting to go over the funding. It was the first time Gina had instigated a conversation with Tony in almost two years.

When Tony put down the phone his smile was so bright it lit up the room. Everything in his life was going so well it was scary. Not just the fact that Gina was back in his life. Maybe not in the way that he wanted but just the fact that they were sharing a common interest and working together to achieve a goal had Tony's spirits sky high. His arduous training schedule wasn't even bothering him. In fact he was enjoying the workouts and it was showing. Tony was looking like a man a lot younger than his years and what was more important, he felt it. He was ready for Halloween night and was anxious to climb into the ring. There was only one thought in Tony's mind and that was to win.

Tony worked out like a man possessed. Whenever Andy said one more Tony would do three. He felt the power of God now even when he was just training. Tony was more convinced than ever that God gave him this power so he could become a fighter, do good deeds with the money and to spread his word.

Dominic wore a never-ending smile these days and the whole gym was always abuzz. This was a big deal for all the fighters at Dominic's and all were helping Tony to be the best that he could be. There has never been a single fighter out of this gym to fight for a championship and if Tony beat the Russian it looked and sounded like he was a shoo-in to be the first. Even Joe and Sam were spending time at the gym watching Tony work, answering questions, and simply helping do whatever they could. The media was becoming a big part of Tony's life and he was using it to the fullest. He spread the word of the

Lord at every opportunity and he was feeling real good about it.

It was the middle of October. The fight was just a couple of weeks away and Tony was ready. He finished a vigorous work out and was walking out of the gym when he looked up and saw Gina standing at the front door.

"Gina, what are you doing here?"

"I was wondering if you had any plans for lunch, if you eat lunch that is? I was in the neighborhood and thought I'd stop by."

"If I had eaten ten minutes ago I'd eat again just so I could be with you."

"Tony, you say the sweetest things."

"I mean those things!"

"I know you do. And thank you. Well are you hungry?"

"Let's go."

Tony and Gina walked across the street to one of the many dozens of restaurants that are located on the Hill. This one, Jacqueline's, was a nice little family restaurant two doors down from Father Bakers Orphanage and cattycorner from Juney & Richies, the best bakery on the Hill.

They sat at the table that's in the front window, ordered some ice tea, and perused the menu. Gina ordered the veal parmesan and a salad and Tony went for the Italian steak sandwich. After ordering, something happened that made Tony's heart skip a beat. Gina reached out and held his hand. Tony tried to act like nothing was going on but he was ecstatic. What was going on here? Was Gina going to say something bad? Why was she holding his hand? Tony held his breath as Gina started to speak.

"Tony, I've been giving something a whole lot of thought. I'm very afraid but I can't help how I feel. Here's the thing. I love you! I've tried very hard not to but I can't help it. I love you! And I just don't know what to do about it. Don't say anything until I get this all out. I know how you feel about me and I'm aware of what you want to happen but as I've said, I'm really not sure what I want to happen. I want to talk about it. I want to talk without you pressuring me. I'm sorry that I'm acting so strange about it. After all, I've done all I can to keep distance between us, but it's not working. This might be the worse timing in the world but I can't help it. I'm sorry. I just don't know what to do."

Tony answered Gina with one of the most passionate kisses this world may ever have known. She hesitated for just a second before the kiss but was a willing participant as soon as their lips met. Afterward they stared at each other, neither saying a word. He wanted to say something but was too afraid.

After more silence than there should have been Tony said, "Gina, as much as I want to just grab you, run off with you, and never let you out of my sight, I know we have to think here before we act. I love you too. I love you so much that I don't have the words to express it. I think, I think—". Tony stopped.

"Well, what are you thinking," she replied.

"I don't know what I'm thinking, other than I'm the happiest man in the world. I'm thinking maybe we could go for a long walk, hold hands, and just talk. I'm thinking we could end up at St. Ambrose and we could have a talk with Father Tom. He knows all the answers. What do you think about that?"

"Actually I've been talking to him a little about this so I think that's a real good idea."

"That son of a gun. He hasn't said a word about anything to me," he responded.

"Well, they were private conversations."

"You're right. I don't care anyway. All I know is you're here with me, we're holding hands, and we're talking. However this happened doesn't matter. All that matters is that we're together. I love you Gina!"

"You already said that."

"I'm going to say it every chance I get and I hope that's every day for the rest of our lives."

Tony and Gina finished their meal. Tony paid, left a tip that would choke a horse, and they went for their walk. Not much was said. They just walked and held hands and enjoyed each other's company.

Tom smiled from ear to ear when he saw his two friends walk into his office, hand in hand. The three of them hugged. Tears formed in Tony's eyes as he hugged his friend. Tony already loved this man but this was far beyond the call of duty. He would have fought a street gang for this guy with only a dull spoon for a weapon. All Tom had to do was ask and Tony would have done anything for him. The three of them sat and talked. Not so much about the past but about the future.

It was determined that Tony and Gina had suffered enough without each other and that it was nothing short of a pity that they waited so long before they put themselves in this position. No blame was mentioned for anything. Only the future was important. After a short time it was agreed that it would be a good idea for them to proceed slowly. They decided to date. They were going to go out Saturday night for a start.

Tony asked Gina for two special dates. The first was to accompany him to New York to attend the big fight. He explained that her family was going to be there and she could be with them while he was tied up with the rigmarole of the fight. She agreed that she would like to go but was a little apprehensive about watching the actual fight. That was settled, she was going. Tony was thrilled.

Secondly he asked if she would accompany him to Joe and Sally's for Sunday sauce. She said that it was too soon for that but she actually is looking forward to seeing them all. Tony didn't push. All he said was that they were all coming to New York too and that she would see all of them there. She said great she was anxious to spend some time with Sally and Betty again but the Sunday sauce thing was just a little too much, too soon. They agreed again.

Tom excused himself when they started that conversation and returned to catch the couple as they consummated the conversation with a kiss. All three were happy. It seemed a long ordeal was coming to an end. The three hugged. As they got ready to leave Tony turned to his friend and said, "I don't know how we can thank you."

"You don't have to. I didn't do anything but bring both of you to your senses. You two belong together, everybody knows that. It's just that it took a little time for the two of you to see it. God bless you both."

"He already has Tom, he already has."

Tony and Gina talked a bit more as they walked back to Gina's car. Tony explained that she was the most important thing in his life right now but he was obligated to give the best effort he could with the upcoming fight and that he wouldn't be able to spend as much time with her as he would like until it was over. She knew that and told him that she would wait until the fight was over but she didn't want to. She told him that she was aware of his commitment and that he wouldn't have much time.

She also explained that she too was extremely busy what with the Girl's Home coming to fruition and that seeing him Saturday would be just perfect. They got to Gina's car. They kissed goodbye. Tony didn't want to part. He wanted to follow her wherever she was going. He wanted to make passionate love to her, but he knew better. They had a plan and a schedule and he was going to follow the rules. He didn't want anything to happen that could screw this up. He waved as she pulled away. He looked up to the heaven and said, "Thank you God."

He had been looking for a place to live for the last month or so but as of that second that stopped. He was thinking he'd let Gina do that now. Anything she wanted, anyplace she wanted it didn't matter to him. He didn't want to put the cart before the horse, it just felt right.

Then something struck Tony as he stood there in front of the gym. Is it possible that with all this happening to him, with all that God had just bestowed upon him, was it possible that he may have just lost the power? Is it possible kept running through his mind. He immediately ran into the gym and headed over to the punching bag. Paulie Jay was working the bag when Tony almost frantically yelled, "Paulie, move for a second."

The whole place went quiet when Tony yelled. Tony drew back his right and let it go.

POW, the leather bag exploded and twenty-five mouths dropped. You can bet that not a soul in the house said a word. They were all dumbfounded.

Paulie turned to Tony and asked, "Man, Tony, what did that bag do to you? I ain't never seen nothin' like that."

"It's nothing Paul, I just wanted to see something. That's all."

"Well, I hope you never want to see something like that with me. That's for sure."

"Don't worry pal, that would never happen. Plus, that bag can't hit back like you. You think I'm stupid or something."

"No Tony, I think you're the best puncher in the world. That's what I think. And looking at these other guys, I think they think so too." Paulie laughed, "Man, you are unbelievable. I know I wouldn't wanna be that Russian dude. That I can promise you."

Tony patted Paulie on the back and walked out to cheers. "Go get 'em Tony—-You're the man buddy—-Awesome—-God bless you Tony." The place was buzzing like it never had before. Nic came out of the office and stopped Tony just before he got to the door.

"What's going on here? What the hell are you doing?"

"Nothing Nic, I guess I'm just happy and I felt like letting out a little excess energy. I think I just got back together with my wife."

"You gotta be kidding. Congratulations, buddy. I'm happy for you. But you know we got a fight here in two weeks. You know sex weakens the legs."

"Stop it will you. I'm winning this fight. Believe me. He'll have to kill me to beat me."

"Don't say crap like that. I know you're gonna win. You'd better win. I've been talkin' to every guy I know setting up a title match if you do. So don't let me down now. I need Minderoff down. You understand the importance of this fight."

"Now who's the one kidding? He's going down. This guy is definitely going down."

Tony shook hands with Nic and headed out. There was one place he had to go and he couldn't wait to get there. He was on his way to Clayton to tell his brother, and he was wearing a perpetual smile. This was a great day for the Russo family. Tony Russo was back and this time there was no stopping him.

"Look out New York, I'm coming, and I'm bringing the power of the Lord with me!"

Chapter 25

American Airlines flight 231 from St. Louis to New York landed at Kennedy Airport Thursday October 29th at 1:30 p.m. Tony and his entourage deplaned and headed directly to the Hotel New Yorker located just two blocks from Madison Square Garden. Tony's group included Nic and his entire staff along with Tony's family, Joe, Sally, Betty, Sam, Gina, her mother, father, her brother Tom. Father Tom and the handball guys Tony T., Mike, Steve, Mark, Frank, Jim, and George rounded off the rather large group. It was a party-like atmosphere and all were having a great time.

It was so exciting for everybody, after all Tony was fighting at Madison square Garden. Who could have possibly in their wildest dreams ever imagined they would be in this position? But here they all were and to say that they were excited was an absolute understatement.

On top of everything else everyone to the last person was equally

as thrilled at the fact that Tony and Gina were on the mend. Babe
Rancuso was acting like a kid in a candy shop for the last two weeks,
ever since his daughter broke the news about her and Tony. Babe loved
Tony like he was his own son and the loss of his son-in-law was a heavy
burden that he had borne. Now that they were getting back together the
entire Rancuso family was elated. Both the Russo family and the
Rancuso family were, Sally and Betty especially. They loved Gina like a
sister and having her back in their lives was nothing short of a miracle to
them.

Father Tom and the buddies dropped their luggage in their rooms
and were in the bar before the dust cleared. They were drinking like
sailors on leave and in no time they were bragging and placing bets with
anyone that would take a bet. After a short time there wasn't a person in
the joint that didn't know that these guys were Tony Russo's buddies.
How could they help it? About every five minutes one of the guys would
hold up his glass and toast, "To Tony Russo, the next heavyweight
champion of the world." They were having a blast.

The rest of the group including Tony joined them in the bar and
they all went out for a wonderful dinner. Tony kept saying everything's
on me, but with the likes of this group he might as well have been
talking to the wall. You would have thought these guys were devout
enemies the way they were fighting every time a tab came. It got so bad
over the course of the next few days that guys were giving the waiters
their credit cards when they were being seated, just so they didn't have
to argue over the bill when it came.

It was pretty obvious that all these people were more than friends.
Tony did get the last laugh though, without anyone's knowledge he had
paid for all the rooms when he had the rooms booked. He knew his
family and friends would never have allowed that if they knew. His
mom and dad along with a few of their friends from Florida got in late

Thursday.

When he saw them all together Tony was emphatic about this being his treat. He told them that he just wanted them to enjoy themselves, the fact that they came up with his parents was a favor to him and he would be quite put out if they didn't allow him to treat. He was met with a bunch of opposition but "Please" turned out to be the exact word to say, and it worked.

Tony was around as much as he could but he also had numerous obligations to perform. Including the weigh in and of course the media. Gina hung with Tony wherever he went. It made an experience that couldn't have been better for Tony, better.

She started drifting away the closer it got to fight time. Gina knew Tony needed to have his mind on what he was doing. She was very aware that in a short time Tony would be risking his life. There wasn't any other way to put it, and she couldn't get that out of her mind. A few hours before Tony had to go to the Garden to get ready, Gina kissed him, wished him good luck, and made sure he knew that she wasn't going anywhere. That she just wanted him to concentrate on the task at hand. He kissed her back, but to be honest the fight had never been out of his mind from the second he stepped foot on New York soil. He wasn't actually scared, but there was no doubt that he was nervous about what could happen. Valerie Minderoff was a great fighter, of that there was no question.

The only question in Tony's mind was could he beat him. In less than six hours he would to find out.

The crowd was filing in and the buzz grew louder and louder. Madison Square Garden was an accommodating facility and all that entered were about to be entertained.

218

Minderoff, even though he spoke little English, had been able to get his point across concerning his view of this fight. "Russo hit hard but he no can punch when he is on his back, and he is on his back before the end of round three." The Russian champ stuck to his prediction thought the week and stepped into the ring a confident fighter.

Tony stepped through the ropes and glared at his opponent. There wasn't even a glimpse of a smile on his face. He was ready for a war. The crowd was ready too, and the buzz reached a crescendo when the announcer called out the names of the combatants. No one in the house cheered any louder than the Russo entourage when he called out Tony's name.

Everyone in the place was yelling something as the referee gave the final instructions to the fighters, everyone except Gina. She sat quietly in her seat. Fear shown prominently on her face. She understood why Tony was doing what he was doing but couldn't help but feel the pain he was about to endure. While all around her cheered and laughed, a small tear dripped down her face.

Nic and Andy spouted words of encouragement to Tony when the bell starting round one sounded. Minderoff screamed like a man possessed, coming out fast and furious. He landed a nice combination before Tony even had his bearings. Tony countered with a few left jabs trying to stay off the Russians charge, but Minderoff was relentless.

The round ended with the Russian landing a right that drew blood. Round one was a good round for the Russian champ and a bad one for Tony.

"What are you doing in there? You're standing flat-footed and this guy's taking it to you. Stick and move, and throw some damn punches will you," shouted Andy as he squirted water in his fighter's mouth.

"He's good Andy. And he's fast."

"So are you, go out there and let him taste that right hand. Bust him up Tony. Go get him."

Ding.

Round two started with the Russian taking a round house left to the jaw, followed by a right hand cross that if landed would have ended this fight. Instead the miss left Tony vulnerable to a left hook. It was a big punch and it staggered Tony. Right hook, left cross, right hook, Tony's back hit the ropes. He hooked an arm over the top rope and hung there trying to stay on his feet but the Russian was relentless and threw a combination of punches that found Tony lying on his back and staring into the bright lights.

Tony heard the ref scream out "Five" and with all his strength pushed himself to his feet. The referee stared into Tony's eyes, touched his gloves together, and signaled the fighters to continue. Valerie attacked with enthusiasm, as he smelled the blood of his opponent. One more shot and this fight was over. He was almost right. As he stepped in for the kill Tony threw a blind right over hand shot that caught the Russian on the shoulder. He dropped to a knee in disbelief, his left arm numbed by the blow. The ref started counting but the Russian stood up immediately. Shocked by the sheer power of the punch he stayed away from Tony for the few seconds that remained in round two.

Minderoff didn't realize that Tony was out on his feet and just about any blow would have put him down for the count. But Tony entered a new ingredient to the mix. The Russian was scared. He didn't believe the stories of Tony's power but he just had a taste of it and he believed now, man did he believe.

Gina was flat out crying when the round ended. Babe held her hand but realized this was painful for his daughter and asked if she wanted him to take her to the dressing room until the fight was over. She mustered up a smile and refused the offer. This time she was going to stay. Even though each punch hurt her, she was going to stay.

It was just then that she realized just how deep her love for her husband was. She told herself that she was sure Tony meant everything he was saying and she admitted she felt exactly the same. These facts struck home like one of Tony's right hands and she truly realized that they would never be apart again. Not for a day.

The next few rounds passed uneventfully. Tony regained his composure and was satisfied just trading jabs with the now cautious Russian champ. The momentum had shifted and Tony, once the hunted, had become the hunter.

He stalked his opponent looking for the opening that could end this thing. With a minute and thirty-one seconds left in round six his chance came. Minderoff got aggressive. He attacked Tony with a flurry of punches going under the assumption that Tony couldn't punch when he's ducking and backing up.

Valerie landed a four-punch combination, not doing much damage but definitely kept Tony on his heels. The Russian saw an opening, and threw what he thought was a fight-ending left hook. This time it was his turn to swing and miss and that was costly. After missing badly he was off balance and the whole left side of his face was unprotected. Tony's right hand hook didn't miss.

He landed what might have been the best right hand he had ever thrown. Bad news for the Russian and for the three or four people he landed on in the third row. Minderoff looked like he just bounced on a trampoline the way he flew over the ropes. The first knockout of Tony's career was a punch that knocked his opponent over the ropes but this wasn't just over the ropes, this guy looked like he was shot out of a cannon. It was amazing. The crowd screamed so loud that they almost took the roof off of the building.

Tony rushed to the ropes and threw a leg through the middle rope trying to get out to check on his opponent. By the time Tony hit the floor, Valerie was moving. Tony climbed back into the ring, the referee signaled the fight over, and raised Tony's arm in victory.

The place was in frenzy, and with that punch Tony's reputation was legitimized. Everything that was being said about him and his powerful punch was just made clear to the whole world. If anyone doubted his punch before, they doubted no more. The media rushed Tony like hungry people at an all you can eat seafood bar. Almost before the referee released Tony's arm there were a dozen microphones in Tony's face.

Questions were being shouted at Tony but they were falling on deaf ears. Tony was busy making sure Valerie was all right. He was standing in the Russian's corner and after Minderoff's corner men helped him back into the ring, Tony was there to meet him.

"You alright, buddy?"

"You're great, what a punch, you knocked me on my ass, you're great. I never been hit like that before. You're great," said Minderoff sticking out his gloved hand to shake the one that just knock him into the third row of the Garden.

Tony turned to meet the media. The first one Tony recognized was HBO's Paul Paulina.

"Tony, great fight. What a punch. It looked like Minderoff high jumped over the ropes. I've never seen anything like it. Can you tell us about that punch?"

"Thanks Paul. I just want to say everything is possible with God in your life. I can't take credit for what happens in my life, because nothing happens without the Lord's help. I want to thank my Lord God for making all this possible. All you out there, trust in the Lord, he loves us all." Tony kissed his glove and held it to the heavens.

"As far as the fight, Minderoff is tough. He had me twice but I was able to weather the storm. He tried to take my head off with a big left.

Lucky for me, he missed. It turned into some bad luck for him 'cause when he missed he left himself wide open for a right hand and I landed a sweet one. He was so off balance that when I hit him that's why he ended up in the seats."

"Not quite Tony. He ended up in the third row. He flew over the top rope and looked like a paper airplane when he sailed over it. This fight is going to be talked about for a long time, a very long time. Tony this puts you in line for a title shot. What do you think about the champ, Mark Piper? And what do you think your chances are against him?"

"Man, I'm still bleeding from this fight. I am not ready to talk about any other fight but if I was, I'd be telling Piper he'd better get ready for a war. I'd like to shout out a Happy Halloween to everybody out there, especially the good folks in my hometown of St. Louis, Missouri."

Tony's entire entourage was allowed into his dressing room. Everyone was in great spirits. Joe was the lead cheerleader and the handball guys were near crazy with happiness. Father Tom stood in the corner simply enjoying the whole experience. Tony acknowledged them all and shared their joy even though he was hurting. He won the fight but he was hit hard and often and needed a little rest.

Gina stared at Tony the entire time and after everyone else extended his or her congratulations she approached Tony and said. "Tony, I don't think I can watch another one of these. Thank God you're all right. How do you feel?"

"I feel like I just got hit by a bus, but that'll go away. I'm happy. That's how I feel. Happy. Happy I won but happier cause you were here. I love you Gina."

"Baby, I love you too. As I watched you up there all I could think about was just how much. I think it's time we do something about it."

The small dressing room was getting smaller as the crowd kept piling in and Nic was getting aggravated.

"OK, everybody out of here. I gotta check out my fighter. You people wait outside and we'll signal you back in once we take care of our fighter here."

Tony added, "Why don't you all go back to the hotel and I'll meet you guys there. I got the press conference and then I'll shoot right over after that. Don't get drunk till I get there. I think I just might join you tonight, non-alcoholic beverages of course. Thanks for coming. I love all you guys."

A cheer went up from the whole group, and they started moving towards the exit.

"Wait, Gina, why don't you stay honey?"

"OK,

"I'll catch up with all of you later. I'm staying with my husband."

Tony smiled a painful smile but just the same it was ear to ear. That was the first time in a very long time he heard Gina call him her husband, and it felt great. She stayed with Tony for the rest of the night's agenda and the two of them were acting like it was their wedding night. As far as Tony was concerned everything was perfect.

While Tony was addressing the media, Nic was on the phone. He was gonna strike while the iron was hot. Tony and Gina left and headed back to the hotel and by the time he got there Nic had sealed the deal. He wasn't gonna say anything to Tony quite yet. He wanted to make sure his friend and family had at least the night to enjoy this win.

He would wait until the morning to tell him that in just a short two months he would be fighting Mark (The Viper) Piper on pay for view in what they were going to call The Holiday Bash for the heavyweight championship of the world. All the numbers weren't finalized but Tony who tonight alone made as much money as two normal men make in their lifetimes was going to make even more, so much more that the numbers were mind-boggling. When the smoke cleared from this next fight Tony who was already a very rich man, was going to be, a very very rich man!

Before Tony and Gina met their friends at the bar they had a stop to make at the hotel's restaurant. When they stepped into the room almost everyone immediately recognized him and he was given a nice round of applause. He was pretty easy to recognize, after all how many people looked like they just got hit numerous times in the face with a baseball bat. It was truly official: Tony Russo was a celebrity. He looked around and saw the people he was looking for, a table full of retirees. They were easy to find because the beam that was shining from both of his parents filled the room. They were the proudest mother and father on earth. Tony and Gina walked over and kissed them both.

"This is my son," Big Tony shouted with enthusiasm.

"I've got a feeling your friends already knew that Pop."

"I know that son. I just wanted the people around us to hear that. I'm so proud of you my boy." And Big Tony hugged his boy and kissed him full on the mouth.

"I'm proud too Anthony but don't ever make me see one of those things again. I almost had a heart attack three or four times," added his mother and she kissed him too. "I am so happy to see you, Gina. I missed you honey." And along with those sentiments came a kiss from both of them as well.

"Oh Mom, I missed both of you too. It took a brick wall, as usual, to fall on him or in this case a couple of hundred brick walls but here we are again and Mom don't worry everything is as perfect as can be."

"Oh honey. Tony is right when he says believe in the Lord. I prayed and prayed and here you are."

"Everybody eat and drink to your heart's content. And don't worry for a second about the way I look right now 'cause it looks much

225

worse than it feels and it goes away fast. I'm talking kind of directly to you about that Mom.

"Thanks for coming and thank you all for the friendship you've shown my parents."

"Don't let anyone of my friends trick you into letting them pay for anything. Charge all this to the room, I told you all that everything while you're here is on me. OK Dad."

"Too late, your brother already beat you to the punch.

"Hey that was funny what I said. He already paid for this when he stopped to say hello."

"He can't let me win at anything, can he? Where is he? He's gonna have a fight on his hands."

"I think maybe you've done enough fighting for one day, son," added his mother. "He said they'd all be waiting for you two in the bar and to send you over when you showed up."

"OK thanks Mom, love you guys.

"Enjoy everybody we'll catch you later."

Gina and Tony kissed their parents again and started to leave. "Tony!

"Yeah Mom."

"No drinking!!" she said like he was still a little boy. Because to her, he still was.

"Yes, mother," he said shaking his head and laughing. "Bye all," said Gina waving as they left.

The couple walked over to the bar where the festivities were in full bloom. He walked into a crescendo of cheers. The celebration was now in full swing.

Chapter 26

"Two million dollars! Did you say twenty-five million dollars? Are you kidding me?"

"Did I stutter? That's right. But just in case you forgot pal, some of that's mine, right off the top."

"No way, you THIEF!!!" Tony said laughing. "Nic, you deserve it all."

"Tony, I would have gone on this ride for free. I knew it the first time I saw that punch. I was absolutely sure we'd be where we are and I was right. You are one special fighter Tony; in fact you're one special man. It's a privilege just knowing you."

"Nic, you're forcing me to pull out all the stops here but here goes. Ditto!"

Both men laughed. You know the kind of laugh someone gets when they just find out they've won the lottery. That's the laugh they were having because they just did.

"Now down to business. The fight is in Vegas on December 21st. I know it's short notice but I didn't argue, after all you're already in shape. I figure it's to our advantage. They want to have it then because of the holidays. They're already calling the thing The Holiday Bash.

"They'll be hyping the pay for view immediately cause they want to take full advantage. In fact you're going to see the commercials starting today. They said they weren't planning on wasting any time. I know what they'll do. They will hit the media with all they got. They will attack you in every way they can to try and build animosity between the two of you. That sells. Not us, let's stay away from the media. I want to keep a low profile. Keep things to ourselves until just about fight time. Say nothing. Don't answer questions about the fight at all except how thrilled you are for the opportunity. Yes, don't ask, I know you're going to talk about your God stuff but just try and do what I'm telling you about a low profile. Then we'll come out hard with something to boost interest and increase the gate just before fight time. How's that sound?"

"It sounds like you're thinking about the gate and I'm thinking about Mark Piper. I've studied this guy Nic, and from what I see I'm not sure I can even stay in the ring with him. He's fast as lightning and he's got a punch like a mule. I don't know, Pal. You're the one biting off but I'm the one who's got to chew. I just hope you didn't bite off too much."

"Stop whining you cry baby. You're the toughest man in the world. I wish you'd realize that."

"It's funny Nic, I don't feel that tough. What I feel is blessed. I just hope I'm not pushing the envelope. I'm going to be tagged one of these times and I'm going to wake up in the hospital or maybe not even wake up. If I die, I'm blaming you."

"You ain't gonna die, you wussie. Now shut up, go find Andy, and let's get started. You're on your way to becoming the next Heavyweight Champion of the World."

Tony and Gina were back together as though their split never happened. They were invited again to stay with Gina's parents but everyday Gina and her mother went out house shopping. When Tony got home from his training session just a week after they got back from the fight, Gina was smiling with that kind of guess-what smile.

"You found a house, didn't you?"

"Tony, it's so beautiful. It's a two story with five bedrooms, five baths, a workout room, a billiard room, and a wonderful pool with a guesthouse. The kitchen is to die for. I love it. Can we go look at it? I really don't want to lose it."

"Where is it?"

"It's in Wildwood, twenty-five minutes from downtown, and about ten minutes from here. And it's well under the amount you said we could spend."

"Honey, I don't care what you spend. Just make sure it's the house you want. I'd live in a cardboard box as long as you lived there with me. So I really don't care."

"Don't say that, it's our house and I want it to be ours. Not mine. There isn't any mine, there's only ours."

"Do you really love the house?"

"Yes, Tony, I really love this house. Anyone would."

"Then, call the realtor. How soon can we get in?"

"It's vacant, and Heather Danniello, the realtor, said we could probably close immediately since there won't be a loan involved. Well, as long as everything goes smoothly with the inspection and the title search."

"Then call Heather, or whatever her name is, and tell her we'd like to look at it tonight. I don't necessarily have to see it but if it will make

Paul Tripi

you happy we'll go look at it and write a contract on it."

Gina hugged Tony and kissed him full on his mouth. "Let's go now. I can't wait for you to see it. She's waiting for my call."

Within a few weeks the deal was signed, sealed, delivered, and they were in. Gina had purchased all new furniture. Not all of it had been delivered as of yet, but for all intents and purposes they were in. And there was still a week before Thanksgiving.

Gina was already planning a feast. She was so happy. Tony saw the look on her face when she told him that they were having everyone over for the holiday and when she danced out of the room he lifted his head up to the heavens and for the umpteenth time said, "I know I've been saying this too much lately but thank you God, thank you for everything."

Tony called Sally. She had wanted to join in on the wonderful things Tony and Gina were doing with the poor and the handicapped and Tony knew it. He had this plan that he had been kind of thinking about for the last few months and he knew that the entire family, especially Sally, would want to take part in it.

So, when he was talking to Father Tom after mass on Sunday, he asked if the church had some kind of a list of people in the parish that didn't have the price of a meal, especially a Thanksgiving meal. Tom gave Tony a list and told him he knew these people could certainly use some help. Tony took his list and gathered more names from other churches in the area. He and his family then put together a Thanksgiving meal menu consisting of a fifteen pound turkey, five pounds of potatoes, five pounds of sweet potatoes, a giant box of ready to make stuffing, cranberry sauce, canned gravy, and a big can of corn and had it all delivered in bulk to St. Ambrose's gymnasium. Then Tony, Gina, Joe, Sally, Betty, Sam, and the Rancusos worked all day Tuesday putting it together and all day Wednesday delivering them. 500 in all. It was a labor of love and for the first time the family got a chance to feel the way Tony felt when he was helping needy people. They felt great. It was the first year of many that the family would do this. It became a family tradition. When Tony led the prayer at their family Thanksgiving meal he said it but he didn't need to because they all felt it, "It is far better to give than to receive."

The next few weeks Tony immersed himself in his boxing. Gina on the other hand was busy with the girls' home. The original plan had been expanded, after all Tony had a big payday in New York and as usual he was passing some more of it on. Father Tom was working hand and hand with Gina and they were already ahead of schedule. Life in the new Russo home was just about perfect.

Mark Piper's camp was trying to dig up as much dirt as they could on Tony. They were looking for whatever they could in order to start some controversy. Problem was everything they found was nothing but good.

So they were forced to try and put a nickname on him that would aggravate him and build a rivalry. Starting that day anytime they talked about Tony they called him Grandpa Russo. If he can't land the right hand he can't win. They were confident that if the fight went over ten rounds you could stick a fork in the old man. He has more chance throwing up then he has throwing punches. Every day a new dig.

When asked about what was being said about him Tony responded with, "Everything they're saying is true. I don't even have a chance against a great fighter like Piper. With God's help I'll do my best. God bless everyone in Piper's camp and God bless America." Mark's camp became more agitated every time Tony responded in that manner. The more they tried to get Tony's goat the more angry they got. They just couldn't get to him. A week before the fight, sentiment was going in favor of Russo and much to the surprise of the entire boxing community so was the betting. A fight that should have been four or five to one in

231

favor of the champion was even money. Tony's reputation was complete.

The same group that partied in New York gathered at Lambert Field in St. Louis waiting to hop aboard their flight to Las Vegas. Father Tom laid his hands on Tony and blessed him, turned and blessed the rest, and they all boarded. The handball guys started gambling as soon as they got seated. Mike, Tony T., Frank, Steve, Mark, Jim, and George each threw five dollars in a pot, picked an exact time the wheels of the plane would lift off, synchronized their watches, and waited. It was the first of many bets they would make in the next few days; take a guess on who they were betting on to win the fight!

Tony, Nic, and Andy were still talking strategies as the United Airlines flight departed the gate. They went over the schedule one more time; Tony slid the small sheet of paper in his sport coat pocket, and went back to his seat next to his wife. The Christmas spirit was everywhere. Tony wasn't really thrilled that the fight was taking place at this time of the year, but beggars can't be choosers. He wanted this fight and would have fought it whenever or wherever. He was definitely ready.

The weather was hot and humid, far from the cold weather in St. Louis. It didn't feel like Christmas time at all. Tony was getting ready to walk down to the arena. Gina rubbed his back and gave him as much encouragement as she could. This time it wasn't about spreading the word or the money. This time it was for Tony himself. He wanted this so bad he could taste it.

"Would you be disappointed if I didn't watch this fight?"

"No honey, whatever you want."

"I want to but I can't stand to watch you get hurt."

"OK, I won't get hurt then."

"You promise?"

"I promise. If you don't want to watch then that's OK, but it sure

232

won't be the same when they announce that I'm the new heavyweight champion of the world, without you there."

"Alright, but you promised. No getting hurt." She paused and continued, "How long is this going to go on honey? We have all the money anyone could ever want. If you win would you consider—oh never mind, just go out there and do your best. That's all I've ever asked of you and if you do, that will be good enough for me. Good luck baby."

"Thank you, I could use it. And Gina, God will tell me when I'm supposed to stop. I don't know how or when but until he does, I'll do his bidding. I know what you're asking but it's not in my hands. I don't know if he wants me to win or lose but I don't think he wants me or anyone else for that matter to get hurt. I'll do my best, that I swear, I just don't know if that will be good enough. All I can do is try. But just in case I want you to know that I love you. I love you with all my heart. Now put a big smile on that beautiful face and I'll see you after the fight."

The crowd was subdued waiting for the combatants to enter the ring. Tony came out first and a roar went up. He was wearing red white and green trunks, the colors of the Italian flag but an American flag was embroidered on the belt. He entered the ring, danced around warming up and waited for the champ.

Loud music blasted, a large entourage entered the building and smack dab in the middle walked Mark "The Viper" Piper, the undisputed heavyweight champion of the world. He was wearing a long white beard and walked with a cane. Mocking Tony. It was a mistake. There were a sprinkling of laughter but most thought he was acting stupid. His tactic never did work and it wasn't working now. Tony Russo never gave the impression to anyone that he was old. All he did was knock out every man he faced, and with incredible almost unbelievable finishes. To Tony's surprise the sentiment was for him.

For the first time, it seemed he was the favorite.

This infuriated the champ and he screamed at the crowd. "I'll kill this old man. You'll see. I'll kill him."

He jumped over the ropes and yelled something to Tony. Tony didn't hear a word. He was busy praying. And man he was sincerely meaning every word he was saying. He wasn't praying for the win, he was praying that he wouldn't get seriously hurt.

The two fighters went to the center of the ring. The ref gave them their final instructions. When they touched gloves Piper spit on Tony's and said, "I'm gonna kill you old man. Tonight you die."

Tony yelled back, "I hope you like soup, cause that's the only thing you're gonna be able to eat for a long time. You're going down you loud mouth punk. Talking is over," screamed Tony as he turned to go to his corner.

It took the champ by surprise. He tried to intimidate Tony but turned to go back to his corner with doubts. Tony never said a thing except to praise his opponent but the spit in the face pissed him off. Tony was ready to fight.

It was evident from the opening bell. Tony came out fast. Instantly he landed a right. A glancing blow but it hurt Piper. The viper ran. He said all along he was going to dance around and tire out the old man but this wasn't dancing, the guy was running. As the bell rang Piper knew he lost the round. He had to gather his composure or he was in for a long night.

Round two was much different. Piper stood toe to toe with Tony and both threw punches like there was no tomorrow. The crowd went wild as the two fighters battled for a solid minute and a half. When the bell rang two bloody men walked back to their respective corners. No winner that round. In fact they were both losers. They were yelling things to one another as the ref broke them up.

Round three went about the same; each man took his turn blasting the other. Tony landed but couldn't land the one he needed. Piper hit Tony with a five-punch combo that shook Tony's world. He was shaking off the cobwebs when the bell sounded.

Round three went to the champ. Piper was feeling more and more confident. It showed as he came out to start round four. He blasted Tony before the ringing of the bell had cleared and he didn't stop. Tony was beaten to the punch at every turn. He was holding on at the end of the round and was lucky to have made it through. He was done.

It was just about over for Tony as the referee broke the battlers up but, just as they were ready to turn and go back to their corners Piper made an awful mistake, he spit in Tony's face again. Tony was about ready to drop before that but as he wiped the mixture of spit and blood from his face he turned once more and glared at the champ.

"You OK Tony? You got to stay away from him this round. He is killing you. Dance away and clinch every time you can. You hear me?"

"You ready to go home, Andy, because he's going down. He's going down. That son of a bitch spit on me for the last time."

Tony lit out of the corner like a bottle rocket and hit Mark Piper with a left hook that his manager felt. Two more lefts and Piper was on the run. Tony chased him around the ring but Piper was too elusive. It was a smart move too by the champ 'cause when the bell rang ending round five, Tony was tired.

Round six. Tony got up slow from his stool. Piper noticed it and came running right at him. He ran across the ring, cocked his right hand and just before he let it fly Tony, who was faking how tired he was unleashed the big dog. He caught Piper right under his chin. Piper looked like a puppet on a string as he slid still standing all the way back to his corner. His arms caught the top rope and he hung there, out cold.

It was over. Tony was the new heavyweight champion of the

world. Tony dropped to his knees put his head into his gloves and then looked up to the heavens. Andy and Nic were on Tony like flies on a dead squirrel. Nic picked him up and hugged him as hard as he could.

"You're the heavyweight champion of the world pal, the heavyweight champion of the world."

The ring filled immediately, everyone wanting a piece of Tony. Tony was looking around frantically and finally found who he was looking for. She was trying to get into the ring but the police were not letting anyone in.

Tony yelled, "Let her in officer, she's my wife," but Gina had already pushed her way past him and jumped into the ring to embrace her husband.

"Are you alright?"

"Never better honey, never better. Baby, I'm the champion of the world. I can't believe it, I'm the champion of the world."

"I love you Tony. I love you."

Chapter 27

The remainder of the night was spent with all forms of media. Tony had a microphone in front of his face for hours. God's message was certainly conveyed that night. Finally Nic stepped in.

"That's all. You guys got all you're getting tonight. Let this man celebrate a little will you."

Tony thanked them all, grabbed Gina by the hand, and they left. They knew their family and friends would be waiting for them and they couldn't wait to share the joy with them. It was one great, unbelievable night for all involved and the happy couple didn't want to waste a minute of it.

The next morning it was straight to the airport. Tony and Gina had enough of Las Vegas for a while and after all, their mission had been accomplished. In fact every mission Tony ever had in his life seemed accomplished. Gina and Tony flew hand in hand. Not much was said, there was no need, life was just about as good as it could be for the Russos as they headed home to enjoy the holidays.

The next few days Tony and Gina spent traveling all over the city. Hospitals, old folks' homes, orphanages, homeless shelters, every place they could think of where they could find people who could use some help and some Christmas spirit. Tony passed out hundred dollar bills everywhere he went. Although his face was still battered from the fight, he managed a smile a "Merry Christmas", and a "God be with you" to all the needy people he encountered.

He had Joe and Sam rent a truck and met them at the Warehouse of Toys. They filled the truck up and along with their wives spent half the day at the orphanage across the street from Nic's place, Father Bakers, making all the kids happier than they've ever been.

The Russos hugged each other in the street in front of the Home. Joe and Sam insisted on giving Tony some money to help with the cost of the toys and being the good man that Tony was he took it. Tony knew that if he had refused he would have cheated them all out of the joy of giving.

They made plans for their Christmas Eve; it was going to be at Joe and Sally's. Their parents were arriving in the morning and as usual were staying at Joe's. Tony wanted them to stay at his new place but the older Russos were creatures of habit and they wanted to stay where they usually stayed when visiting their children. There was never any arguing over such matters. When their dad spoke that was the law and that was it so Christmas Eve was at Joe's, period. No discussion.

They left the orphanage and everyone headed back to their cars, Joe took the truck back and Tony and Gina stood looking at the building full of children. They couldn't help but feel some sadness creep into their hearts. They both realized it was a feeling that would never go away.

"I think it's time we go see Father Tom now," said Tony smiling and grabbing his wife's hand.

"Let's go, I'm going to enjoy this as much as you," said Gina.

Tony and Gina drove over to the church in their brand new Chevrolet Tahoe, parked it in front of the rectory and went in to see Father Tom. Tom was in his office as usual.

"How you feeling Champ?" he said as soon as he saw the couple at his door.

"I don't think it's possible to feel any better buddy, I've been out making as many people happy as I can and I'm enjoying every minute of it. Matter of fact I have something for the church here. Do you have it honey?"

"It's in the glove compartment."

"I'll go get it for you Tom."

"What do you have? Whatever it is, I can tell you right now, it's not necessary."

"We'll see, come with us."

The three of them went out to the car. Tony reached into the glove compartment and was digging around when Tom said, "What in the world do you have in there?"

Tony pulled out a check, handed it to Father Tom and said, "A new wing for the rectory."

It was a check for $200,000.00.

"No way. I will not accept this."

"You can't refuse. It's a Christmas gift for all the priests here at St. Ambrose and it's very impolite to refuse a Christmas gift. Now don't make me fight you, I'm still sore from the fight I had the other night."

"I don't know what to say."

"Don't say anything. It's me who has something to say. Thank you. Thank you for my life. Thank you for my wife. Thank you for being my friend. There isn't anything in the world I wouldn't do for you anything. All you have to do is ask. God bless you Tom."

"Bless me? Bless me? Bless you!" joked Father Tom. "No I mean that, bless you both. You deserve one another. You might be the kindest people I've ever met in my life. I can't thank you enough for this generous gift. I accept on behalf of all us priests here at St. Ambrose. This is wonderful. What a Christmas this is."

"Well, there is one way you can pay us back," said Tony reaching into his pocket. "You can drive us home in this new truck of yours," he said smiling as he handed Tom the keys to the new Tahoe.

"NO. NO. NO. I mean it. Don't you dare," he said pushing away Tony's hand.

"You were right Gina we will have to take a cab home." Tony threw the keys into the truck. "Tom the title is in your name and it's in the glove box. Have a Merry Christmas buddy. Taxi, *loud whistle,* taxi."

"Come over here you two." Tom hugged his friends. "Give me those keys. There is obviously no sense in arguing with either of you, plus I just can't say no to this beautiful machine. I love it. Thank you. Thank you both so very much!"

They all jumped into the Tahoe and away they went. All three as happy as can be. And the giving didn't end there.

Christmas Eve at Joe and Sally Russo's was always a special event for the family. They had enough food to feed a small army, and it tasted so good there wouldn't be a person in that army that wouldn't love to be there. Big Tony played the piano and the whole family sang Christmas carols. It was great.

Then they passed out presents. First the kids and believe me they were spoiled by all, then the adults. Their gifts to one another were also way too extravagant. But these people loved each other and it showed. When all the gifts were handed out and opened Tony and Gina stood up and said, "We have a special gift for each of you." Gina reached into her purse and pulled out a Christmas card for each family. Tony gave a card to his mom; Gina gave Sally and Betty their cards. They all opened them in unison. There wasn't a word said. Everyone to a person was stunned. In the cards were checks for one million dollars.

"What the hell do you think you're doing? We can't accept this," said Joe speaking for everyone.

"I don't want to hear one word about this. And that's that.

"Every person I've ever known always says the same thing, if I ever win the lottery I'd give everyone in my family a million dollars before I did anything. Well, I sort of won the lottery so shut your pie hole and come over here and hug us. But before you do I do have to tell you that this is not a gift.

"This is a paycheck for being assistant trainers. That means that you guys pay the taxes on this money. It's better than a gift tax anyway. Merry Christmas. And that's the end of that."

What could they say? They didn't give them any choice. In seconds all were hugging and there wasn't a dry eye in the house. Tony's dad, Sam, and Joe, each at different times did talk to Tony and said that even though they truly appreciated what he had done they all agreed that it was just too much. Mom, Sally, and Betty did the same to Gina.

"Would you all please stop. You're taking all the fun out of the best thing we've ever done in our lives. Look we have all the money we can ever spend. Why can't we share it if we want? Now the next one of you who says something about this money is going to get a shot like you have never seen before, I mean it. That goes for you too Mom, I'll give you such a punch you won't believe it."

"Bring it on tough guy," she replied. "I'm not afraid of you," she said making a fist.

Tony laughed and hugged his mother and whispered, "I love you Mom. Go see the world. Do everything you've always wanted to do. I've got a bunch of money left. This is just a drop in the bucket. I am not done yet. I'm the heavyweight champion of the world Mom. The heavyweight champion of the world."

Tony spent the rest of the week resting. They had a quiet New Years Eve and had the family for dinner at the house for New Years Day. It was a very nice day and quite uneventful. Exactly what Tony wanted. You see with fame comes the loss of privacy and Tony was a private man. Family time was more than important, it was a necessity, and Tony was now cherishing the time he spent with his family and friends more and more. Fame is a give and take situation and Tony was learning exactly that.

The following Monday after New Year's Day Tony went back to work. He walked into the gym to a round of cheers, pats on the back, and handshakes. He thanked them all for their support, reached into the box he was carrying under his arm, and pulled out the heavyweight championship belt. He held it in the air and yelled, "We won."

The place went even more crazy. He made them all feel like they were part of this win, and to Tony, they were. Nic came out of his office; Tony walked over to him, and handed him the belt.

"Put this where you think it belongs, Nic. The fact is without you it wouldn't be here."

Nic took the belt into his hands, kissed it, and handed it back to Tony.

"The belt is where it belongs, buddy, it belongs with you. You've earned it. Now we'll see if you can keep the damn thing."

"Don't tell me you've got another fight set up already."

"Not yet. I'm gonna let this all set in first then I'll milk this thing dry. You need a rest. You've been fighting too much and too often and I think we'll enjoy this for a while."

"Well I'm gonna work out. I'm sore and I'm old and if I don't keep these old bones working they'll stop working."

"Then get after it. You're my meal ticket, you know."

"Yeah, you need more money like I need another hole in my head." Tony turned to walk to the locker room, after a few steps he turned again, "Hey Nic, thanks again for everything. You are truly the man."

Nic just smiled and pointed at Tony with his finger looking like a gun. "Go work out you big galoot."

Tony walked out of the gym to an unbelievable commotion. Fire alarms were sounding. People were screaming and running all over the place. Black smoke was bellowing from across the street and the visibility was near zero. Father Baker's orphanage was on fire and the fire trucks were not on site as yet.

Tony panicked like everyone else and didn't have any idea of what to do. He ran across the street as fast as his legs would carry him. There were a number of people standing around all in mass confusion. Chaos, bedlam and pandemonium would be the words that would best describe the scene.

A woman was screaming and pointing to two men holding and running with a bench towards the steel doors of the small Chapel connecting the church to the orphanage. They obviously had intentions of using the bench as a battering ram hoping to open the heat swollen metal doors. The men hit those doors with all their might and all they accomplished was to turn that wooden bench into splinters.

At the same time, the woman who screamed and pointed finished her rant with, "There are children in that chapel." Immediately, Tony took off running towards the chapel and on the dead run looked down at his right hand and screamed to the two guys at the door, "Get out of the way." He continued on the run towards those doors, drew back that powerful right arm of his and with all his strength and power, he hit them. The sound from that punch made a noise like a small explosion. There were two others sounds that went along with that, a creaking noise, which was the sound of the doors starting to open, and a cracking noise, which was the sound of the bones in Tony's arm breaking.

Even though the pain shooting through his body was excruciating Tony drew back his arm again. When he hit the door a second time, the pain dropped him to his knees, but the doors opened. The two men standing behind Tony rushed into the smoke infested chapel. Tony got to his feet and joined them.

They gathered up the children and like cattle drove them to the doors. Tony turned and saw a small figure squatting down in the corner. He rushed over scooped up what turned out to be a young, scared, little girl, and raced out of the building. As he ran, the little girl wrapped her arms around Tony's neck and squeezed with all her might.

"What's your name?" he said cradling his precious cargo in his arms, trying to comfort her.

"Jodi," she said crying but so sweetly it melted Tony's heart.

"How old are you Jodi?" he asked trying to keep her calm. "Five years old," she replied.

Tony hugged her even harder and as they ran from the flames he looked up through the smoke filled air to the heaven and with tear choked words said out loud, "Thank you God, thank you!!!!"

The smoke over his head seemed to part. A beam of sunshine shone down on Tony and it was warm. "**NO ANTHONY, THANK YOU!!**"

Tony was dumbfounded. Did he just hear what he thought he heard? He did! My Dear Lord he did! Oh my God that was it. That was it. In that one moment everything became crystal clear. The power, the power he received didn't have a thing to do with spreading the word, and nothing to do with the money to help others, or boxing or anything else. It was all about this. Saving these children. He stood there stupefied. The pain in his arm was gone. More than likely so was the power. He didn't care. He held Jodi tightly.

He reached into his pocket, pulled out his cell phone and called Gina. He told her about the fire and the chapel and the children, and about Jodi. The how, the why, and his part in it, was never mentioned. After she was positive he was all right she asked about the little girl. They talked for a few more moments, and they hung up. Tony held on to Jodi for dear life. His and Gina's conversation was short but overwhelming, and maybe even life changing. Tony had no intention of letting Jodi go and according to what Gina said on the phone, neither did she.

Gina rushed to the orphanage as fast as she could, squeezed through the barriers the fire department and police had erected and frantically searched for her husband. She found him holding a beautiful little girl in his arms and talking to some official-looking people. It turned out Tony never did put little Jodi down. You see when the smoke cleared, and I mean that figuratively, Tony and Gina finished the conversation Tony started with the staff at Father Bakers. It seems that Tony and Gina had some paperwork they needed to fill out.

Tony, Gina, and Jodi Russo, a happy family, with a happy life.

The end—or is it?

Made in the USA
Middletown, DE
26 April 2019